Getting to Goal

Eli Celata

Getting to Goal by Eli Celata

Chapter One

Keeping the room dark, I traced the familiar steps from my bed to my desk. My dad always got up early. Fishermen rose hours before the sun, so on those rare days when I managed to wake before his alarm, I did my best to stay quiet. He deserved the rest. Soon enough, he would be on his boat, checking cages and casting his nets. Most of the money came from lobster these days, but he always caught fish for us.

Since my brother, Brandon, died, I laid out my close at night - like he used to do - tugging on sweatpants in the dark with whatever sports bra I'd managed to dig out of my drawer. They were all the same style. I'd gotten them in bulk after my last growth spurt. Tugging on my brother's old Boston Marathon t-shirt and a hoodie, I slung my sports bag over one shoulder and crossed it over with my school satchel. I kept my stick by the door with my shoes, so shuffling down the stairs, careful not to knock the rails or slam the bags against the walls, I flicked on the coffee maker on my way to the backdoor.

Dad always said we had the money for two sticks - one for school and one for home, but I never found another stick I liked, so I kept Brandon's old stick by the door and stored my actual stick in the rink. I could always use Brandon's if I needed. Wasn't like he ever used it much. He was the swimmer. Always on his own on purpose when competing and otherwise. After he died, the whole school talked about what a tragedy it was. Swarms went to the counselor's offices, but I think they were just scared because someone as healthy as Brandon getting cancer stole away their illusion of invincibility.

I never thought I was invincible. Brandon said I was too practical. He wasn't a dreamer either, but he probably hadn't expected the cancer any more than the rest of them had. Mom hadn't died of cancer, after all. Dad always used to say Mom's family went two ways. Either they died young on drugs, or they lived to be a hundred. Brandon didn't do drugs.

Biking to practice along the back shore was my favorite part of the day. Only fishermen seemed to get up well before dawn in Port Edmond. Well, at least after the first of November. My breath curled white around me, leaving my skin to prickle with the cold when I glided downhill, but it wasn't bad enough yet to need a jacket despite the frost covering the ground. Only tourists and private school kids wore jackets in Port Edmond before the first snow that stuck. We'd had sprinklings on Halloween, but they didn't last the day.

In the quiet and dark of pre-dawn twilight, only the churning ocean and the occasional squeak of my bike's brakes made any sound. All the street lights glimmered. A snaking trail of light along the shore where soft sand beaches would fill with colorful towels and bodies in the summer, but as winter crept steadily closer, only the birds would venture there in the dark. Even the dedicated surfers would wait until after sunrise. Coves and crevices where the soft tan sand became rough rocks were the best for those. Their waves crashed in curls, growing with the tide. But before dawn, it was just me and the beach - not even a single footprint marking that another person had ever been there. The night tides had washed them all away.

An hour took me almost to dawn, and though the rink remained dark, a single car sat in the parking lot. Gliding up beside it, I knocked on the window.

"Morning, Beni," Mike grumbled. He'd been up probably just long enough to drive across the street from his house. With eyes clenched shut, he trudged to the door with his coffee in hand. "Don't you have actual practice this afternoon?"

"Yeah."

Twisting the key, he glanced back at me. "Congrats on making varsity, by the way."

"Thanks."

And that was exactly why I had to practice twice as hard. I had skated and handled my stick well enough to be varsity last year as a freshman, but people had always been a little weird about a girl on the ice hockey team. While the school rules stated any team which did not have both a men's and a women's side had to consider players of the opposite sex, almost nobody actually ever used the rule. Probably why it was still around. Each year, staying on the team was an uphill battle. Now that I made it to varsity, I had to make sure they had no reason to get rid of me. Freshman year without my friends was a nightmare.

Flicking on the lights, Mike headed to get the rink ready for their actual opening while I went through the women's locker room, turning on the lights and doing a quick survey to make sure everything was in order for opening before heading toward the closest rink. Dropping my gear on one of the benches, I couldn't help but wish the women's side had more lockers. Figure skaters and the younger girls' teams took the bulk, so only shorter term were available, and while Mike wouldn't care if I ditched my equipment in one longer than the couple hours I used for games and practices, it didn't feel right. Besides, my gym locker was big enough to store my gear during the day. I didn't have much time before school and getting Mike to wake up daily at six-thirty in the morning was hard enough when the first lessons didn't otherwise start until after nine.

Skates on, I headed onto the ice. I did my handling drills before bed. Mornings were for sprints. Biking warmed me up, so I went straight into racing across the ice. Short side to side first followed by the long ways. If I could get from a defensive position to the opposite goal faster than the other players, I had a better chance of actually having the puck during the game. None of the guys would avoid passing to me if necessary, but when they thought of who could get them out of a pinch, I wasn't their first choice unless I was the one right in their faces - but that was last year. This year should've been like middle school. Sean, Geoffrey, and Ryan liked me well enough. Sean and Geoffrey were my best friends, and Ryan was nice to everybody. Maybe Ryan being the captain this year would change things. He was two years older than the three of us, but if Ryan welcomed me in like usual, maybe everybody else would too.

"You've got school!" Mike yelled. "You're old man will blame me if you're late."

Gliding back to him, I let the chill of the rink settle over me. "P.E. first period anyway."

He rolled his eyes. They flashed white like he was possessed for a moment before he rubbed the base of his nose. It was always a gamble. The more exhausted he was, the less likely it was I'd get lectured for overworking myself. Time didn't stretch on infinitely. Finite, I had to grab it and hold tight. Every minute needed to matter.

"If you underperform at your first varsity practice, nobody's gonna take you seriously." Mike walked away with a wave before I could reply.

Still, I grumbled, "I won't underperform."

Tall as my teammates, if not taller, I had trained for endurance from my first time on the ice. Speed and strength mattered, but too tall and too big, I had those naturally. Endurance mattered. While everybody else ended practices in puddles, I had to be capable of going twice as long. Besides, if I didn't practice as much as usual, my hands got twitchy. Anxious and filled with too much energy, leaving me a clumsy mess more likely to cause a pile up when going to slam my opponent into the boards. Pile ups with blades on feet were never a good idea.

Port Edmond Public High School stood two blocks and all downhill from the rink. Cliffs and beaches made up Port Edmond, so when old folks complained about walking uphill both ways, everyone just laughed because there wasn't anybody in Edmond who didn't have to do that. Even the private school kids at St. Raphael's

Academy had to go uphill. Probably the point of building it on one of the highest points in the area. - so they could walk uphill and look down their noses at the rest of us. Least, that's what Brandon used to say.

Buses rumbled down the street, heading toward the front, but I guided my bike around the side where the racks stood by the stairs which led up to the hall between the science hall and the gyms. Some walkers mulled about with their cells in their hands, but they left enough room on the sidewalk for me to slide right up into place.

"Beni!" My name burst through the noise as Sean half-leapt down the stairs at me. Geoffrey - as usual - followed behind him.

"Hey, Sean."

Leaning against the rails, he grinned like the Cheshire Cat. "First day on varsity! Are you excited?"

I clicked the lock on my bike, and the gap between his question and my move to answer was just long enough that Geoffrey answered instead, "She'd probably be more excited if she had been brought up with the rest of us - when she should have been in the first place."

"Coach Carr is a jerk." Sean nodded sagely.

I shrugged. Complaining wouldn't change it. "I'm on the team now."

For each step I took, Sean took two. Even with that, he barely reached my height. Geoffrey never seemed to care, but he was taller than Sean, and it always seemed like everybody was fine being shorter as long as they weren't the shortest one in the group. Unlike a lot of guys, Sean - for all his jumping on stairs and stretching as tall as possible whenever standing next to me - hadn't ever turned his problem with my height back around on me, so I kept my regular slouch. Saving that inch or two for when someone tried to use me as fodder for their wheezing ego probably wasn't the nicest thing to do, but a few inches also seemed to make me less intimidating so it was a win-win.

As we mulled through the quickly filling halls, Sean rambled on about how much I'd enjoy being on varsity. All the while, he kept his shoulders back and chest up. Each step bounced on his toes.

"Are you hitting your locker before gym?" Geoffrey asked when we reached a split in the halls. When I nodded, he stepped back, sidling around from my left to stand with Sean. "See you in the weight room then."

"Coach Maglione has the girls on basketball while you guys do weight lifting," I said.

Sean snorted. "She won't care if you ditch with us."

Shaking my head, I reminded him, "First day on varsity. Not really the time to make waves."

"I guess, but it's not like Coach Carr is a gym teacher. He's history. If Maglione is cool with it, it'll be fine. Besides, first period for guys is Coach Doug. He's like - what - two years out of school? Whatever Maglione says goes," Geoffrey argued, and honestly, the idea tempted me.

"I'll ask."

Cheering, Sean beamed. "O'Connor bet me five bucks the football guys in first could outlift the hockey." Moonwalking toward the gym, he sang, "We're gonna crush him!"

Geoffrey shook his head, but with a wave, he trailed after Sean, leaving me to fight my way upstream through the busy halls to my locker. Taller than most by almost a head, it wasn't that hard to navigate. People darted around me. Even with their faces in their phones or half-turned to speak to their friends, I wasn't an easy person to miss.

When I got to the gym, Maglione frowned when I jogged over to her with my hockey bag still on my shoulder. "Early morning practice, Beni?"

"Yeah, and I was hoping you wouldn't mind me joining the guy's class today?" I asked, and the few girls mulling around the gymnasium, stretching out before class or feigning stretches, snickered.

9

"If Beni gets to go to weights, can I?" Emily Baker called.

Maglione scoffed. "Beni'll actually participate."

"I participate!" Emily retorted, but her boots, skirt, and still in place jewelry said she had no intention of participating whether with the girls or guys side. "Anyway, it's not fair if you let Beni go and not any of the rest of us!"

"If anyone else wants to go, is dressed appropriately for gym, and is willing to have Coach De Monte sign off on their circuit completion, then they can go." Maglione didn't even bother to look up from her clipboard as she spoke, but I tugged out my notebook and a pencil.

"Thanks, Coach."

"They're doing a deadlift contest today. Show them what a woman can do, Ms. Seaver," she commanded, and with a quick smile, I ducked into the locker room, tossing my bag into my locker before jogging over to the weight room.

Sean waited with Geoffrey and Thomas. O'Connor and his crew stretched, flexing and punching each other as they taunted the trio of hockey players in their midst. Thomas was still junior varsity, but he apparently counted, which didn't mean much. Fast with high endurance - his talents would've only been useful in a run. In the weight room, we could probably all deadlift him without blinking.

"Hey, Coach Doug," I greeted.

Dark haired with the sort of chocolate brown eyes and tan skin girls used to pale and light eyes swooned over, Coach Doug De Monte hadn't been in Port Edmond long. The rare out-of-towner who moved into the area, he'd shown up from the city with his certificates and a southern drawl. When he helped out with the girl's soccer team, all the other women's side sports were jealous. Despite his face, he took his job seriously, and he'd never made a comment on how tall I was or how much bigger I was than the other girls, so he was fine by me.

"Morning, Beni, Maglione let you join our side today then?" he asked, and when I nodded, he grinned. "Good. You might actually be able to make Kevin actually work for it."

That left me a bit less than pleased. Not that I would say anything, but when my expression smoothed to a frown, Sean bopped over, smacking me on the back with another of his too toothy grins.

"Might?" he scoffed. "Beni's gonna kick O'Connor's ass!"

"Like a girl's gonna beat me!" the footballer in question roared. He had his sneer firmly in place, but he eyed me like he did whenever I walked into the room in the gym. "Can't believe hockey needs to bring in a girl to help them win."

"Well, Thomas beat your guys at the mile. Beni and I out-swam your lot. Sean took home the win on pull-ups. Pretty sure we've been running circles around you," Geoffrey counted out the victories on his fingers. "Oh, and our soccer team won against yours, but - I mean, we did have Andy Gibbs and Malcolm who are the star forwards, so..."

"Ugh, shut up, Statham," O'Connor grumbled.

"Yeah," one of his teammates - wide receiver by the name of Henry - said. "Put all that hot air into lifting. We're gonna destroy you!"

"While I appreciate the enthusiasm, keep your language clean!" Couch Doug commanded, and as the rest of the class went about their circuits, he set the two sides up where he'd prepped an area of the weight room for deadlifts. "Anyone does improper form, they're out. Nobody's leaving here injured, got it?"

"Yes, sir," we said in unison.

One by one, we lifted. Each rise in the weight shifted the order until Thomas was the first out, followed by Sean and then Henry. We kept going until we reached one hundred and eighty pounds with only O'Connor and I left. At two hundred, he huffed with a glare. By two-fifty,

Coach watched us nervously, and Sean - sent off to do his circuits - froze in place with two uneven free weights in his hands.

"Might as well quit while you're ahead, Seaver. You might be a beast, but you can't keep up with me," O'Connor jeered.

"Jump to three hundred?" I offered instead.

Couch Doug frowned, glancing between the two of us. "Either of you lift that high before?"

"Yes," we both replied, but he crossed his arms.

"You two have kept good form, but class is over in ten. I'm not having one of you walk out of here with an injury." His eyes slid to me. "And you just made varsity, Beni. Nobody here should be risking injury just to pad their egoes, or you'll end up kicked off your team."

"I can lift three hundred," I retorted, but he kept on frowning.

"I think I'll call it a draw. Stretch it out and clean up," he ordered. Before either of us could argue, he headed down the length of the gym to correct another student's form.

Kicking the wall, O'Connor huffed, "Don't think this means anything. Coach Doug saved you today."

"Whatever."

His eyes narrowed at my dismissal. If he intended to start up a fight, I wouldn't stop him, but Mike and Couch Doug kept repeating how it was my first varsity practice today - first official one at least, so I had to keep my nose clean. Whatever he thought, O'Connor stormed off, leaving me to put back the weights as the rest of the guys had been kicked off to do circuits when they had dropped out of the contest.

Dropping his free weights back into place, Sean jogged over to help. "Plus side, we didn't lose."

"Why does everyone think I'm going to screw up practice today?" I mumbled as I put the bar back into place.

"You've never messed up a practice." Nose wrinkling, he scratched the back of his head. "And who is 'everyone?'"

"Mike, this morning. Coach Doug just then. My dad. First thing he said was congratulations, then he warned me not to be surprised if Coach Carr knocked me back to J.V. for the stupidest reason." I rolled my shoulders half in a shrug and half to stretch out my muscles. "You don't think he'll do that, right?"

"Coach Carr? Nah. That guy likes winning too much."

"And he doesn't bring people up lightly," Geoffrey added, joining us at the end of the weight room. "If he brought you up, you'd have to do something really embarrassing for him to admit he overestimated you."

"Time to hit the showers!" Coach Doug called, and with a grateful smile aimed their way, I headed out to the girl's locker room.

Chapter Two

"Again!" Coach Carr bellowed.

His voice echoed across the rink as we raced across the ice, sprinting as if our lives depended upon it. Stopwatch in hand, he waited until the last person crossed the finish line to click his tongue against his teeth. Sean took the first couple. Focusing on him helped, but by the fifth go, Sean's endurance faltered, leaving Ryan and me to compete for the prime spot. Not knowing how long this would go on, I stuck to Ryan's pacing. He wasn't competitive enough with his own teammates to try to exhaust himself to be first. Probably why the guys made him captain. The most handsome and popular guy on the team - Ryan just had that sort of feel about him. He made me feel special. No matter how many times the other players used to bully me, he treated me like somebody worth knowing.

Shoving his stopwatch into his pocket, Carr sneered, "Is that all you've got? I've seen PeeWees go faster than this! I see I'm gonna have to whip you all into shape again this year." His eyes slid to Sean. "Galliger, you're in charge of morning runs this season. Fast means nothing without endurance!" He called out a list of names who would be joining Sean. "If I trusted any of you to do this on your own, I wouldn't have to listen to your groaning," he shouted, cutting any grumbling before it could even start.

Drills followed. Nobody had time to cause trouble for me, and as long as I kept my head down, Carr didn't need to think of me as anything else but another annoying teen for him to get to Nationals. By the end, when we scrimmaged, I believed I had managed my first varsity practice without issue.

Charging toward goal, I passed to Sean, and having recovered a bit, he wove between the other players, but for all his speed, Ryan caught up to him. I struggled to get open, but Andre - Ryan's best friend and probably the best player on our team - kept on top of me the entire time.

Even behind his mask, I could see his smirk. With his golden curls and bright blue eyes, he might have been Michaelangelo's vision of the perfect angel. His personality was more like Satan. Every good quality in Ryan found its inverse in Andre. Ryan continuously offered other's help while Andre taunted them for their mistakes. When complimented, Ryan would dismiss his talents, turning the conversation around to talk about something the other person had done well. Andre loved talking about himself. Half of what I heard from him involved him praising his own abilities. The other half involved jokes about how I looked like a guy - or a giant.

"You know, we've got a bet going," Andre told me. I shoved him aside, but he glided right back into my path. "About how long Coach Carr'll keep you on the team."

Anything I said would get turned back around on me. Speaking wasn't my strong suit. Especially in the moment. Silence worked best. On the rare chance I had a good one-liner ready to go, odds were the situation had happened so many times I had no choice but to think it over to the point of creating a response. Determined not to screw up, I focused on the scrimmage.

Then Coach Carr roared my name: "Seaver! Stop dancing with Page! You're a head taller! Smash him into the boards!"

So I did. Ducking, I pulled my elbow into my side and slammed my full weight into his chest. Andre stumbled, falling backwards. I raced to get into position where Sean could pass me the puck, but before I could get there, Ryan had out-maneuvered and outlasted Sean, stealing the puck and rushing our goal. As the puck glided into the net, Coach blew his whistle, and that was it.

"Hit the showers!" he commanded. Pointing at me, he added, "Seaver, get over here!"

Skating over to him, I removed my helmet. "Yes, coach?"

"You're big." Not exactly what I was hoping to hear, but not nearly as bad as I had thought. "Someone gets up in your face - slam 'em. If they can't handle getting hit by you, they shouldn't be on this team. I don't give a shit if you end up in the penalty box. Be a beast. Got it?"

"Yes, sir."

He gave a sharp nod. "Hit the locker room."

In a daze, I glided away toward the women's locker. I had done it. Hungry and tired - undoubtedly going to be sore in the morning - I hadn't screwed up. Despite Andre's jeering, nobody had done anything or said anything horrible. Maybe my thoughts leaned too negative. I had made varsity. They saw how well I could play, and it wasn't like this was my first year skating with any of them. Coming up from PeeWee hockey, I had been on the rink since I was five. Eleven years with me - they had to be bored with being jerks.

Showered and dressed, I chucked my bag over my shoulders and headed out. Sean and Geoffrey waited. Both glanced at me then at each other, and dread pooled in my gut.

"What?" I asked.

Forcing a grin, Sean held his hand out for a high five. "You rocked it! I seriously thought Andre was gonna puke. He complained about his side the whole time we were in the showers."

"Probably still complaining about it," Geoffrey added.

"He's already got a bet going. Not like Ryan'll let him do anything too bad," I said.

Sean pursed his lips. "Yeah…"

My shoulders slumped. "What?"

"Somebody cut your bike's tires," Geoffrey informed me.

Cut tires. I could handle that. As long as I could get the bike home, I could probably patch them. If not, I'd work a few extra shifts for Mike or helping the neighbors. Tires were fine.

"Okay." I nodded. "Mind if I catch a ride with one of you?"

"My mom's bringing the bike rack." Sean's nose wrinkled. "They also spray-painted it neon pink."

"Seriously?" The word left my mouth before I could catch myself. Taking a deep breath, I shook my head. "Pink's fine. It's just a color. As long as they didn't cut the brakes or screw with the chain, I can live with a pink bike once I get the tires fixed."

Patting me on the back, Geoffrey headed toward the front where my maimed and newly painted bike sat. They had managed not just to spray paint the bike. Half the bike stand was pink. Some of the sidewalk too. It streaked across the wheels, and while it was bright enough to give me a headache, I didn't mind pink. My skin seemed splotchy if I wore it, but on a bike, pink failed to matter.

Somebody had punctured both tires, but they jabbed them rather than sliced, so the cuts were small. My dad had stuff to repair his car's tires in the garage. More than likely, bike tires worked the same. No chain damage. My breaklines were intact. Probably have to wait a day or two to be certain the tires had set, but I could run to school rather than bike. Mike would be happy. No early wake-up call tomorrow.

"It's still wet, isn't it?" Like an idiot, I reached out and touched it. Yep, still wet. "I'll talk to Mike. I don't want your mom's bike rack getting ruined."

Sean shrugged. "Don't think she'll care."

"If you leave it, somebody might steal it," Geoffrey suggested, but the corner of his lip curled at the sight of it. Nobody would want a damaged, vandalized bike.

I shrugged. "It's fine. I've got to tell Mike I can't come early until it's fixed anyway."

Jogging back inside, I headed over to the front counter. Mike leaned on his elbows, speaking in a low voice to two guys about my age. Both had golden blond hair - darker than Andre's. One was about my height. The other sat in a wheelchair, so I didn't have a good idea how tall he'd be, but while the first one kept a bored expression - flat line of the mouth and glazed look in the eyes, the guy in the wheelchair smiled brightly.

"Not that I don't adore being near my brother," he told Mike, "but I could get a better view of the game from higher up in the stands."

Mike hummed. "That seems like a lot of effort."

"And your alternatives seem like a lawsuit waiting to happen," the meaner looking one snapped.

"Hey now, Richie Rich, not all of us have our daddies paving the way. I'm out here in the cold cruel world of capitalism," Mike complained - despite his massive trust fund and his inherited chain of apartment complexes. "Couldn't your old man pay for a ramp to be added? Though having it done during the season might be bad. You should've brought it up sooner."

Narrowing his eyes, the mean one drawled, "Unfortunately, our rich daddy wasn't thrilled with the idea of his recently released from the hospital son coming to a chilly rink when he'd just woken from a coma."

"Man, that was too easy." Slapping the counter, Mike stood up, grinning in my direction before confessing, "I just wanted to hear you say 'rich daddy.' I've already got Jim working out how to add a ramp in the staff hall, so both rink's upper seats can be reached. Glad to see you out and about, Tanner."

The guy in the wheelchair, Tanner, shook his head. "You're going to give Jackson a heart attack one of these days."

Both Tanner and Mike chuckled, but the meaner of the two, Jackson, scoffed. "Practice starts in ten. You going to laugh with your friend here? Or are you coming with me?"

Tanner shrugged. "If I stay here, I can guilt Mike into giving me free food."

"Bull - I'm building you a ramp. My conscience is clean. Not like I'm the jerk who ran you over." Mike stepped toward me. "What's up, Beni?"

Gesturing with my thumb over my shoulder, I opened my mouth to explain, but Jackson cut me off, slamming his fist against the counter. "What did you say?"

"Oh, drop it. If I can't joke about it, what's the point of my fractured spine?" Tanner cheerfully asked.

"It's not a joke," Jackson growled. His eyes slid to me. "Shit - you're a girl."

In sweatpants and a hoodie once more, I understood his confusion. Or more correctly, so many had said the exact same followed by some variant of 'you're huge' that I didn't find any reason to respond.

"Somebody punctured my tires and spray-painted my bike. Mind if I leave it here and pick it up after school tomorrow?" I cringed as the rest of the disaster came into mind. "I'll help clean the rack and sidewalk too."

With his usual nonchalance, Mike released a long drawn out sigh that verged on a yawn. "Does this mean I can sleep in tomorrow?"

"Yeah. Maybe longer. I don't know how much work it'll be to fix the tires." An itching feeling tickled at the side of my head, and when I glanced over, both guys were still there. Hands folded in his lap, Tanner looked up at what I could only assume was his twin with a smirk. Jackson stared at me as if I were a bruise he couldn't remember getting. "Anyway, I'm getting a ride with Sean, so I'll let you know."

"Sure, sure!" Mike waved me off.

As I turned to go, Jackson grumbled, "You're a girl."

Part of me wanted to say 'yeah, and what of it?' The other part just wanted to go home. Dad would ask about the bike, and I'd get another rant on how disappointed he was in our education system, how Mike wasn't a responsible owner and should have cameras outside to catch these sorts of things when they happen, and how no matter what I do the universe screwed people like us over. Winter always made him tense. Any time he couldn't spend the majority of the day on the water left him off kilter, so maybe if I rushed home, he wouldn't realize I didn't have my bike.

Per usual, I listened to common sense, leaving the two golden boys at the front desk. Sean's mom had pulled up. No sense making her wait longer than necessary.

Chapter Three

By our traditional pre-season game against
the Lions, I had patched my tires two more times.
Andre kept his jeers to himself, so that was an
improvement. The Lions were local legends. They
played for one of the local private schools. We had
three in the area: girls, boys, and co-ed. Only the
boys had a varsity ice hockey team. Girls and co-ed
stopped in middle school. Which made it all the
more embarrassing that I hadn't recognized Jackson
Duke. Duke led St. Raphael's Academy to
Nationals every year he'd been on the team. Not
that they had been doing poorly before then. They
went more often than not, but two years earlier, they
had to fight for it against our school. They were
Division 1 North while we were Division 1 South.
The two schools closest to each other on either side
of the line. Win or lose, the traditional pre-season
game only counted for ego.

The crimson and gold of the St. Raphael
Lions' uniforms weren't the only thing that set them
apart from our blue and gray. Rumors said they
boarded, but true or not, most of their students were
from summer folks who maintained homes up here
that stayed empty during the majority of the school
year. They recruited our best members too. More
than once, they had come around asking about

Andre and Ryan, but Ryan's family - rich as they were - had a thing about privilege. A belief that private school made a man soft, and if Ryan didn't go, Andre wasn't going either. Although he was a jerk, he was a loyal friend.

Jackson's team also used the rink right after us, and he reserved the rink - just for him - in the half-hour before, which meant every time I had to stay late to handle my bike issues, he and his brother were around, pushing about the ramp because Mike's contractor buddies didn't moving fast enough. Neither of them spoke to me, but Jackson gave me those same looks. The *you're a girl* sort of looks. They said enough.

In their crimson and gold, Duke and his teammates wove across the ice.

"Freaking pricks," Lincoln grumbled.

Shuffling on the bench, the rest of the team shifted - restless as the two teams slid into formation. Victor took center with Sean gliding to his right and Kendall on his left. With Geoffrey as right defenseman and Derek in goal, the other new starter was our left defenseman - Joseph 'Joe' Dale. While the rest of the team had their game faces on - concentration and a rage built on two years of scoreless defeats, Joe grinned. His smile practically glowed beneath his helmet, and I couldn't help but feel happy for him even if I wanted to be on the ice too.

"Keep prepped," Coach commanded as the referee held the puck above Victor's and Jackson's crossed sticks. "Page, Caldwell, Seaver - you three are on next."

I nodded, keeping my eyes on the puck. In a collision of force, the deep inhalation as the puck dropped broke into a slicing clash of sticks and the crisp grating of ice beneath blades.

Victor never had a chance. Kendall had better stick work, but one-on-one against Jackson, Kendall wasn't even close to keeping up. On the ice, Jackson wasn't just a progeny. He was practically clairvoyant. If someone managed possession in the short amount of time he allowed the puck to remain with a teammate, Jackson flew like a fury to reclaim it. Dodging checks and guiding the puck back to his control, he was untouchable.

In his crimson jersey, he raced toward the goal. Even fully rested, Sean barely kept up, but he couldn't get his stick around to knock the puck away, and as small as Sean was, any attempt at checking would only send him flying.

"Get on him, Dale!" Coach roared.

And Joe tried. He stormed up as Geoffrey backed off to prep near the goal with Derek, but our only hope was Jackson passing, and his teamwork was his weakest skill. Unless he had to, he would keep the puck on him. Sean stayed to Jackson's left as Joe came up on his right, but the moment before the three collided, Jackson shifted his skates, slowing as Sean twisted only to have Joe barrel right into him while Jackson sent his first shot straight at goal.

Derek dropped, knocking the puck back off his pads to Geoffrey, who passed it along to Andre as Sean disentangled from Joe. A player with a gold BAKER on the back of his jersey checked Geoffrey, but he had managed to get a clean pass to Kendall who headed back toward the opposite team's side.

"Minute in, nobody's scored. That's an improvement," Lincoln said, but he wrung his hands, twisting them around his stick, and like a curse, Jackson swept the puck.

Passing up to Baker when Victor and Sean blockaded him, Jackson raced into position to receive it back, and before we passed the second minute mark - the St. Raphael Lions scored. Their entire bench pumped their fists. Chanting 'Duke, Duke, Duke,' they finished with a double-tap of their sticks as the crowd - deck in their own crimson - screamed their support. At the very top of the stands, Tanner yelled the loudest. Despite the crowd, he was hard to miss with a painted face and their school's flag waving from where he'd attached it to the back of his wheelchair.

"Line switch! Move - move - move!" Coach Carr called.

All three of us pushed forward. The second they drew close, we flew out onto the ice, taking over. On the plus side, it was only one point. We still had time in the first period, and they had scored five in the first period last year.

I slid into position on Ryan's right. Across the ice, Baker blinked as if confused by me, but he didn't say anything. This round, Ryan cleared the puck to Andre. We headed into their end, and Baker fell behind as I glided up toward goal. As their defense blocked Ryan, he passed to Andre, but Jackson stole the puck. Like before, Jackson veered toward his left, heading down my area. However, while Sean had kept if not outpaced Jackson, I had held back as Andre and Ryan took the puck up, so a gap remained, letting me shift course. Speed hadn't worked to stop him, but an immovable object?

I blocked his route, keeping my body between him and the goal as our sticks tangled. Both struggled to get the puck, but remaining low, keeping my backward footwork strong, I slowed us enough for Ryan to come up alongside. His stick entered the fray, and Jackson couldn't keep pace with both of us on top of him. Given no choice, he could have passed backward, but Andre fielded Baker, and Geoffrey moved up to keep guard on the other forward. Well-trained instincts moved him, but he hadn't prepared to be blockaded.

And then I had the puck.

Ryan blocked Jackson from immediately chasing, and a few feet of space built between us. Their red jerseys flashed. They faded until my mind only saw them as traps to be avoided, and while they were the best team in the region, their traditional pre-season game stuck them against us for a reason.

Up the side, I charged. Andre raced, slowing only to keep from going offside before he sought to get into position for a pass and an attempt on goal, but Jackson Duke wasn't about to sit back.

When he slammed into me - shoving me up against the boards, adrenaline flooded my system, and I shifted my weight to push right back. We swerved. Serpentining from the boards away and back, dodging his teammates and mine. None of them could get close enough to get the puck. Each time I had it, Jackson prevented me from clearing it away. I managed to do the same, but the longer we remained locked together, the more certain I became that sooner or later, he'd be the one to clear the puck if left up to stick work alone.

Clenching my teeth, I didn't give myself time to debate. I caught his stick with mine, swinging us around to slam my shoulder into his chest. It wasn't a dirty hit. Even if the referees hadn't been right on our tails, they could have seen it was clean, but while Jackson had my height, he didn't have my bulk. Like Sean focused on speed, Jackson trained on twitch reflex - a mix of speed and technique. No matter how much I trained, brute force served as my natural leaning. I avoided it. Focused on technique everyday. I could outmaneuver most guys on my team, but Jackson - he was a league above. Which left me no choice but to check.

When he slammed into the boards, his eyes widened. I didn't wait to see if he dropped. Eyes forward. Everything zoomed in on the goal. Before I could even process what had happened, a snapshot flicked the puck. A buzz sounded. I had scored! The whole bench cheered.

Geoffrey crowed. "Way to go, Beni!"

Gliding alongside me, Ryan held up his glove for a high five. "First goal of the game!"

A whistle blew, and all eyes turned to the sound. My last hit hadn't been against the boards. Even if Jackson managed to skirt the issue when he slammed me, I didn't want to risk the same. We had enough tension getting stuck together that long without some sort of penalty being called. But the whistle wasn't for a penalty. I hadn't looked back, but Jackson hadn't gotten back up. He waved away his teammates, but every moment had him wrapping his arms around his chest, grabbing at his padding.

"Shit. How hard did you hit him?" Geoffrey asked.

Shoving my head down, Ryan pushed me back toward our side. "He's just stunned. Been a while say anybody checked the Duke."

A whistle blew. The referee signaled time out, and a flurry of panic took over as we glided to the bench. Our eyes shifted between each other and Jackson. Baker stood beside him, offering a hand, but Jackson waved him away for a moment until the other forward - Williamson - joined them.

"Beni," Sean called, holding out my water bottle. "He's fine."

Shoving up my helmet, I let it balance on my head as I drank. "I didn't think I hit him that hard."

"He's exaggerating. Probably wants a penalty," Geoffrey assured me.

Andre hummed softly. His lips curved up. "Not bad, Seaver."

Elbowing his best friend, Ryan laughed. "We're tied up. Haven't managed a score in the first period in the last three years against the Lions."

"Odds are Duke won't stay down long," Coach drawled. "They've built their offense around him, and they haven't switched their defense line yet this period."

He paused. His eyes leapt to the clock where the time out was counting down before dropping to where Jackson skated off the ice. The moment he entered his bench, a crowd fussed over him. Up in the stands, his brother shifted, rolling this way and that as if debating charging right down the stairs and crashing to get to his brother. Nobody on his side seemed to notice.

"Get that second goal!" Coach Carr commanded.

As I headed back into position, I waved to my dad to catch his attention. All it took was a gesture toward the opposite side, and he gave a curt nod, heading up to help. With that taken care of, my head returned to the game.

Playing the Lions without Jackson was like playing a completely different team - a good team but one with an entirely new gameplan. They knew how to work together. Offense - when they got the puck - handled it well. Their defense fell short, but every team had its weakness, and if they had been going up against any other team, they wouldn't have been bad at all. But Coach hadn't been exaggerating. They built their team around Jackson.

Even if they knew the moves without him, they had two years without needing to use them in a game. Still - they worked well enough for it to take until two minutes to the end of the period to score.

"Andre!" Ryan cheered.

Bumping gloves in celebration with his best friend, Andre twirled across the ice before sliding into the bench as Sean switched in for him. "We've got time for you to get one next time we're in."

Smacking me on the back as he passed, Andre added, "Or are Seaver and I carrying you this game?"

Ryan rolled his eyes as he jumped the boards, switching out, so Victor could take the ice flanked by Sean and Kendall. Movement from the Lions' bench caught my eye. My dad stood with Tanner. Jackson sat, leaning against the side of the bench, but Tanner seemed far less worried than before, but what really caught my attention was Ariadne. In a bright blue dress and leggings, she sat on the bleacher closest to Tanner's chair. Her hand rested on his shoulder. Unlike her brother, Andre, Ariadne was a genuinely good person. Popular, beautiful, smart - more often than I cared to admit, I thought about how much easier my life would be if I were more like her. So, her helping my dad and Tanner made sense, but the way she leaned in -

something itched in my mind. A stupid sort of protest. She was Ryan's girlfriend.

Which was ridiculous. Her being his girlfriend didn't prevent her from helping someone else or caring about another person's wellbeing. That was just my own envy. Ducking my head, I ground my teeth, determined to shove the thought right out of my head. Scoring had Andre being nice to me. Maybe if we won the game, my bike would be safe.

Chapter Four

Ryan never scored a goal. We won regardless. Everyone screamed, surrounding Andre and chanting before they headed back into the locker room - and I into another. I couldn't hear the chanting. Back in sweatpants after a shower, I debated rushing out, but the idea of being out there - waiting while they celebrated in the guy's locker room caused my stomach to curl into knots. Growling, I shoved my gear into my bag, slamming the locker shut. Nobody got anywhere being a coward.

"Beni!" My dad wrapped his arms around me, pulling me into a tight hug before I could get two feet out of the women's locker room. "Tied the game up! That's my girl!" he shifted as if trying to ruffle my hair before realizing what he was doing. "Come on. Where do you want to eat? Anywhere you want. My treat!" Before I could reply, he backed away, tapping his forehead with the heel of his hand. "What am I saying? Team's probably going out to eat to celebrate."

"I don't - "

Pulling out his wallet, he pulled out a couple of bills, handing them to me even as I refused. "Here! I know it's not a school night, but I want you back by ten."

"What? Dad - "

He didn't give me any time to refuse. Patting me on the back, my dad pointed over to the guy's locker room. Sean and Geoffrey came out with their bags over their shoulders. Jumping around - pumping his fists in the air, Sean chatted animatedly before his eyes caught sight of my dad and me.

"Beni! We are the champions!" Sean bellowed. Running over, he launched himself at me. An arm wrapped around me as he rocked side to side. "You should hear it. Coach kept talking you up - 'Seaver took Duke out of the game. Seaver saved the day.'"

"'You idiots needed a girl to win a game,'" Geoffrey mumbled, scuffing his foot against the floor.

Dad frowned, setting his hands on his hips. "Meaning he made my daughter's life harder? Fantastic. Where's that son-of-a..."

The rest of my high school life flashed before my eyes. Coach Carr used me as both the carrot and the stick. Pushing us to band together as a team only for every success I had to be used as a tool to flog them. My dad would have a heart attack. Grabbing his arm, I stopped him in his tracks.

"Dad! It's fine. Geoff's just kidding," I said.

Sean grinned, knocking elbows with Geoffrey. "Yeah - even Andre talked about how we're guaranteed to go to Nationals this year."

"'I finally have someone decent to work with.'" Geoffrey said with air quotes.

Still frowning, my dad sighed. "Fine." Looking toward me, he let his arms fall to his side. "So you kids are all going out to eat?"

"Yeah, whenever we win, we hit up Charlie's." Sean beamed.

Nodding, he pointed to me. "Ten, Beni. Not a minute later."

"Yes, sir."

With a pat to my shoulder, he headed toward the door, leaving me behind as the rest of the team started to come out. When he vanished into the crowd, Sean deflated, "Man, did you have to?"

Geoffrey just shrugged. "We're heading over to Charlie's with Lincoln. Derek's driving."

If I wanted to smash my ego, I would've asked where everyone else was going. Instead, I nodded. "Sure. Sounds good."

"Derek takes long showers, and I'm hungry. Anybody else up for nachos to pre-game burgers?" Sean called, already racing off to the concession stand before Geoffrey or I could reply.

"I swear. Hollow leg," Geoffrey huffed.

As we trudged after Sean, I scanned the rink. My eyes immediately caught on Tanner. He parked at a table next to Jackson - already showered and dressed in casual clothes. His golden hair - darkened by water - dripped onto his henley. Dressed in a suit, an older man sat next to Jackson. Like both brothers, the man had blonde hair and a Disney prince jawline.

"I'm fine!" Jackson raged, but he winced when he shoved his chair back.

The man, probably their father, scoffed. "You likely have multiple rib fractures. Do you know how long those will take to heal?" He adjusted his suit jacket, glaring down at the chairs and the table. "I'm parked out front. We're not talking about this here. Get moving."

"About that…" Tanner dragged out his words, glancing between his father and his brother. "I'm feeling peckish. We've got - what? A half hour drive back home?"

His dad stood - keys already in hand. "You'll be fine."

Tanner rolled his eyes, unlocking the break on his wheelchair. Backing up, he swiveled around toward the concession stand, nearly bumping into Sean who dodged around with his nachos as Geoffrey collapsed back into a seat at one of the tables. The quick dodge, unfortunately, drew

Tanner's attention our way. His eyes widened. Glancing back to his dad then to me, he quickly shifted course.

"You know what? You're right. I'm good. Let's head - "

"You!" Their father pointed at me. Stalking towards us, he demanded, "Are you Beni Seaver?"

Turning invisible wasn't a possibility. "Yes?"

"A girl? On a men's hockey team?" His lip curled as he studied me.

Chomping away on nachos, Sean snorted. "Yeah. You gotta problem with that?"

"Dad! Just leave it," Jackson growled.

He shoved back from the table, wincing. Gritting his teeth, Jackson reached for his bag when Tanner slapped his hand away, pulling it up onto his lap. The two brothers stared off, but their father continued to glare down at me as if I should explode for having dared to check his son.

"Yes. I am a woman on my school's only hockey team. It's completely within regulations - as was the hit I landed on your son." Staring him down, I kept my face as blank as possible as I added, "Any other questions?"

With a scoff, he grabbed the bag off Tanner's lap and stormed out the front. Jackson followed quickly after, but Tanner paused as he glided by our table.

"Probably not the best choice, but you've got balls." He tilted his head back. His sparkling white teeth flashed. "I like you." And with that, he rolled away.

Chapter Five

"He's back," Geoffrey said.

Weaving around me, he gestured up to the high stand on the opposite side of the rink. Sure enough - for the second practice in a row, Tanner sat up on his high row, watching our practice from his perch.

"Didn't Coach kick him out last time?" Lincoln grumbled. "Why is he even trying? We don't officially play against them until States, right?"

Up in the stands, Tanner grinned. Likely having caught that we were watching him. Raising a hand, he wiggled his gloved fingers.

Huffing, I slid the puck back and forth from side to side. "Just leave it."

"Ah - seriously? He's back?" Ryan skidded to a stop right across from me. Tilting up his helmet, he panted. His broad chest heaving as he stared up at Tanner - who did his mocking finger wave again. "Sheesh - he's gonna get into trouble if he keeps this up."

"Maybe he's plotting revenge!" Sean suggested.

Ryan snorted - somehow managing to make the expression both dismissive and graceful as he ended it on a broad grin. "Tanner? Revenge? Yeah - I doubt Beni's on the top of his list."

"Who knows? Who cares?" Andre drawled, knocking his shoulder into Ryan's. "If he doesn't want his special little ramp covered in tacks, he needs to stop coming."

Of course, Andre's solution was violence. If Ryan decided to ditch the public school for St. Raphael's, Andre would've left us all behind in a heartbeat, but for now, he could sneer and mock anyone and everyone involved.

Still, Andre's animosity seemed to inspire Joe. He charged to the opposite side of the rink, yelling, "Hey! Dickweed! Get lost!"

Tanner tilted up his chin. The same move both he and his father seem to go to when they wanted to look down their noses at people. He raised both hands, offering Joe the bird twice over.

"Yeah, that'll end well," Geoffrey grumbled.

Tearing off his gloves, Joe slammed them down on the ice. "Oh, that's it!"

Joe tugged open the door, climbing into the opposing team's bench. He raced, sliding and stumbling as he stormed after Tanner, who stayed where he sat. Joe's skates and padding caught him up, leaving him falling flat on his face more often than not. Tanner calmly watched.

"Joe!" Ryan called. "Leave him alone!"

"Should we get Coach?" Sean asked, but Coach Carr stood by the goal with Derek and Matthieu - our other goalie. He hadn't even glanced up to see what the noise was all about, so odds were he expected Ryan to deal with it as captain.

Geoffrey snorted. He didn't manage to make it look nearly as cool as Ryan had. "Joe practically did the same yesterday."

"Then why's the idiot back?" Andre glowered. His eyes narrowed for a moment then a dawning expression of surprise grew on his face as Tanner waved at me again. "Oh! No way!"

"Crap, Joe's gonna give himself a concussion." Ryan raced off, neatly getting through the bench and up toward Joe without any mishaps.

Andre, however, smirked. "So...Beni? All grown up and flirting with boys?"

"What?" I sputtered.

Spinning to stand between Tanner and me, he gestured to Tanner with his thumb. "What? Is he a masochist? Saw you barrel over that dandy brother of his and just couldn't stay away?"

"He did say he liked her," Sean - the traitor - noted, rubbing his chin as he squinted up at Tanner. "Well, guess if he's got a crush, not like he'd do anything sketchy."

"Sketchy? How could he? Beni's a beast,"
Andre said. He patted my shoulder, but the gesture
wasn't friendly.

"Nothing is going on. He's screwing with
our heads," I grumbled, shrugging off his hand.
"Come on. Ryan has Joe. If Coach cared, he'd have
said something already."

"What are you idiots gawking at? Sprints!
Now!" Coach bellowed as if to emphasize how right
I was. His usual glower turned to Joe, who Ryan
had by the collar. "Captain, keep your players on
the ice! You're wasting my time!"

"Yes, sir!" Ryan called.

***

Slinging my bag over my shoulder, I
groaned. Couch had run us into the ground. From
heel to hip, my legs ached. Practice tomorrow
morning balanced on the edge of the table, and that
was before I considered the bike ride home. Gritting
my teeth, I leaned back and forth. My hip popped.
Stretching, I shook off my shoulders before shoving
the door open.

"No." The word jumped out of my mouth
before I could stop it.

Sitting there - apparently waiting for me -
Tanner smiled. "Hey, Beni!"

I wanted to tell him I couldn't deal with whatever plot he had. There was no way he liked me. Not in the way Andre thought. Liked the way I didn't let his jerk of a dad give me crap - sure. Thought my skills on the ice were decent - probably. Enjoyed my reactions - maybe even thought they were entertaining, maybe. Liked me? I was almost six foot. I hand an inch on his brother. Some guys liked tall girls, but liking tall girls didn't mean they liked me. I lived in jeans and sweats. Not the sporty, athletic model type either. I aimed toward baggy.

Gritting my teeth, I kept my head down and headed toward the bike rack. Tanner spun his wheels, easily keeping up with me. "Just - stop."

He cocked a brow. "Not that watching you practice isn't entertaining. I've started a betting pool on how long it'll take for that buzz cut defenseman to get up the stairs - "

"Joe Dale."

"Joe Dale? Huh - not the name I'd've imagined. Looked like a Richard - ya know, a -"

Throwing open the door, I let it slam behind me, cutting him off. He could hit the button, but it gave me just enough time to get through the second set. Unfortunately, the bike rack stood empty. My bag dropped off my shoulder onto the ground. Biking home would've been bad enough. Walking?

"Well that sucks for you."

Grimacing, I glanced over at Tanner who rolled up beside me. He flashed me a commercial white grin. The urge to punch him twisted in my gut, but it wasn't like he stole my bike. Well...

"No," he held up his hands, "I didn't do it."

Crossing my arms, I frowned. "I didn't accuse you of anything."

"Most people probably tell you that you've got a stone face, but your eyes are pretty expressive. Anyway, as I was saying, I thought you'd be interested to know why I was watching when I came the first day, but you just skedaddled off," Tanner explained. He folded his hands on his lap. "So - you good for us to talk now?"

"Okay - now I'm going to ask if you stole my bike."

Shaking his head, Tanner sighed. "I'm not that desperate."

"What exactly is this?" I asked.

"Me being a big enough man to ask for help. You see, a little over a year ago, these," he gestured down at his legs, "stopped working thanks to a lower lumbar spinal injury. I'm healing. Nerves still work. Long odds on me walking again without assistance. Definitely no future for me as an athlete anymore - not that I've ever had the chance anyways. Two left feet. I could do basics, but really, that's Jackson. Which is weird, really, considering."

Picking up my bag, I spun on my heels. Whatever he wanted to talk to me about, I wasn't dealing with whatever word vomit he intended to send my way. I had a lab I needed to finish. Plus, this was a late night. If I didn't cook, Dad would probably go to bed without eating anything.

"You know, I have a car!"

Spinning around, I frowned. "I'd be surprised. But your dad's loaded."

"Yeah, something about it being a therapy thing. This all happened due to a drunk driver, so...yeah, anyway. I have a car," he repeated. "Jackson's in practice for another hour. I can give you a ride?"

Walking seemed the best option. I had no reason to trust Tanner wouldn't do anything, or that he didn't have some weird ulterior motive. Actually, by all counts, I had no doubt he had an ulterior motive. His ranting just kept blocking me from figuring it out.

"Can I get a reason why first?"

He shrugged. "Really? Can't I just offer it out of the goodness of my heart? Do you know how boring it is to watch Jackson practice? The Lions? They're so predictable. Finally have something interesting. Of course I'm going to pick it over like a mad man. There's other girls in the league. Not a lot. None in New England except that one up in Maine, but I mean - it's Maine."

"You got a point somewhere in there?"

Digging his keys out of his pocket, he jangled them. "Have keys. Will drive. Friends?"

"Why?"

"Cause I think you're interesting. Because I'm bored out of my gourd. Come on."

He didn't bother waiting for my response. Instead, he rolled away, heading to the side of the nicest car in the lot. Sore and without my bike, I didn't have the ego to storm through the pain and walk home when a ride was available. Sean and Geoffrey had left. They both probably saw the empty bike rack and assumed I had already headed out. Even if Tanner tried something, I was bigger than him, and a least one camera had to have caught me leaving with him, so I followed.

"Chuck your bag in the trunk," he instructed, clicking the button on his key to pop the lid. As I did, he lifted himself into the car, folding his chair and sticking it into the back. "Come on, Seaver! Don't want your teammates to see you drive off with the enemy."

I rolled my eyes. "Not exactly the enemy."

Before my buckle even fully clicked, Tanner peeled out of the parking spot. "Where to?"

I gave him my address, telling him to turn right out of the lot. I expected chatter. He hadn't exactly struck me as a quiet car partner, but as he headed up the hill toward my house, he hummed along to the radio - upbeat popular pop hits - and kept his eyes on the road. All his controls - brakes and gas - were modified to be done by hand.

We were half-way to my house when he turned off the radio. "See, I can do companionable silence. Not that hard. So let's be friends."

"Didn't think people actually asked that."

"What? To be friends? It cuts to the chase. Life's short. Why waste time screwing around? I want to be friends. If you do too, we can cut to the chase and actually get some fun in before I'm off to MIT, and you head out to..." he trailed off, glancing my way, "Wisconsin? Madison has the best program, right? Maybe Boston? Yeah - probably Boston. It's only you and your dad, right?"

"Hopefully, yeah..."

"Boston College, Boston University, Northeastern...just a few choices, I suppose." I nodded, and he smiled, turning into my driveway. "Have you considered Harvard?" Before I could even respond - talk about how expensive it was and how unlikely it was they would be interested in someone who was a B student, he parked, turning his keen eyes onto me. "I'm going to MIT. If we're headed to the same city, might as well make some friends ahead of time."

Arguing with him didn't make sense. Tanner Duke came from stock that got their way, and if someone tried to stop him, his father could buy them off. He had enough money to buy the town a hundred times over, so anything I did to dissuade him would only push his interest more. My best bet for peace was to agree. Eventually, he would grow bored. Guys like him always did.

"Sure," I said, climbing out of the car. "Friends."

Flashing his pearly whites, he popped his trunk, waving to me after I grabbed my bag and headed past his window toward my front door. "See you tomorrow, friend."

And he flew out of my driveway like nothing in the world could hurt him.

Chapter Six

With my shoes in hand, I crept down the stairs, hoping not to wake my dad, so he wouldn't know I had to leave a half hour earlier to run to the rink. Wherever my bike had ended up, I had to get it back before he noticed. Best case, I could take an extra shift from Mike on the weekends and buy a new one before he realized what had happened. The last thing I needed was my dad demanding we go down to the police station and actually report what had happened. Odds were, whoever had taken it had either lawyers for parents (Andre) or enough money to bury us (anyone from St. Raphael's).

Easing the door shut behind me, I slipped on my shoes and slung my bags over either shoulder before ducking out from around the back and up along the side of the garage - where a car idled on the street. A grinning Tanner in the driver's seat as he waved.

"What are you doing here?" I hissed when he rolled his window down.

The blond shrugged. "No bike. Mike said you help him open. Thought you might like a ride."

"At the ass-crack of dawn," another voice grumbled from the back seat.

Tanner cringed. "Sorry. Had to bring the idiot."

"Had to?" Jackson scoffed, sitting up to glare at his brother. "If the beast gets early access to the ice, it's only fair if I do too."

Grinding my teeth, I managed to hold my tongue. A dull ache thrummed in my calves. A ride to the rink would keep it from getting worse before I could stretch it out properly, but putting up with Jackson hit my thresholds. Tanner - at least - was helpful. His brother - not so much.

"Forgive him. He hasn't had his morning caffeine," Tanner implored.

With a glare at Jackson, Tanner gestured between his brother and the door. He couldn't exactly reach across the seats. At his brother's beckon and with a put upon sigh, Jackson reached forward, popping the door open.

"Your carriage awaits, my lady," he drawled with a smarmy quirk of his brow. It made his sneer almost look like a smirk.

Adjusting my bags, I nodded at the trunk. Tanner shrugged. "Just shove them in the back with Jackson. Maybe we'll bury him alive and get some peace and quiet."

"Ha ha - so funny," Jackson slid to the driver's side seat in the back, reaching out his hands. "Hand it over, Seaver."   biting back my pride, I opened the door, kneeling on the passenger's side seat as I shoved one bag and then the other into

Jackson's open arms where he stacked them behind my seat.

"What do you carry in these things? Rocks? Don't you use one of the rink lockers?" he complained.

Buckling in, I waited until Tanner pulled away and flicked on his lights to answer. "Better to take my gear home and keep it clean. Most of the lockers on the women's side are reserved anyway."

"Probably all taken by the figure skaters. Their teachers have connections across the area - even the magnet schools and the women's side up at our sister school goes through them. They aren't as good as the Lions record-wise, but we've had at least a handful try out for the Olympics," Tanner added - his eyes never leaving the road. "But what about the employee lockers?"

"Like they'd be big enough for hockey gear," Jackson scoffed.

Slouching back in his seat, Jackson thumped his head against the window, groaning. His practices went way later than our own, and if I remembered correctly, St. Raphael's started later in the day by an hour, meaning he would be doubling his private practice time at least. And people were worried I might over exhaust myself.

By car, we'd get to the rink more than forty minutes early. Which meant either waking Mike, a terrible idea by any sensible person's standards, or waiting in the lot. If the two brothers thought I had a key or any power to get into the rink earlier than our agreed upon time, they overestimated me.

When Tanner pulled into the dark lot, Jackson shoved away from the door. "Where the hell is Mike?"

"Language," Tanner said, clucking his tongue, but his lips twisted into a grin.

"Probably sleeping," I admitted. "He doesn't get here for another," I glanced at the clock, "Forty-two minutes."

"What? Then why did you get up this early? Seriously, Tanner?" Flopping over onto my bags, he grumbled, "I'm taking a freaking nap. I can't believe this. You owe me so much."

Rolling his eyes, Tanner gestured back at his brother with his thumb. "Drama queen."

"Screw you. I'm a freaking king!"

I shrugged, wanting to give Jackson credit for at least admitting his theatrics, but the words caught in my throat as I debated how to deal with the extra time. Especially with Jackson sprawled on my stuff.

Before I could say anything, Tanner unbuckled, turning to smack his brother's knee. "Hey! Hand me my chair."

"It's under the bags," Jackson reminded him, but he got quickly to work shoving my bags forward at me.

With them on my lap, he couldn't hand over the chair, so opening the door and stepping out with them wasn't just what I wanted to do - it was what made things easiest. When I glanced at Tanner as he lifted his collapsed chair over, swinging it outside his own door, he winked at my appreciative smile.

"Jolly giant," Jackson called, holding out his hands. "Toss them back."

"Just lay down if you're tired," Tanner commanded. In a practiced motion, he lifted himself and settled into his wheelchair.

I adjusted my bag, shutting the door with my hip. "Need to stretch anyway."

Jackson's eyes narrowed, flicking over to his brother than back to me. His arms dropped to rest on the side of the passenger's seat as he slouched forward. While the two looked so similar at first glance, their expressions were nothing alike. A tension remained firmly between Jackson's brow. Somehow making all his expressions either bored or condescending.

"And you need your bags for that?" he drawled with a slight upward twitch of the corner of his upper lip.

"She wants her bags. Shut it," Tanner
immediately commanded, and as he shut his door
like a period to finalize his statement, Jackson
kicked open the passenger's side back door, gliding
out like syrup. "Come on, Jackson. Don't be a jerk.
If you want to sleep, the backseat is plenty comfy."

"What if I want to sleep on the sidewalk like
a hobo? Make my own newspaper blanket," he
mocked in a way only someone who never had to
worry about his next meal could manage.
As the two brothers glowered at each other, I set my
bags down on the sidewalk. Shifting my hips side to
side, when the lull of silence grew too long.

"No way. Sprints from here to the far side of
the lot and back!" Jackson yelled.

Tanner sent me a pleading look around his
brother, so I didn't even wait for an agreement. I
just took off. If nothing else, competing would be a
good exercise pre-gym. It wasn't like the weight
room took much effort.

***

Headlights passed over us as Mike pulled
into the parking lot. His brakes squealed with the
turn, and he rolled into his usual spot. As the lights
flickered before turning off, he opened the door - a
coffee in hand. Moseying up to the door, Mike

scanned the three of us before settling on me. "Beni, you left your bike here last night."

"What?" I gaped.

"Yeah, it's in my office. Taking up space because I'm the nicest guy ever," Mike said. He ran a hand through his messy hair. "It's exhausting being this saintly."

My shoulders dropped as my mind raced. "How did it get in your office?"

Blinking rapidly, he stared at me as if I had grown a second head, but before he answered, his eyes slid to Tanner and Jackson. Rolling his eyes, he shook his head.

"And I thought you had no social skills," he finally announced, patting me on the shoulder as he turned to unlock the doors. "Plus side - you've got a personal chauffeur. Does this mean I can sleep in ten more minutes?"

Glancing back at Tanner, I swallowed my immediate desire to demand answers at his completely nonplussed expression. Jackson, however, glared at Mike like he could set him on fire.

"Not my chauffeur. One time situation," I said.

Jackson snorted - rough and indelicate. "Like I'm letting you get early access to the rink alone."

"You're on our way," Tanner lied as if I didn't know where the St. Raphael's dormitories were. Everyone knew. They put themselves up on a hill. It made their denials of recruiting outside their district all the more ridiculous. As if he could read my disbelief in my face, he stared me down. "We don't board."

"Why waste a perfectly good house with two pools and a full-time chef?" His brother added as if I needed the reminder that their family was ridiculously wealthy. "The spread we get every day could even feed someone as big as you."

"She's an inch taller than you, Jackson. In a year or two, you'll probably be taller," Tanner informed his brother, rolling around us and through the front door as Mike held it open for him.

Jackson huffed. "She's a brick wall. I'm not going to get nearly as broad."

"Not with that attitude, you aren't," Mike cut in, pushing Jackson back when he tried to follow after Tanner. Letting me through first, he gave Jackson an insincere smile and then tripped him when he finally let him pass.

"Seriously?" Jackson cried.

"Whoopsie daisy! How clumsy of me!" Mike drummed his fingers against his lips, affecting a high-pitched giggle as he sauntered over to his office and the lights.

"Should just purchase the freaking rink," Jackson grumbled, brushing himself off.

"Yeah - sound investment. You'd probably live here too. Whole house to myself…" Tanner hummed.

Rolling his eyes, Jackson adjusted his sports bag. "You'd miss me."

A flash of bright white nearly blinded me as Tanner fluttered his eyelashes at me. "Oh, Beni-dear, would you come visit me? I'd be so lonely all on my lonesome with no one complaining to me about who is slacking at practice or how the cook doesn't keep the protein drinks stocked well enough or how they can't find a way to talk to -"

Jackson grabbed his brother's chair by the back, shoving him toward the entrance to the ramp between the two main rinks. "Shut up!"

"What are you? In middle school?" Tanner asked, sticking his tongue out before he glided off toward the ramp. "Come on, Beni. You and I are going to have some fun one-on-one time without that idiot."

Grumbling beneath his breath, Jackson stormed off toward the men's locker room as I headed toward the rink. While they had driven me here, there was no reason for them to bring me over to school. Luckily, I had my bike back, so not exactly a time crunch.

"Where's your padding?" Tanner called when I dumped my bags in the bench area.

Kicking off my shoes, I pulled on my skates as I replied, "I've got gym first period. No sense showering twice in a row."

"Still, how is your hair not brittle?" he commented, rubbing a lock of his own between his fingers. "Mine has a fit when I wash it two days in a row - let alone twice in the same day, every day."

"I come from oilier stock, I guess."

Grinning, Tanner folded his hands on his lap. "See. So much better without Jackson. Look us at banter!"

The chill of the rink settled over me as I glided onto the ice. Smoothed from the end of day clean-up, it was untouched. Crisp and clean and all mine. Cutting an oblong oval, I kept my pace slow and steady. Overworking risked injury. I needed to just clear my head. Put aside whatever weirdness went on yesterday and this morning. Push aside thoughts of Tanner and Jackson. Nothing else mattered. Just me and the ice.

Chapter Seven

With my bike returned, I got to school on time and with no sign that I hadn't been alone earlier in the morning. I hadn't given Tanner time for more than a wave of a goodbye, so there was still a chance he would show up tomorrow morning with his jerkier brother in tow. Any hope I had my day would return to an approximation of normal failed miserably within the first five minutes of gym.

Waffling about the free weights, Sean asked, "So what did younger Duke want anyway?"

"What?" I didn't bother looking up from where I spotted Geoffrey on the bench press. "I don't know."

"Come on! Did he ask you out?" Sean weaseled, wiggling his eyebrows as he grinned teasingly at me.

"He probably just wanted to tell her off for smashing up his brother," Geoffrey suggested as he lowered the bar to his chest. "Lincoln saw him at Charlie's last night. Said he looked stiff."

"Maybe baby Duke is lonely. Stuck-up golden boy like Jackson at home, guy needs to get friends from a rival school if he doesn't want them fawning over perfect Jackson," Joe piped in, pitching his voice.

"He did ask if I wanted to hang out," I finally admitted.

Taking my place on the bench as we switched, I adjusted my grip on the bar and staunchly ignored their stares. They didn't have to know he gave me a ride home. Nobody but Mike saw me with them this morning. I could keep my head down. Keep their interest starved. Get through the rest of the period and hope hanging out in the morning meant Tanner wouldn't show up to practice.

Geoffrey, however, pulled me aside at the end of class. "Andre saw you get into Tanner's car after practice"

"Somebody moved my bike into Mike's office. I thought it was stolen," I told him. "He gave me a ride home."

"Which is fine, but..." he glanced around as if not wanting someone to overhear us as he whispered, "Apparently, Tanner's been flirting with Ariadne. Ryan doesn't know, and if he did, he wouldn't go after the kid - I mean, he's a complete push-over off the ice, but Andre's pissed. Not at you. Probably hopes Tanner'll go after you instead."

"What?" My eyes narrowed.

Geoffrey shook his head. "It's crazy. I know, but you know how Andre is."

"Which means what exactly?"

Crossing his arms over his chest, he sighed. "He's all about picking sides. If Ariadne dumps Ryan for Tanner, he could end up going to St. Raphael's. His parents wanted him there anyways."

"He's not going to just ditch his best friend," I argued, shocked that I even had to say that. The two of those were impossibly codependent.

"He could, and then our chances at beating them at States goes poof!"

"What do you want me to do about it?" I asked.

I already expected the answer, but I wanted him to earn the punch in the arm I had on lock as a response. He didn't disappoint.

"Flirt back."

I slammed my fist into his upper arm. Hard enough to hurt but not bad enough to cause more damage than a nasty bruise. "I'm not leading him on."

"Why? Cause Ryan'll be free if he gets dumped?" Geoffrey grunted, and before I could deny my crush, he added, "There's a line of girls a mile long for him. You're my best friend, but the odds are better for us going to Nationals with Andre than you dating Ryan if he leaves."

I didn't punch him again though he deserved it. He already rubbed the bruise from the first, so guilt brewed in my stomach, but faced with the horror of having someone not only realize my crush but remind me how much of a long shot it was absolutely wrecked my day. Especially as it was Geoffrey. He never pulled back on the harsh truths with me. Still, both of us avoided the sore subjects.

Unable to bring myself to lash out, I raised my shoulders and walked away. He didn't call out. No last minute apologies. I shouldn't have expected one. Geoffrey wanted to go to Nationals. Not losing our best player made sense, and if I thought I could actually help, I would've, yet the idea that I had to flirt back when Tanner wasn't even flirting with me was insulting. I wasn't some bait. A skirt to toss out to mislead the competition. I had scored first. I got Jackson Duke out of the game. I wasn't going to play distraction because I was a girl.

***

As if Tanner sensed my bad mood, he stayed away. The stands were clear at practice, and Andre jumped on everyone. He slammed Joe into the boards, screamed at Lincoln for missing a shot, and nearly punched out Derek. Not that he could take Derek. The guy had fifty pounds on him and way more padding, but he looked ready to try until Coach kicked him off the ice.

"What's the matter with you?" Coach Carr demanded. "Get the hell off my ice, and if this isn't fixed by tomorrow, don't bother showing up!"

We all stared in horror at that. Missing practice before a game meant the person couldn't play. With our next game against Northview High School, we didn't need him to win, but the idea of it hit too close to home, and Geoffrey cocked a brow, staring at me pointedly.

When Andre left, Ryan glided forward. "I'll talk to him, Coach."

"Chit-chat on your own time," Carr growled. "You all have twenty more minutes left. Get out there!"

Ryan shifted. His eyes followed Andre's cursing retreat into the locker room, but he sunk as if unbearably weighed down before going back into position. Everyone rushed - tense and awkward in the last stretch. When Coach finally blew the whistle - berating us, Ryan raced off the ice.

"Guess he was pissed his boyfriend wasn't here," Joe spat, rubbing at his side.

Derek tapped him on the butt with his stick. "Shut it, Dale. We all have bad days."

Hanging back on the ice, Geoffrey glided in front of me, and Sean fell into line beside him. The defenseman sighed. "Told you so, Seaver."

"What?" Sean asked.

"I don't know - maybe Joe's right," I retorted. "Seems like a pretty big fit over some guy flirting with his sister not even being here."

"Because if he isn't here, where is he?" Geoffrey pointed out.

Sean's nose wrinkled. "Probably with his brother. Like normal."

Good old Sean. Could always count on him for the optimist's vantage point. I shrugged, heading toward the woman's side. "Not my business."

"It will be if Andre decides to join the Lions!"

Sean scoffed. "You are so clueless. Andre's not going to St. Raphael's."

"How would you know?" Geoffrey demanded.

A smarmy smile spread across Sean's face. Giving a single shoulder shrug, he told us, "I've got my sources," and ducked into the guy's locker room.

Watching him go, Geoffrey rolled his eyes. "That idiot thinks he knows something."

"And maybe he does."

"Or maybe I'm right," he returned.

I gritted my teeth. Enough was enough. I had to put up with Andre and his gang. They might have given me some slack since I scored, but that could change at any time. I wasn't about to let my friend put me through a guilt trip for not jumping on a grenade.

"If you think I can't compete with the girls who will go after Ryan after Ariadne dumps him, what would make you think I'd have a chance competing against her?" I demanded, and Geoffrey balked, gaping like a fish.

Throwing my hands up, I hit the showers, leaving him there. The day had gone on long enough, and there was no telling if tomorrow's beginning would be any less strange.

Chapter Eight

"Morning," Tanner greeted me with unnecessary cheer.

Sitting in the driver's seat, he leaned out the window from where he blocked my driveway. With my bike in hand, I walked around him, determined to leave him and this ridiculous change behind. Geoffrey and I hadn't made up after practice, and the more often they followed me around, the greater chance someone would notice. I didn't need Geoffrey breathing down my neck. Or worse, Andre.

"Hey!" he hissed, driving after me. "Come on. This is stupid."

From the back seat, Jackson groaned. "Being up this early is stupid."

"You realize I can just drive ahead, wait in the parking lot, and get in when you arrive!" Tanner yelled as he followed me as I pedaled down the street.

The fresh salt air swept cold and crisp around me. I could almost entirely drown out the rumble of his engine, and the frustrated huff as Tanner kept close behind. If he wanted to follow, that was his prerogative. I had no intention of acknowledging them or dealing with the trouble the Duke brothers would bring my way. Geoffrey might've been a prick for telling me to flirt for the sake of our team, but I had no intention of letting Tanner get whatever it was he actually wanted. Extra skate time for his brother. Some sort of psychological attack. It didn't matter. I just needed to keep my head down.

Rolling down his window, Jackson yelled, "He's not going to give up."

"We can stick the bike in the trunk," Tanner offered.

Jackson huffed. "If it would've fit, I wouldn't have put the stupid bike rack on the back."

Glancing over, I sighed, rolling my eyes. There was, in fact, a Lion's red and gold bike rack on the back. "Is everything you two have color coordinated?"

"I prefer blue, personally. Brings out the color of my eyes," Tanner drawled.

Jackson snorted, but his gaze weighed on me as he leaned on his arm, looking half-asleep as he slouched. "You look good in blue."

"I do, don't I?" the younger brother preened as they drove and I rode along the back shore. "Maybe you should go play for Beni's team. Their colors are blue, aren't they?"

Scoffing, Jackson grumbled, "I meant her, you idiot."

"Really, Jackson, now you're just embarrassing yourself. Of course we're talking about her uniform. It'd be weird if I wore it."

They bantered back and forth the entire way. A comment here and there which almost sounded like something for me to respond to, but even if I stayed silent, they played it off, keeping the volley going until we arrived at the rink. Mike wasn't there yet, so as I locked up my bike, I had no hope of running away.

"You know, you should save up your energy. In my car or by bike, we all ended up here together," Tanner told me as he rolled up beside the bike rack.

The muscles in my jaw tensed. A tension headache bloomed at the base of my skull. Brandon used to say I didn't deal well with change. Not the best trait for a fisherman's daughter. Things changed with the season. But it was always the changes at home that made me want everything else to be steady. Not the same. Steady. If things stayed the same, I couldn't progress. I would still be on the junior varsity team.

I stood up, taking off and putting back on the elastic at the end of my braid. Not really because it needed adjusting. Just as something to do. "Why are you doing this?" I asked.

"You're interesting."

A perfect valid answer by someone used to making friends easily. "I don't find you interesting," I retorted. "If your brother wants to practice early. Just show up around now. He can talk it over with Mike."

Tanner snorted. "Jackson doesn't know what he wants. It's either an hour now or an hour after school. I like having an hour without him. He gets to stay late to get his work done. I get some time with my school friends -"

"With Ariadne?"

He blinked rapidly, studying me as if I had suddenly grown a second head. "What?"

"Guys on my team think you're going after her. If you are, they'll go after you. She's dating our captain," I informed him as Mike's headlights shined over us as he pulled into the parking space beside Tanner's car.

His brows peaked, but for once, he stumbled for words, seemingly flabbergasted. Maybe I shouldn't have said anything. Odds were that Andre's problems were something else, and the whole thing was just rumors. I hadn't seen him flirting with Ariadne, but I also hadn't seen her around Ryan recently.

They both sat together at lunch, but they hadn't been holding hands. No sickeningly sweet small, chaste kisses. His arm always used to be around her shoulder, and he constantly brought flowers and jewelry for her. A day keeping an eye out wasn't much data, but as much as I didn't like Geoffrey's solutions, I trusted - to some degree - that he had observed something. Maybe not exactly what he thought - but enough for there to be something there.

And the small part of me who felt something was happening there panicked. Tanner remained gobsmacked. Staring at me as if he was a computer that had blue-screened, he sat there as I walked away, heading into the rink behind Mike.

As the door shut behind me, I could hear Jackson ask, "What's wrong with you?"

73

But the door bounced, slamming closed, and I wasn't sure I wanted to hear the answer.

Chapter Nine

When I ended my morning practice, Tanner wasn't in his raised area in the stands. However, once I got out of the locker room, any hope I had to avoid the Duke brothers crashed and burned. Jackson leaned against the wall outside. Pushing off it, he sauntered over - his bag slung over his shoulders and his hands in his pockets.

"Where's your brother?" I asked.

He shrugged. "Probably in the car calling your captain's girlfriend."

"I kind of hoped my friends were wrong."

Again, another shrug. "Honestly, odds are any rumor about Tanner that would get his butt kicked by ninety percent of people is true. I mean, he's been waking me up ridiculously early." When I cocked a brow, he rolled his eyes. "Two hours earlier. I should've known it had to do with some girl."

Adjusting my satchel, I headed toward the door. "Whatever. Not my problem."

Jackson snorted, falling into step with me. "Apparently, it is."

"Why? Cause you show up in the morning? Not really."

"Wow. High praise. Here I thought you found my presence inconvenient," the blond grumbled, running a hand through his damp hair. He pulled at the strands, shifting and styling it with the practiced ease of someone who had once spent a great deal of time in front of a mirror to perfect the action until he could do it by muscle memory.

Shoving the door open, I headed to my bike, expecting him to head to his brother's car, but he trudged after me, watching as I crouched to undo the lock around my bike. Inhaling, I stood. "What?"

He held up his hands. Palms faced me as if I was some sort of beast he had to calm down despite cornering. "I have a car."

"Great. So use it," I retorted.

"True. No more early mornings…" he said, nodding along as if I had commented on it. Rolling my eyes, I lifted my bike out of the rack. "I'm not trying to brag, Seaver. I'm offering you a ride."

Brows furrowing, I climbed onto my bike. "If I don't want a ride from Tanner, what makes you think I want one from you?"

Jackon scoffed, stepping back as I guided my bike in a small loop. "Obviously, I'm better looking than him." My eyes narrowed, and I pressed down, glided a bit away. He jogged to catch up. "Come on, Seaver. I'm the best player in the league. Top rated in the United States. Schools have been chasing me for years. You're good, but training with me would take you to another level."

He wasn't wrong. Even if we threw out checks, just practicing with him would be incredible. If Andre hadn't always been so indifferent to me, working with him would have been similar. Not as distracting as Ryan. But it made no sense. Andre - the best player on my team - had to be forced to pair with me. Not because he was still out to make my life miserable. He just didn't care about me. I wasn't on his radar. Whenever he had a chance, he stuck to Ryan. I mean, I understood. Given the chance, I would've spent as much time with our captain as I could, and the few times when Ryan could, he paired with me - more than happy to help the odd man out on the team. Jackson wasn't Andre - and he certainly wasn't Ryan.

"And what would you get out of it?" I asked.

Studying me, he frowned. "Nobody's ever caught me. If I want to go pro, I've got to either get used to getting wrecked or train to make sure I never do. No one on my team is going to hit me. Anybody else I ask on another team would aim to hospitalize me."

"And I'm too nice to?"

His lips quirked into a smirk. "Not exactly."

Unable to find a good reason to say no, I informed him, "I'd be a legend at school if I landed you in the ICU."

"You'd hate it."

Biting my lip, I glared out at the parking lot. Sure enough - sitting in his idling car - Tanner ranted, hands flailing, hopefully at someone on his cell phone. Whether he spoke with Ariadne or someone else, Tanner hadn't denied something was going on between him and another guy's girlfriend. Going after her was wrong. Her cheating on Ryan was wrong. Moreover, it was absurd. I liked Tanner. His dry wit and determination won me over though I couldn't trust his enthusiasm, but Ryan was amazing. Captain of the hockey team. Incredibly nice. Smart. Gorgeous. Everybody liked him, and he wasn't the sort of jerkish tool that a lot of the guys in my high school were.

I had thought Ariadne was similar - model-like beauty, soft-spoken and caring. She seemed his perfect match. Maybe they were too similar, but Ryan deserved to be let down easy. To be broken up with before Ariadne went after someone else. Andre - as much of a jerk as he was - deserved to not be tugged around by his sister too.

But that wasn't my responsibility. I couldn't control Ariadne or Tanner. Best choice, I removed myself from the situation, but Ryan - the guy I liked - happened to be dead center. Which meant I had to figure out if he was worth the oncoming pain. Being around Tanner seemed like taking his side. Even if I wanted nothing to do with him. Even if he just kept following me around like he was now - everyone, especially Andre, would think I was on Team Tanner.

Agreeing to accept Jackson as my training partner? Early mornings - almost zero chance anyone would realize what we were doing. Even if we were caught, he was the top rated player in the league. Mike liked him. Knew him personally and would let him keep coming even if I refused to share a rink with him. Just as many excuses popped up for practicing with Jackson - more even - than dealing with Tanner.

"Fine. Just you. Ten minutes before Mike gets here."

Bright and broad, his smile almost blinded me. "Don't forget it, Seaver. Tomorrow, I'm going to show you how to train like a god!"

I huffed, shaking my head as I rode off, leaving him and his ridiculousness behind. However, as I paused, prepping to turn out of the parking lot, I glanced over my shoulder. Jackson drummed on Tanner's door, and though I couldn't see his face, Tanner's eyes widened - jaw dropping before he grinned widely as well and offered his hand in a high five. Frowning, I turned my eyes back to the road. I was better off not knowing what they were thinking. Odds were this wouldn't end well for me.

Chapter Ten

"That's not how you - has no one every taught you the basics? Just because you can handle getting hit doesn't mean you should let me catch up with you!" Jackson yelled, dodging around me.

The urge to smash my stick into his own grew. It wouldn't be pretty. Neither him or his brother had said for certain what his issue was, but when I slammed into him in the first game, he went down like a lead balloon. If I chased after him - smashed into him - sent him onto his back on the ice, would he be able to get back up? More and more, I wanted to test it. Maybe only a little bit. Just to shut him up.

Grinding my teeth, I headed back into place. We aligned. Him on one side. Me on the other. "You need to read me," Jackson told me. "See where I'm going to go before I do."

"Wouldn't this work better if we trained with each other rather than against?" I asked.

He snorted, clapping his stick against mine before lunging forward. Tugging the puck close, I swerved. I raced across the ice, charging down the ice. Laughing, he chased me. Which meant I wasn't going fast enough. Still laughing, he caught up to me. Jackson stole the puck. Flying down the ice, the

St. Raphael Lion flew from one side to the other, and every time I almost caught up - he'd push that little bit harder - fly that much more ahead, and every time, the thought cycled around my head. If I didn't hesitate, I could knock him down. A hip check would do it. Knock him off his game enough for me to steal the puck and get a head start racing down to score. If I did it right, I might even manage it without shattering his ribs or whatever damage I had caused the first time around. Or I could get faster.

"Come on, Seaver, if you aren't going to knock me, you better outpace me," Jackson called, knocking the puck into the goal. He threw up his hands, cheering - playing out the applause of a crowd that wasn't there. Jackson spun loops around me. "What? You afraid you're going to break me? I'm not that fragile, Seaver."

"Says the guy who had to be out the first two weeks of the season after I knocked him down," I retorted.

His brows furrowed beneath his helmet. "Two weeks? You think that's bad. I got hit back when I first started by a tank who could barely keep his skates straight. Landed on top of me. Three times my weight. Four inches on me. Multiple fractures - ribs, collar bone, broken femur - sprained wrist. It sucked. Out for the season."

Snorting, I pulled the puck from the goal, grumbling, "And your dad let you keep playing?"

"God no - he was too busy setting up a hospital in Kenya and running a surgery with spotty internet to care what I was doing." Sliding into place across from me, he skated in figure eights. "My mom pulled me aside. She was a pediatric surgeon. Without a contact sport, my life would be a hundred percent normal."

"But you wanted to play one of the most aggressive sports. Sticks and full body contact - knives strapped to your feet," I joked back.

He snorted. "Think blades will cut you up just as easily as me."

"Yeah, but I can take a hit."

"Sure. Fine, you can take a hit. But can you skate with bruised ribs? Outskate everybody else with a broken toe because some dipshit decided to shove a weight back where it wasn't supposed to be and didn't think getting a five pound on somebody's foot was a problem," Jackson told me, taking the puck - passing it back and forth to himself. "It sucks. People tip-toeing around me. Why do you think I'm stuck practicing with you?"

Off he skated to the center. We started over, playing until Mike announced the time - ten minutes later than I should have left - over the loudspeaker.

83

"I can drive you," Jackson offered, but I brushed him off.

If Geoffrey freaked about me hanging out with Tanner, the whole team would completely lose their minds if they saw me spending any time with the star player for the St. Raphael's Lions. That didn't mean that Geoffrey didn't give me a knowing look when I ran into the weight room right as the bell rang.

Chapter Eleven

Our third game of the season should've been an easy win. Score-wise, anybody might think it was if they hadn't been there, but sitting on the bench waiting for my turn on the ice, I would've chewed my nails off if it weren't for my gloves. Tanner - the idiot - sat watching. Ryan noticed. Then Andre noticed. Then Andre noticed Ryan notice, and probably also the way his sister was sitting in the row closest to Tanner, and the tentative camaraderie which had reformed slowly since Andre got kicked out of practice completely broke.

"Get your head in the game, Dixon!" Coach Carr roared when Ollie chased Lowell's right wing. Turning on me, he growled, "Page, Caldwell, Seaver - switch in!"

Change signaled, I raced out as Ollie practically fell into the box. Lowell wasn't a tough team. They had some decent players, but their coach hadn't ever played hockey. He was a stand-in. A lot of the local teams were like that. Not a lot of the local players ended up teachers, and the ones who didn't get as far away from the area as possible usually ended up in jobs where they didn't exactly have the time to help - like my dad.

Ollie, Peter, and Graham had started first. Coach probably thought it would be a good chance for them to get more time on the ice, but Lowell had upped their game. Even worse, when my line took the ice, Andre and Ryan were trainwrecks. Usually, the two of them worked together like a well-oiled machine, but they stumbled. Completely wrecked. Despite that, we won. Ten to two, but the whole thing was a mess. Enough that I got dragged into the guys locker room for the coach's end game rage.

"Pathetic," he spat. "That's all I see. An offense that stumbled their way to victory on the back of its youngest players. And defensemen, look at your goalie." Derek's face flushed like a tomato. He almost never shared a goal, but between the second and third period, Coach Carr pulled him, and he still didn't look great. Red and sweaty, he panted in the corner, half out of his gear. Matthieu sprawled, having already drained two bottles of water. "They ran themselves ragged covering your sorry behinds. This was a pathetic, disgusting performance. If I ever see this again, I will drop you all from the team. And you," Coach rounded on Ryan. "You're supposed to be the captain. Lead by example! If you and Page want to squabble, do it off the ice. Whatever problem you have, fix it"

Bowing his head, Ryan murmured, "Yes, sir."

Coach Carr shook his head. Shoving his clipboard under his arm, he clucked his tongue. "Get changed and get yourselves sorted."

"Yes, sir," the team cried in unison.

Following the coach out, I headed toward the women's side when he reached out to stop me. "Seaver - I know the guy've been hard on you, but today, you showed me how serious you are. If any of them give you trouble, let me know."

Oh. That was dangerous. An invitation to snitch. That would definitely go over well with my teammates. On the other hand, his statement meant a lot. Having him on my side eased my fear about getting kicked off the team. As long as I never slacked, I had a spot which paved my way to scholarship opportunities, ensuring one less obstacle between college and me. Brandon would say to lean positive.

"Thanks, coach," I said, ducking into the locker room.

I tried to be quick. My dad wasn't around, and this wasn't the sort of game we'd go out to eat after - even to commiserate. All I wanted was to grab my bike and ride off the night, but when I got out with my gear over one shoulder, I found Andre waiting instead. Nobody else hung around. Not that I could see. No sign of Tanner or anybody that would rile him. Assuming he was waiting for somebody else, I headed toward the door. He darted forward. Blocking my path, he stood as tall as he could - still an inch and then some shorter than me. Andre was lithe. Not tiny or anything. Just on the shorter end and all lean muscle.

"Seaver," he growled. "What was he doing at our game?"

My brows furrowed, and like an idiot, I said, "Your sister probably knows more than I do."

Andre gritted his teeth. The muscles in his jaw spasmed as he took a deep breath. His nostrils flared. "What."

It wasn't a question. This was an attempt to give me a chance to rephrase what I had said, or more accurately, to backtrack like nobody's business, but what was I supposed to say? "If you've got a problem with Tanner, take it up with him. I'm not his keeper. I'm not even his friend."

"Then why's he keep showing up here?" Andre demanded.

"Cause it screws with your head? How am I supposed to know?"

His fingers tightened - knuckles whitening around his stick as he stretched, trying to stand tall enough to stare down on me. Slouching, I tried to give him some reassurance I wasn't looking for a fight, but ducking that little bit didn't really even up our heights. Like a kettle brewing, I could almost see the steam rising off him. Then he blew.

Rounding on one of the support pillars, he slammed his stick into it again and again. "Just for once in your stupid life, why don't you think about somebody else!? Only ever helps until it's inconvenient! Son of a - doesn't even care - ruining everything!"

Andre never made my list of the most put together people. Fashionable. Yes. Intelligent and athletic. Sure. Popular. Definitely. But he wore his emotions on his sleeve. If he hated a person, they knew it. When he bullied me, I never had to wonder who or why. He didn't have to pretend. As long as he wasn't directly caught or confessed in front of the wrong person, he could pop my tires and screw with my gears over and over without consequence - which is why it had been such a relief to think I'd won myself a place on his good side. Or even his neutral side. However, watching him lose his mind and destroy his stick, a realization struck me. None of this rage moved my way.

Maybe I should have taken the chance and ducked out. Grabbing my bike, I might've been half way home before he calmed enough to recognize he was alone, but for better or worse, we played on the same team. My best chance to make that as enjoyable as possible - as successful as possible -

meant I ought to reach out and help him. Or, at the very least, get Ryan to do so for me. Just thinking it made my stomach churn. Bile and bitter rose in my throat. My dad would be so ashamed of me. People, he always said, should help each other because it is the right thing to do. Brandon would've understood. My brother always put actions over thoughts. Thoughts got away from you. Actions didn't.

"Hey, stop," I called, grabbing his arm.

When he whipped around toward me, tears lined his eyes. Not the pretty kind. The sort with snot right behind. "Get lost, Seaver!"

"You just wrecked your stick," I pointed out. "Do you want to talk about it?"

His lips twitched, curling into a sneer. "Why would I want to talk to *you* about anything?"

"Because you don't have anyone else to?"

Not the nicest thing to say. Accurate though. Everybody else had split loyalties. Most people liked Ryan or Ariadne over him. Not that they didn't like Andre. People thought he was clever and funny, but when two people had an argument, people assumed clever caused the problem. Especially when the other person was nice, and Ryan was genuinely the nicest guy. Even offering my ear, I doubted there was anything Andre might've said that would've made me take his side.

Ryan wouldn't have done anything mean. He didn't have it in him.

Andre scoffed. Grabbing the remains of his stick, he stormed over to the trash shoving it inside before marching right out without a backward glance.

Shrugging, I adjusted my bag. I shouldn't have been surprised to find my tires slashed. Trying to be nice, I shoved my nose where it wasn't wanted, and walking out into the cold night air, I sighed, deflating. "Seriously?"

The door opened behind me, and I stepped out of the way, glancing over at Ryan. His dark brown hair dripped down his neck. With his hair slicked back, he looked like a model despite his hoodie and sweats. His dark eyes scanned the scene, taking in my face then the clean cuts on my poor tires - right through the earlier patches.

"Shit, Andre, you freaking drama queen," Ryan grumbled, rubbing his hands over his face. Inhaling and releasing a slow breath, he shook his head. "Let me guess, the splinters in the lobby were from his stick." When I nodded, he set his hands on his hips, glaring up at the sky with a heavy sigh. "Great. That's...great." Adjusting his bag, he nodded toward his car. "Come on, Beni. I'll give you a ride home. I think your bike will fit in the back of my car."

"Thanks."

We managed to get it in without much problem after he put the back seats down. In the dark seclusion of his car, silence reigned only in the small gap between me giving him my address and us turning out of the lot.

"I'm sorry you're having to go through this. He's not actually angry at you," Ryan told me. His hands shifted, clenching along the wheel. "Sometimes, he's - he's not the best at expressing himself, and with things rocky between me and Ariadne…" he trailed off with another sigh. "Do you have a boyfriend?"

I blinked, taken aback by the sudden question. "No."

"Yeah - that's probably smart. Dating just - it's balancing egos. I thought I was okay at that. People like me," Ryan said, and the way he said it - like a fact as straightforward as saying the sky was blue - somehow managed to keep him from sounding like an arrogant jerk. "I'm the youngest of three, and my brothers - do you remember them? I think you met them when you came around with Brandon when you were little, right?"

"A couple times."

Ryan smiled a small and fragile sort of wistful look. "I always liked your brother. Got a little jealous, honestly, that he liked Scott better." A laugh - sharp and nothing like the rich warm sound of his usual tone - echoed in the car. "He was probably the only one."

Scott was the second eldest. Skinny and gaunt, he had a sharp mind and a worldview that bordered on dangerously black and white. Worse, their eldest brother, Isaac, and their father somehow managed to be much more absolute in their morality. Honestly, if I didn't know better, I would've doubted anybody - even Brandon - could like Scott over Ryan. I never knew why Brandon liked Scott. That was just another way he got us out of the house when Mom got sick. Ensured food before he figured out how to use the oven. They didn't do much. Brandon, Ryan, and I would do our homework at their kitchen table, and Scott would skulk around. He always finished first and never helped anyone.

"Maybe you should break up then," I suggested, barely speaking above a whisper because just thinking this seemed to be jumping head first into the fire Geoffrey predicted. "I mean, if you feel like that."

Ryan hummed. A long trailing note which he held. The longer the note lasted, the more my stomach twisted. Turning into my driveway, he set the car to park and as he turned off the engine, he finally said, "I don't think I'm ready to give up yet."

93

A beat passed, and I pushed open the door. "I think I can get it if you unlock the back doors."

But Ryan had already gotten out, pulling my bike out and carrying it over to the garage where he set it down. "I'll pay for the tires. Just let me know what they'll cost."

"Thanks," I murmured, waving as he drove off into the night.

Chapter Twelve

Whatever I expected to come from Ryan driving me home - which was nothing, I expected nothing, Ariadne stopping me in the hall on the following Monday as I headed to my locker during the middle of my lunch period wasn't anywhere in the ballpark. She didn't even have the same lunch block as me.

"Beni! How are you?" she asked, gliding over to me. Her smile was perfect as if she practiced it. Not too much teeth. Wide enough to be sincere but not so wide as to seem manic. All her teeth - like her brother's and the Dukes' - shined a picture-perfect white.

I glanced around, but nobody else was in the hall. "I'm good. You?"

"I'm well," Ariadne returned.

Maybe if that was it, I could've dismissed the whole thing, but she waited, watching as I switched out my notebooks. Spinning the combination lock, I shrugged. "Can I help you with something?"

"There is a little something I wanted to chat with you about," she said, and wrapping an arm around mine, she dragged me down the hall. "I'm so glad I caught you. I've been wanting to speak with you for a while now."

"You have?"

Her light blue eyes met mine as her brows furrowed as if to convey some extreme sincerity, but my stomach twisted with unease. "Of course,

Beni. I know you and I haven't always been close, but I've always admired how determined and hard-working you are."

"Thanks…"

"Ryan does too. He was so happy when you made the team," she informed me. Her eyes shifted to look out one of the hall windows. "Andre was rather jealous. He felt that way about Brandon too. You know Ryan adored your brother, don't you?"

I had no idea. Brandon got on with everyone, so Ryan hadn't been anybody particularly special except that I had liked Ryan, and he happened to be Scott's brother. I might have noticed Ryan looking at Brandon like he hung the moon, but a lot of people looked at him like that. For all he isolated himself in sports, people gathered around him. He always had a pithy one-liner and a carefree smile ready to go.

With a shrug, I said, "I had an idea."

Her smile returned, twice as bright. "I always did wonder, you know, what might have happened if Brandon hadn't died."

My heart thundered in my chest. Every ounce of me screamed not to have to talk about this with someone like her. Someone who kept everything light and nice and not at all how I felt when I thought about Brandon and how unfair it was that he was gone.

If she noticed I stiffened, she didn't stop. "They were already dating by then, but Andre went on and on about how Ryan was going to leave him for Brandon. His self-esteem is surprisingly low."

My brain stopped. White noise bounced around my head, and she tugged me with shocking strength to the window where she pointed out at the community garden. Almost nobody came around to the little patch of ground between the newer section of the school above the cafeteria and the old art rooms. The construction effort for the new music wing had created an awkward area visible only from a few second story windows. Back in the 60s, they'd put in a garden in an attempt to stop people from smoking, but practically nobody went back there, and the student council fenced it off. Ryan, as the president, had the key, so I wouldn't have been surprised to see him or Andre.

Ryan rested against the wall, and Andre leaned around him with arms on either side of his friend. Somehow despite being shorter, he seemed to take up enough room to almost completely obscure Ryan.

One domino fell in my mind, and then an entire wave of realizations poured over me. Ryan was gay. He and Andre were dating, but they couldn't tell anybody. The why was obvious. Ryan's family were fanatically homophobic. Ariadne - knowing all this - must have been pretending to be his girlfriend, which meant that she couldn't date Tanner - who she might actually want to date because she didn't have the perfect boyfriend everyone thought she had. If Ariadne dumped Ryan for Tanner, his family would get on his case until he'd found another girlfriend - which would require an actual girlfriend or risk getting found out because his family - especially his eldest brother and dad, would immediately suspect Andre.

Everyone suspected Andre. He wasn't exactly shy about his opinions. Never dated. No interest in girls at all. Dressed way better than any of the other boys in the school. He'd been taunted about it once or twice, but he never confirmed or denied. Probably couldn't, or Ryan wouldn't be able to spend time with him outside of school and practice.

It was so twisted. Bad enough to know I had no chance with the guy I'd liked for years, but I had always known that. Worse was knowing I never realized someone I cared for was suffering. Just because nobody knifed his tires, I assumed his life was perfect. Which was exactly what he had wanted. What he needed. Like Geoffrey kept harping about -

"Does Geoffrey know?" I cringed. "Sorry - that's not - he's just been on my case, and I thought -"

Ariadne laughed. "God, I hope not. I mean, usually they're a bit better about hiding than this."

"Then why are you telling me?"

She sighed, playing with her long brown hair. "Tanner and I have been…seeing each other for a few months now. Before school even started. We met over the summer. There was a lecture series on politics and public health that their school hosted, and we clicked." Her lips curled into a smile as if she just couldn't help but be happy thinking about him. "He's a genius. I swear, it's ridiculous."

The guy did skip a grade while recovering from a fractured spine, so I couldn't argue with her there. Imagining him as a doctor - at his father's hospital or anywhere else - didn't exactly fit. I couldn't imagine him with even close to decent bedside manner.

Lowering her gaze, she fluttered her long lashes, and before she spoke, I cringed, knowing she wanted a favor. Nothing good would come of this.

"Unfortunately, we can't date or spend any time together publicly without people talking," Ariadne explained. "I know it's a big favor - but would you be willing to date Ryan?"

I blinked. Her pleading eyes kept staring up at me, but she couldn't have asked what I think she did. "Date - who?"

"Ryan. I had thought we could fake double date, but that doesn't solve the problem of Tanner and I wanting to go out together publicly," she told me with the same practiced smile which she had used to approach me at my locker. "But if you date Ryan, he's got someone else in his corner. Scott was friends with Brandon, and you were at their house a lot when you were younger, so nobody will think it's weird that he starts dating you after we break up."

"That's stupid." I winced. "Sorry. But it is. We're in completely different worlds here."

Her smile never broke despite my exclamation. "Which is why it will work. It's like all those songs. I'm the gorgeous woman with a life plan of my own that has no interest in hockey or anything else Ryan likes frankly, but you - you're on the team. Plus, you have a crush on him!"

"How did you -"

"I'm not an idiot, Beni. I did my research. I might've known your brother, but I didn't know you, so I couldn't be sure you were as kind as him," Ariadne said, taking my hands in hers. "You're a good person, and if it were anybody else, I wouldn't trust my brother and one of my closest friends to them. I love those two. Please - just think about it."

And before I could answer, she left me there - standing frozen in the hall with what I never believed I could have in the way I would never want it. Stepping back, I headed back to the cafeteria. The revelation stirring around my head like poison. It stuck there the rest of the day, and even after nothing happened in practice - a surprisingly calm one - the first we had without Andre going after someone in a while, I couldn't help but wonder what Brandon would've done, and why that didn't help make either choice any more appealing.

It haunted me into the next day as well. Waking up, I stumbled out of bed. My usual smooth routine sent me somehow falling up the stairs. A groggy goodbye from my Dad caused me to upturn my book bag. If he realized the car outside wasn't one of my friends that he knew, I'd never hear the end of it, but I didn't want him to worry. It wasn't like Jackson was anybody he needed to know about anyway, so I stuffed everything back in and ran out to the jerk's frustrated face and flashing lights.

"Stop that," I hissed.

"You know-" Jackson drawled, dragging out the word as I stuck my bags in the back and climbed into the car. "It would be easier if I had your cell number."

"I don't have a cell phone."

His eyebrows rose. "Seriously? What are you? Eighty?"

Buckling up, I glared at him. "My dad's not a big tech fan."

"So what? You have like - a landline? Aren't those more expensive nowadays. Tell me you at least have the internet," he demanded, pulling out from where he'd parked alongside the road in front of my house.

My shoulders rose as I sunk down in the seat. We did. Have the internet that is. Brandon had set that up before the end. When he got sick, he wasn't up for doing work at Ryan's house with Scott, so he had asked - not wanting to fall behind when he first thought it would just be a few months until he bounced back. Like he could bounce back from a highly aggressive stage four cancer that almost immediately took his leg. My dad couldn't say no, so Brandon got a laptop - which meant I had a laptop.

Pulling into the rink, he reached over, popping open the glovebox. "Here," he said, tossing me a cell. I immediately moved to open the glovebox to shove it back in when he blocked me. "Come on," he insisted. "It's not like I need it."

"And it's not like I can afford a phone plan on what Mike pays me," I retorted.

"It's prepaid."

Glaring down at the electronic rectangle, I grumbled, "Why do you have a prepaid phone?"

"Cause I'm a spy - I dunno, cause I got bored of my old phone, and my dad didn't want to buy me a new one. Then that one got scratched, and my dad finally relented," he drawled, reaching over to flip the phone to point as a dinky scratch on the back like someone had keyed it. "See?"

A voice that sounded like Brandon suggested he had guessed I didn't have a cell and bought this just for me. Keyed it and made up some stupid story. But guys like Jackson Duke didn't do things like that for girls they did like as more than friends let alone people they begrudgingly practiced with, so their annoying younger brother could get some alone time with the girlfriend of their rival team's captain. Even thinking it all out sounded absurd.

If the story actually was made up, Geoffrey would say the phone was a way to bribe me or to spy on the team, but even if I texted Sean or anybody, we weren't going to be saying anything Jackson could use to do any more damage to the team. It wasn't like we knew anything life-changing. Well, anything Jackson couldn't get from Tanner.

"Thanks."

With a snort, Jackson kicked open his door. "Sheesh, don't sound so suspicious."

"I'm not. Really, I mean it. Thanks," I repeated, and for all the first half was a lie, I did appreciate it. "So is it to the end of the month?"

"Unlimited talk, text, data - I think there's like ten or more months on it," Jackson replied, tugging his bag from the back. I leaned against the car, staring at him until his gaze met mine. Huffing, he rolled his eyes. "What? I get it. I'm a spoiled rich boy. Come on - they sell them at Walmart. Seriously. It's embarrassing that you haven't saved up for one."

They were hundreds of dollars, and all my money had gone to tire repairs and hockey, but talking to him about that opened up a Pandora's Box I wanted to avoid. We didn't discuss it further, but half-way through our practice time, he picked up the puck from the goal, glaring at me.

"Are you still harping on the phone? I had an extra phone. I gave it to you. It's not a big deal!" he yelled, waving his stick in the air.

Picking at the tape on my stick, I sighed. "That's not it."

"Then what?"

I couldn't tell him. Nobody could know. It wasn't my secret to tell, and worst case, if Jackson wanted to screw with Ryan, that would be the perfect material. But who else could I talk to? Geoffrey would instantly realize - reading between the lines and making everything so much worse. On the other hand, Sean sucked at keeping secrets. The few other friends I had weren't the sort I'd confide secrets in. Passing friends. In class only, never invite out sort of friends.

"I like this guy…" I told him then groaned when he wriggled his brow. "Shut up. He's got a girlfriend."

"And you want to make him jealous?" Jackson joked, skating in circles around me.

Shaking my head, I sighed. "He's not supposed to be dating his girlfriend. Racist dad or whatever. They want me to cover for him. Fake girlfriend for his family."

Stopping in front of me, his green eyes scanned over my face. The weight of his gaze burned into me, and I quickly looked away. After a moment of silence, he slid forward, reaching out, but his glove paused an inch above my shoulder.

"Can I hug you?" Tired and anxious, I shrugged, and he pulled me into a one-armed hug. "That sucks."

I patted him on the back, mumbling, "It's not like I thought I had a chance, but…"

"Salt in the wound," he said, pulling back to nod before he gave my upper arm one last reassuring squeeze. "Well, movies say if you do it, he'll fall for you. Can't say it's ever worked for me."

"You fake dated somebody?" I asked, trying to push the attention off me.

With a shrug, he smirked. "Maybe. Might even tell you about it if you can score."

"It better be a good story."

His eyes sparkled as he dropped the puck between our sticks. "You'll just have to find out."

Chapter Thirteen

Restraining from flashing his car lights, Jackson looked me up and down when I climbed into the passenger's side seat the next day. His lips twitched up on one side. With a derisive snort, Jackson asked, "What are you - six feet?"

"Five eleven."

People balked at my height, and my doctor kept saying I had another inch or two in me. While I stood a good three inches taller than the next girl my height in the school - a senior without risk of further growth, I never minded being tall. I cared about being tall and big. Buffer than most guys. Sometimes, I took pride in it. Beating them in deadlift contests or anything gym class related, but outside of athletics, the big caused me more trouble than the height. Clothes existed for tall girls. Clothes existed for athletic girls, big girls - but muscled and tall - I had better luck in Brandon's old things than at the women's section in the mall.

And, predictably, Jackson headed straight for that weak spot. "You dress like you're trying out for Rocky VII."

"Really?" I rolled my eyes, crossing my arms. "You're insulting sweats and a hoodie?"

"Just saying - you could mix things up."

"We're hitting the ice then I've got PE. I'm not wasting time changing in and out of my school clothes when I don't need to," I informed him. Riling me might've been his entertainment for the ride, but he couldn't rile common sense.

Gesturing at his own clothes - fitted joggers and a wicking long sleeve shirt, Jackson replied, "You can dress smart and look good."

Like a divine blessing, we rolled to a stop right across from a new billboard, but not just any billboard, this one had the face of a certain local hockey star in the exact same outfit. They had smoothed his tan, hiding the freckles on his nose and completely took out the scar on his chin. Most days, I didn't notice it, but blow up, the lighter rough line should've stuck out.

"All your smart and good looks come from your modeling gigs?" I joked, grinning as his lips pressed into a thin line as if he had completely forgotten the billboard was going up.

It wasn't the first. Almost all the local sports shops used him to get people to come in. He was a household name, and everybody knew he'd be professional some day. Scouts filled the seats at his end of year games, and even Ryan played that little bit harder when there was a chance at scholarships or even a team offer riding on how close a player came to keeping up with Jackson Duke.

"Better than dressing in your dad's hand-me downs," he huffed.

I laughed - not finding his grumbling nearly as intimidating with that giant billboard in my head. The subject dropped - for a while, reemerging when we got onto the ice. Fifteen minutes in, he scored the first goal, cheering as he looped me.

"See? Dress right, play right," he chanted.

"Not everyone has sponsors to give them free gear."

"It's not free," he retorted.

I snorted. "Yeah, you had to pose in it first."

"Modeling is a legit career."

"Whatever you say, pretty boy." I had smirked, pleased to finally get one over him as he fumed, and when we lined up at center, I waited until right before we went to add, "Plus, I've got better abs than you anyway."

While he sputtered, I raced across the ice, scoring before he could catch me. I dug the puck out, and when I glanced back, he tugged up his layers to show off his six pack.

"Beat that, Seaver," he sneered.

Some days, I honestly forgot Jackson didn't go to my school. That he honestly didn't know I was that girl - the tall one with more muscles than most of the guys, but he had never seen me in short sleeves. My biceps and shoulders would've given away the game, so when I showed off my own six pack, the sight actually shocked him.

I laughed, gliding back toward the center. "Never doubt my core strength, Duke. I could bench press you if I wanted."

"No shit…" he murmured. Blinking, he chased after me. "Anybody ever told you that you're an absolute beast?"

I'd heard it before. Normally, girls said it with a sneer, and guys said it like they'd just realized they'd stumbled into a zoo. Jackson made it sound like an honor comparable to knighthood. It was stupid how such a little thing from somebody could keep me smiling to the point where it was noticeable.

"You seem happy this morning," Sean commented when he and Geoffrey met me at the bike racks. "What's put a pep in your step?"

"Nothing. Just had a good morning practice," I told him, adjusting my bag.

Rolling his eyes, Geoffrey half-snorted, half-laughed. "Sure - that's it."

Jumping up to the railing, Sean punched Geoffrey's arm. "Stop being dumb."

"I'm not being dumb."

I raised an eyebrow. My gaze shifted between the two. "What's he being dumb about now?'

"Now? Smug jerk thinks you're dating Duke," Sean informed me with a follow-up fake gag.

At his words, I struggled to fight the heat rising to my face. There was no way Jackson liked me like that. He modeled. Honest to goodness modeled on the side - and not just for his dad's hospital. Local sports shops used him, and he even had a couple bigger athletic clothing ads. Jackson was movie-prince sort of handsome. Chiseled and perfectly symmetrical. Not even by accident. He worked hard for it, and the more I knew about his dogged pursuit of a professional hockey career,the more I understood why he was so popular. Girls cheered him. Entire swathes of pretty girls of all kinds - ones with perfect make-up, ones with none at all - he had fans across the spectrum. Popular and hot went together. Popular, hot, and liking an introverted social mess like me? Not so much. I had two close friends, and while I wasn't somebody people went out of their way to avoid, everyone else was sort of classroom specific. They talked to me when I was around, but I wasn't who they went to if they had a choice to pick somebody else.

Scoffing, I rolled my eyes. "Yeah, like that could ever happen."

"I don't know," Geoffrey drawled. "Tanner seems to really like you."

Of course. No way they had meant Jackson. Tanner didn't have his brothers enthusiastic following, and for all they looked similar, he was skinnier with a pale gauntness about him. Without knowing him before the accident, I had no idea if he used to look more like his brother - especially as he had seemingly no interest in any sport or even going outside from what Jackson said.

Ducking my head, I hurried past them into school. "He's about as interested in dating me as you guys."

"I don't know. He was giving me the eye that time during practice," Sean joked, crossing his arms overs his chest as if scandalized.

Geoffrey snorted. "Now who's being dumb."

Even though the topic dropped, my brain buzzed. Jackson Duke - just friend. If that even. Maybe a friendly rival but not someone I shouldn't instantly reply no about dating. Hiding our joint morning practices wasn't some scandalous affair. This wasn't a regency romance. We weren't running into each other because fate had some great plans for our romantic future. Jackson and I practiced together. That was it. Frankly, we only did that because of Tanner, and I only relented to Tanner because of my bike, and relentless pretty much defined him. Thrown together by Tanner. Not exactly a match in the making. Just two hockey players doing one of the player's brother a favor, so he could meet up with his secret girlfriend.

Tanner and Ariadne - those two courted. Any secret affair didn't include me, and my heart only raced because I thought Geoffrey knew about Jackson. About him practicing with me. Nothing else. Just that. No feelings involved. Beyond maybe annoyance.

Except he actually helped me. Even Coach Carr noticed I had improved - and it wasn't like I was a chump before, but Andre wanted me on his team - even over Ryan, which meant I had to be good because when they weren't fighting, they always paired up.

Because they were also in a secret relationship. Which was the reason Tanner and Ariadne had to keep their relationship secret. All leading back to Jackson and me - who only practiced together. To help Tanner - and Ariadne who was helping Ryan and Andre.

All out of sibling love. Jackson helping Tanner. Ariadne helping Andre. I was an accessory to the plot line. Also apparently the only one not

111

being motivated by love or sibling loyalty. I wanted to improve - ensure a scholarship and hopefully free ride to Northeastern, and the more I played against Jackson, the better I got. If I could top out in the guy's side high school league, scouts would have to pay attention to me, which meant my dad didn't have to worry about college. No loans paved the way to a better future. On ice or off. So - selfish but kind of also family motivated because of my dad.So my secret only was a secret to keep other people from getting found out, which meant lying to my friends wasn't a sign of some hidden crush I had on Jackson.

Chapter Fourteen

"You know…we don't have to practice every day," Jackson informed me as he drummed the steering wheel, waiting for me to stick my stuff in the back.

"Why? Are you getting bored?"

Rolling his eyes, he snorted. "As if. You're finally getting good."

"Finally? I seem to recall I knocked you out of play for over a week," I retorted, shutting the door behind me.

Rolling down the street, he waited at the end of my yard to turn on his lights and take off. "Still - practicing everyday - twice a day? Bit overkill."

"We don't do weekends."

"So you claim."

Grinning at him, I leaned back in the passenger's seat. "Games don't count."

"You don't have a game every weekend, and I'm ninety percent sure you're the giant I see running every Sunday," he retorted. His voice dropped low and rolling as he tagged on, "As elusive as Sasquatch - the Port Edmond Giant. Often seen running along the back shore. No one knows why. It has no natural predators."

"It?"

He shrugged. "Don't want to assume."

Smacking his arm, I groaned. "Not all of us are demigods. This mortal has to work for her endurance."

"Mortal?" He gave a noise of derisive disbelief. "Giant. At least half. I've seen your dad, so I know he's jolly and giant - not green though. Very disappointing."

"We're Scandinavian. Brandon hit six foot in middle school," I informed him, and when he gaped, jaw dropping as he turned to stare, I smirked. "Yeah - you want to see a jolly giant, Brandon even painted himself green for Halloween once."

The year he died. My brain waited just until the words had left my mouth to remind me. Brandon's last Halloween pre-diagnosis - his last Halloween period, had been spent painted green faking out kids with candy corn. A few actually liked the stuff, but most had a slightly disgruntled look at receiving it, so when he revealed a big bowl of chocolate, their eyes had lit up.

"A little disappointment makes success sweeter," Brandon used to say. A surprise party when I thought everyone forgot my birthday. Tickets to a midnight showing when he'd said they were all sold out.

A weight on my forearm nearly had me jumping out of my skin, but Jackson stared at me. The car turned off as we sat in the parking lot.

In a quiet voice, he asked, "Does it get easier?"

Most people said it like a statement. It will get easier. They were liars, but Jackson didn't know that yet. His mom had been gone just over a year. Tanner was stuck in a wheelchair. A daily reminder for both of them as if they needed anything more than the gaping hole in their lives where another person - their mother - should have been. Sudden and unexpected. No adjusting. No time to go through any sort of processing. A crash of some drunk, and she was gone.

Maybe it was easier that way. Not to have it dragged out. Watch them fade inside themselves. Brandon struggled so hard. Tried to keep a brave face even after they took his leg. After his body and the treatment ate away his muscle and fat, leaving him skin and bones as his hair fell out. His smile never dropped because if he wasn't brave - nobody else was going to pretend it was okay. Pretending never made it easier.

Dad pretended with Mom. Denial at first. She wasn't forgetting us. Her episodes of losing control of her muscles - lashing out because her body was attacking itself, he pretended everything would get better, and Brandon - back then - told me the truth. Mom wasn't coming home. Mom won't be alive long. He didn't lie. From diagnosis to hospitalization to death - two years. I could barely remember what my mom was like before - who she was except what I've seen in home videos. What I had heard from Brandon or Dad.

Time to watch it happen didn't make the dying easier. At least, I imagined it would've been easier not to hate everyone when the universe hadn't decided to make someone I loved suffer. Someone important.

Arms wrapped around me, pulling me toward Jackson, and when had he even unbuckled? He hugged me tightly. A sob escaped my lips as everything blurred before I buried my face into the shoulder of his stupid designer hoodie. Biting my lip, I clenched my eyes shut, trying to stop the flood, but my brain just kept playing it on a loop: *My mom is dead. My brother is dead.*

A decade ago, I lost my mom, and four years ago, my brother died too - and nothing was easier. Nothing was better. The thoughts hurt. Piercing and painful and too big. I should've gotten used to it. Most of my life, I hadn't had a mother, so honestly, the ache - the rawness was all Brandon. He made the world make sense. Told me I was right when everyone else thought I was weird. His approval always mattered most. And he was gone. My brother was dead, and it wasn't easier.

A small hiccup from Jackson drew me more out of my head than his hug as he murmured a wet, "I really had hoped you'd tell me it did."

My arms wrapped around him, returning the embrace where I had previously only sort of leaned into it. We sat - crying and holding each other - until the bright lights of Mike's car flashed over us. Then, we awkwardly pulled apart.

Jackson smiled sadly. His eyes bloodshot and ringed with red. "We could skip."

"Exercise has endorphins. Supposed to make you feel better," I said.

He shook his head. His blond hair shifting like a halo around his head. "I mean, like, skip school. Call in sick. Grab food and bunker down at my place. Or yours. Or somewhere without people." Jackson's voice pitched, cracking at the last part. "Shit. I don't know how Tanner does it. He's stuck in that stupid chair, and I'm the idiot bawling his eyes out."

"Cause you almost lost him too."

Taking a shaking breath, he shook his head.

"I was supposed to go with Mom."

"Jackson..."

"I've got dyslexia. When I'm stressed, it gets - it gets worse. My dad had been pressuring me to quit hockey, and I had this huge book report to do, but I just couldn't get my brain around the words, so when Mom came to get me cause I'd promised to go grocery shopping with her - I yelled at her. Told her I had enough on my plate, and I told her to take Tanner," Jackson confessed, leaning back into his seat as he stared blankly ahead.

Taking his hand, I squeezed it. "That's not your fault."

"Dad says that too. Says if it was me in the car, I would've died 'cause my - you know..." Jackson collapsed forward, grabbing and holding onto my hand like an anchor. "Tanner said it too. I swear, he's our dad's mini-me."

I had no idea what to say. Tanner's words came to mind. He had asked for a friend, using that as an excuse for why he suddenly popped up in my life and wouldn't let go, but he'd ditched both of us

117

for Ariadne, so while he might have meant what he said, he had meant it about her. Not that I faulted him for it. If she made everything easier, I honestly wished them the best, but sitting in his car, watching Jackson fall apart with guilt and grief, I saw myself - I saw all the bargaining I had done. Wanting my marrow to match, hoping it was a sign when it did, feeling like a failure when it didn't save him. When the cancer had progressed too far, and nothing took - because he wasn't healthy enough to go through it, so my dad hadn't wanted to put me at risk when the doctors said Brandon wouldn't survive either way.

Squeezing his hands with the hand he held, I ran the other through his hair. "I'm really glad you weren't in that car."

Jackson sat back up slowly. His eyes shined, but before he could reply, a knock on the window had us both jumping.

Mike stood outside, leaning against the car. "You coming in? Or you gonna make out in the car more? I'm pretty sure Brandon wouldn't have approved of secret liaisons, but I'm pro-Benson all the way."

Giving us two thumbs up, he grinned before swaggering away. Rubbing at his face, Jackson snorted, laughing quietly. "Come on. I could use some endorphins."

I nodded, following him out of the car.

Chapter Fifteen

The rivalry we had against St. Raphael's meant we lost almost every time, but we always gave them a run for their money in our traditional pre-season game or when we made it to States. Manchester saw us like we saw the Lions. Scores remained low. Their defense held tight. Derek contorted himself, becoming a stone wall. Impenetrable. But they exhausted him by the third. We had one goal up - Andre's.

As long as we maintained that single goal, we'd win. A fine attitude to have after the game but, as a power forward, not the best mentality. If I wanted to get scouted for scholarships, I needed to score. However, my brain has been buzzing since the first period. Jackson and Tanner were both watching.

"Your boyfriend's back, Beni," Joe had snarked, gesturing at Tanner.

Andre sneered. A venomous glower contorting his usual handsome face. "Shut up, Dale. Not her fault Duke's sent his brother to spy." Luckily, they had somehow managed to miss Jackson.

When we'd skated out, Andre had smacked my back, telling me to back him up because he didn't think Joe was up to par if the puck got by us. Definitely not helpful for team camaraderie. Well, if anyone else said it. Somehow, Andre could insult one of the guys by comparison, and they accepted it. Took it as some kind of brotherly joking.

Learning from their example, I had always tried to do the same, but it didn't feel the same. Either way, I wasn't pointing out Jackson didn't need Tanner to spy. He sat right next to my dad, and any time I switched out, my eyes moved from the game to them.

Wearing a beanie and glasses, Jackson leaned close, talking to my dad. My dad nodded. Beyond that, I couldn't figure out what they said. With the game staying close, I couldn't distract myself with them, so I didn't draw anybody else's attention to what was going on behind us. They could focus across the ice on Tanner. He, at least, seemed off-limits outside of glaring. If they realized Jackson Duke sat behind us without his regular muscular backup, a few of the guys wouldn't hesitate to try something. Even if it was just Andre's sharp barbs.

Coming up to the line, I squared my shoulders, pushing the rest of them out of my mind. I couldn't control what happened off the ice. Manchester kept us from scoring the bulk of the third. We spent the period on their side, but as we switched in and out, everyone grew tired.

I raced back onto the ice in the back half of the third. Ryan took the puck, sending it to me. I charged ahead, passing to Andre before getting slammed against the boards. A knotting mess up and back and side to side. Dropping back, Ryan sent the puck forward. Though it was meant for Andre, an opposing defenseman cleared it toward a forward on my side, and I swept passed him, sending the puck straight into the goal.

Cheering, Andre slammed into me, throwing his arm around me as he half-hugged, half-dragged me back toward center. "Five minutes left. Bet I can get another first."

Ryan rolled his eyes. "Get off the ice, Page."

"Sure thing, Caldwell. Maybe you should score next time around. Beni and I are thrashing you," Andre called. He removed his arm from around me as we jumped the boards. "Or maybe Pasternak'll beat you to it too!"

Victor rolled his eyes, sliding into his spot as we took off again. Nobody else scored. Ollie got close, but a Manchester player managed to steal it until Graham got it back. They'd taken it up and down the ice, but nothing came of it.

"Good job!" Coach Carr proclaimed, sending us into the locker rooms.

We'd likely get an earful on Monday when we had our post-game analysis. After the coach had a chance to review how he thought things went. Even in the women's locker, I could hear the guys chanting and cheering. Thank goodness the rink was in our district. Most schools had to take buses home before they could shower, but Port Edmond's public school had the first call to reserve - despite Mike having gone to St. Raphael's. Maybe exactly because of it. He never seemed to have anything positive to say about the place. Plus, as the only girl on the team, I got the women's side all to myself.

After a warm shower, I pulled on my jeans and knit sweater. Quickly braiding my wet hair, I stuffed the rope of its end up into my hat. The temperature took some time to drop fully in Port Edmond, but since last week, most nights dipped into the low forties, and as we headed into the weekend, there were some grumblings about a blizzard.

When I headed out of the women's locker room, Jackson stood a way off, heading out the door. Though I breathed a sigh of relief no one had realized he was here, something squeezed in my chest at the gaggle of unfamiliar faces - all girls about our age - gathered around him. Tanner weaved around his brother, speaking to the girls with a devilish smirk, but Jackson just scowled.

"Hey, Seaver," Joe called. "You coming out to get burgers?"

Friday night - the weekend stretched out, an open possibility. Before I could agree, my dad came up, pulling me into a hug.

"Go on," he said. "I'll take your stuff home."

"You sure?"

"Yeah, just be home before ten." Taking my bags, my dad frowned. "You need money."

"Nah, Mike paid me last week."

All thoughts of Jackson vanished, and I headed off to grab burgers. Sitting in between Sean and Geoffrey, I didn't get a word in between the play by play Ollie recounted or the shouts from

Andre, scolding a player who he thought could've done better.

"You've all lucky to have me," Andre announced, interrupting Ollie acting out the first goal scored in the second period.

Victor snorted, rolling his eyes. "Beni does more than you."

Panic clenched around my heart, but Andre laughed, throwing a fry at our teammate. "We both scored. What were you doing?"

"He isn't wrong," Ryan drawled. "Beni assisted your goal. I got the assist on hers."

Slamming his shoulder into the captain, Andre grumbled, "Shut up, Caldwell."

"We could make it a contest," Sean suggested. "Everybody knows you guys can score. Maybe next game, let's see who gets the most assists."

"In addition to scoring? Then what will the rest of you do?" Andre retorted.

His lips curled into a smirk, and when Ryan rolled his eyes, bumping his shoulder and stealing a fry, the expression softened. Everybody had to know they were dating. At least, everyone on the team. They were so obvious about it. They brushed up against each other. Kept close. Constantly touching, murmuring this and that, but with Derek on Andre's right and Ryan up against the wall, who else could hear between Ollie's rambling and all the broken bits of conversation.

Maybe people just decided not to see. Made assumptions based on the information readily given without looking for more. I hadn't noticed. Not until Ariadne brought it up.

She hadn't asked me again. Hadn't said a word to me. Not that we ran in the same circles most days, but I expected more pressure to do what she wanted. As long as she said nothing to me, I intended to pretend it never happened.

As we all piled into different cars, Ryan called me over, "Hey, Beni. I'll give you and Ollie rides home. You're closer to my house anyway."

"Thanks," I said, sliding in the back beside Ollie, who frowned at Andre.

"Aren't you on the other side of town?" Ollie asked.

Andre rolled his eyes. "Don't worry your little underclassman head. Seniors are continuing the party - location NTK."

"What?" Ollie's nose wrinkled.

"Need to know," Ryan explained, but he didn't add any more detail as he pulled out of the diner's lot.

Ollie crossed his arms, slouching back in the seat. "Seriously? I'm a junior. Come on!"

"May be a junior, but you're pouting like a freshie," Andre teased, punching Ollie in the knee.

"Screw you two, maybe Beni and I will contact the underclassmen. Have a party without the seniors," Ollie retorted.

"Don't drag me into this," I said, holding up my hands and leaning back. "My dad'll kill me if I'm not back by ten."

Itching his palm over his buzz cut, Ollie sighed. "Man, Beni, he seems pretty chill to me. My dad would have a fit if my sister wanted to stay out this late with guys."

"She's on the team. What's he going to do?" Ryan noted, and I nodded, gesturing at him.

"Team spirit," I added.

Ollie snorted, laughing. "Nah, man, my dad would totally think my sister was using that as an excuse or something to see her boyfriend, and aren't you close with Sean and Geoffrey? Like, I've never seen you with another girl."

"I have female friends."

Turning around in his seat, Andre cocked a brow. "Really? Who?"

"Jane Malcolm - we're chem partners too," I offered.

Rolling his eyes, Ollie shook his head. "Come on. Somebody you meet with outside of school."

My mind blanked. "I don't know. Sean and Geoffrey have been my best friends since preschool. I've never really had time to hang with anyone else." And it wasn't like Jackson was a girl or somebody I could readily admit to hanging out with at all.

"See," Ollie exclaimed. "No lady friends."

"What girls do you hang out with, Oliver?" Andre demanded, turning on Ollie as quickly as he'd ganged up on me.

Ollie sputtered. "Plenty!"

"Yeah, but who?" Andre pushed.

"Veronica."

Andre's eyes twinkled in the dim light of the car. "Louis or Mayford?"

"Mayford," Ollie quickly replied.

Humming, Andre shook his head. "Lying like a freshie."

"Don't pick on your teammates," Ryan scolded, pulling up to my house. "Here you go, Beni, and just ignore them. Good friends are hard to come by."

"Hey!" Andre shouted, punching Ryan in the arm.

Ollie burst out laughing, his weird snorting guffaw echoing even as they drove away. Despite it being almost curfew, the lights remained on - and when I headed inside, my dad sat at the kitchen table.

"How'd it go?" He asked, pushing out the other chair with his foot.

Glancing around, I sat down. "Fine. We got burgers."

"So, Jackson Duke…he says you've been helping him practice in the mornings. Would've been nice if you told me," he said.

I shifted in my seat. "It's more like we're helping each other. I've improved a lot because of him."

"I could tell." His blue eyes stared at me, studying my face as if looking for something there he hadn't expected to need to look for in the first place. "This anything I should be worried about?"

"What'd you mean?"

He leaned back, crossing his arms over his chest. "Are you dating the boy?"

My jaw dropped. "What? No. No-no-no. We aren't like that."

His eyes narrowed. "You sure?"

"He's just a friend. We don't even see each other outside the rink," I explained quickly.

Though his lips pursed, he nodded, accepting my words for the moment. Which was ridiculous. Jackson had no interest in me. Ryan might've been more popular because he was genuinely nice, but Jackson modeled. He was internationally famous. Guaranteed to be a big shot NHL player. Even girls at my school - who painted their faces and bad-talked St. Raphael's - would jump at the chance to be with him. Somebody like that wasn't interested in more with me.

Running his hands over his face, he sighed. "Okay." He stood. "Just - just let me know if that changes." The way he said *if* sounded an awful lot like *when.* Still, I nodded. With a returned curt nod, he headed off upstairs with a quiet, "Goodnight then." But I could hear him murmur beneath his breath, "This was supposed to be your job, Mary."

Dad was completely off base. He'd talked to Jackson one time. Sure, we were friends, but there was no way either Duke brother saw me as anything more.

Chapter Sixteen

For all the strange things in my life since Tanner Duke decided to drag me into his and his brother's secret circle, nothing was as surreal as sitting in the Duke household with piles of expensive unused gear in front of me. Jackson kept vanishing upstairs and coming down with armfulls of sticks, padding, workout clothes, and even skates. They honestly lived in another world. Their couch alone probably cost more than all the furniture in our house and my dad's car combined. I'd never been so afraid to touch anything.

"Hey, Leo's making personal pizzas for lunch," Tanner announced, coming back from the kitchen. "What do you want for yours?"

"Whatever's fine."

Snorting, Jackson dug through the piles. "You'll end up with some experimental health-nut shit."

"And that's bad why?" I asked.

Tanner rolled his eyes, but he didn't argue as he tugged out his phone to text their personal chef because the kitchen was too far away - and the walls too thick - for him to just yell. There was even an elevator. Their father had gotten an elevator built in their four story house - not including the basement - after the car accident. Anybody else I knew would've been lucky to have somewhere on the first floor converted into a bedroom.

Throwing himself down on the couch beside me, Jackson sprawled. "I mean, it'll taste fine, but you're not taking advantage of our personal chef properly."

"Leave her alone," Tanner commanded. "Seriously, Jackson? If you're going to take over the floor, push back that chunk of the sectional! How am I supposed to get anywhere?"

Cocking a brow, Jackson scoffed. "Don't you have an affair to conduct?"

The muscles in Tanner's jaw jumped. Crossing his arms, he surveyed the room. I could practically hear the gears in his mind turning to discover a clear route, but the sectional formed an almost perfect square with the only free side being taken by a large fireplace over which a ridiculously large television hung. Every gap had been expertly filled with hockey or general exercise gear. Which I was supposed to go through.

While Tanner plotted, I shifted the gear. "Are you sure you can give this stuff away?"

"If it's not gone by tonight, my dad will be pissed," Jackson informed me. "We have the same skate size, right?" Grabbing a pair of Bauer skates, he tossed the boxes down between us. "You need to get rid of your old ones anyway."

"My old ones are fine," I argued.

Even if it made me feel weird, I couldn't pass up new skates, but I didn't need ones that were several hundred dollars. Rolling up beside me, Tanner leaned over the back of the couch. "Stop freaking out. He's got like a pair for every day of the week."

Putting them down, I lied, "I'm not freaking out."

"Great, then you'll take both," Tanner retorted. Gliding back a few feet, he clicked down the breaks, and grabbing the back of the couch, he swung himself over, landing with a curse followed by a crow of triumph. "Screw you, Jackson!"

His brother rolled his eyes. "You're such an idiot."

"Isn't there somebody on your team -"

"Nope," Jackson interrupted me. He dug through the sticks, picking out a couple and tossing them to one side.

"But what about the - "

He cut me off. "Not a fan."

"You don't even know what I was going to - "

"Say? Yeah, you're super predictable, Beni." Pitching his voice, Jackson gestured with a stick as he said, "I can't possibly accept any sort of help! It would undermine my underdog obsessively independent schtick!"

Grabbing the blade, I tugged the stick out of his grip. "Fine. Give me the stupid stick."

Jackson beamed like he'd just scored a goal. Then his eyes fell to the stick. "Shit - not that one. Give it back." Digging through the pile, he pulled up two others. "These two are better."

"I already have two sticks," I grumbled.

Tanner snickered. "Give the man what he wants. He'll lecture you about appropriate equipment maintenance and stick cycling for the next week if you don't."

"Stick cycling?" Jackson smacked his brother's shins. "Don't be stupid. Extra sticks in case this beast shatters one."

My nose wrinkled despite myself. "I've never shattered a stick."

"Then you obviously haven't been playing hockey right," Tanner retorted. Jackson nodded sagely in agreement, shoving the two sticks at me once more.

Trading off the one stick for the two, I shook my head. "You're both ridiculous."

Jackson merely smirked. A single golden brow cocked up as if to remind me that no matter how absurd I thought he was, he had gotten what he wanted. He and Sean would've gotten on well. The same cocky pleasure when they won something - regardless of how important the argument was. Or maybe that's why they wouldn't have. Sean thought Andre was a jerk, and he acted the same way.

However, even though Tanner laughed along, mocking his brother with the usual dry tone and smarmy smirk, he seemed tired. His body slumped against the cushions. Legs shifting, he pushed the heel of his palm against his thighs as if to remind himself that he could still feel them. Every once in a while, his toes would twitch up.

"You okay?" I asked when Jackson carried off the remainder of the sticks. Apparently, they had a storage pod in the back, and anything Jackson couldn't convince me to take would end up being donated somewhere. Jackson hadn't been specific about where.

With a half-shrug, Tanner sighed. "Yeah. I'm fine."

"You don't seem fine."

Tanner leaned back, resting his head on the couch as he stared at the ceiling. "I'm not great at apologizing. Our dad - he's - he's not really an apology person. He's a 'do better' sort of guy. Jackson either doesn't care, or - if someone he cares about is angry with him, he's a freaking mess. Like - when I was in the hospital, he wouldn't stop bending over backwards no matter how much of a dick I was." Running his hands over his face, he confessed, "I've only really had to apologize to my mom before."

He glanced at me, peeking through his fingers as if waiting for me to speak up. Maybe it was a bit petulant, but I stayed silent. Staring back at him in return, I waited. If I could outwait Geoffrey, Tanner wouldn't beat me. Apologies mattered. Saying the words might not have been enough for his dad, but sometimes, sometimes I just needed to hear it. To know that it wasn't just in my head. To hear that the person recognized what they had done. Otherwise, I'd spend my time worried and waiting for it to happen again. Doing better helped, but it didn't change what had already happened, and that mattered too.

Striding back into the room, Jackson glanced between us. His eyes narrowed as he studied his brother. "You're stalling," he accused.

Tanner groaned. "I'm not."

"Say it then," Jackson demanded. "Man up and apologize."

Frowning, I focused on the pile of hoodies and compression shirts. "Leave it, Jackson. Apologies don't count if somebody forces you to do it."

Glowering at his younger brother, Jackson pointed flared his nostrils and jumped his brows. I tried not to notice Tanner throwing his hands up, but the two weren't exactly trying to be subtle.

Shirts. There were a lot. Jackson and I were about the same size, but my hips were broader, so the smaller shirts wouldn't work. Tossing them aside, I kept my head down until Jackson grabbed a pillow, throwing it at his brother's head.

"Seriously, Jackson, leave it," I grumbled.

Tanner - like the drama king he was - screamed into the pillow before proclaiming, "I am a complete jerk. Ariadne told me what she said to you, and she had the nerve to - " Jackson pointedly cleared his throat, and Tanner groaned. "Point is, I'm a jerk. I'm sorry. I dragged you into this - and honestly, I really do want to be friends. I think we work as friends. You're good people, Beni Seaver, but then I got stupid and caught up because Ariadne Page liked me, which - I mean, come on?"

"Stay on point," Jackson ordered.

Taking the shirts I tossed, Jackson dug through the other piles to remove the other tops of the same size. Both our backs were to Tanner.

135

Maybe that helped. It made it easier to listen to his ranting excuses without rolling my eyes.

"Fine, fine. I'm responsible for my decisions. I ditched you and Jackson, and even though I think it's gone well for everybody involved, I said one thing and did another which was a jerk move. I'm sorry I did that, and I want to start over," Tanner said. Humming slightly, he chuckled. "Frankly, Jackson kind of owes me after -" Jackson whipped around, throwing a balled up shirt at his brother's face. "Shit! Seriously?"

The two of them glared at each other. Rolling my eyes, I shoved Jackson. "Leave it. This isn't on you."

"He's my little brother. It's my fault if he's a dick," Jackson retorted.

Tanner threw the shirt back at his brother. "I screwed up. I get that. I'm sorry."

"Do you?" I asked.

Brows furrowing, he pressed a hand to his chest when I turned to stare him down. "Yeah. Course."

"Great. I don't plan on being any guy's fake girlfriend, so - sorry, but Ariadne's gonna have to deal with the fallout there on her own," I announced, and it felt good. Like a weight vanished from my shoulders.

Ryan and Andre weren't my responsibility. Even if Ryan was nice to me - even if I had spent years crushing on him, I owed him nothing. He hadn't stopped his boyfriend from slashing my tires - or getting his friends to do it. Face to face, sure, he was kind - said the right things, but when it came time to be just decent, he went off and did the easy path. Did I wish he didn't have to hide who he loved? Yes. His family - they were horrible. I didn't need to know they were homophobic to know that. Ryan's family competed on an unreal level. No amount of success measured up to his brothers, and his dad only had snide remarks when Brandon and I used to hang out over their house after school. Involving myself in that mess made zero sense. Maybe if Ryan had asked - or Andre hadn't been such a complete jerk - maybe I wouldn't be resolutely against throwing myself up as a shield for them, but I owed them nothing. I owed Ariadne nothing, and I certainly owed Tanner nothing.

"Good." Jackson smiled, smacking me on my back.

Tanner pursed his lips. "It's like six months until graduation. I think Ryan can live without a girlfriend. There's plenty of reasons not to date."

"They'd just break up when going to college, wanting to play the field, he's gay," Jackson listed out, shoving more short-sleeved and sleeveless tops into my pile. Crouching, he tossed shirts this way and that like a dog determined to bury a bone. "I'm guessing medium pants aren't gonna cut it."

We'd only gone through two of the three piles of clothes. A pile of padding remained as well as a mix of odds and ends from athletic tape to water bottles. Even cutting out the ones that wouldn't fit and the weird colors - bright neons

137

which always made me feel awkward like I had put a spotlight on me, the shirts were enough for me to go through two weeks of twice daily practices without wearing the same shirt twice. A full week of hoodies. Another week of fleece jackets.

"This is ridiculous," I said.

Snickering, Tanner riffled through the accepted pile. "Man, if you think this is a lot, never go in Jackson's walk-in closet. He's got a bureau just for his practice clothes. Note, this is separate from his game day clothes, gym clothes, and casual leisure wear - which is basically joggers and the same crap."

Jackson kicked Tanner. "Shut up. You hoard stationary."

"Which I'll eventually use."

"I use all my clothes!" Jackson retorted.

A laugh escaped me, and Jackson turned a betrayed look to me. "If that was true, I wouldn't be here helping you clean out your 'clothes hoard.'"

Tanner shook his head. "Weirdest dragon ever."

"Oh, shut up," the elder Duke grumbled, returning to his sorting.

Humming, Tanner folded the shirts as he said, "You know - St. Raphael's has a sister school."

"Our Lady of Mercy? Hard not to know. They come to all our games against you guys," I reminded him.

"Our joint charters dictate that if there's an extracurricular activity - or even a class - at one school that isn't offered at the other, a student can petition to take the course - or join the sport - at the other school," Tanner informed us. "So if you went to Our Lady of Mercy, you could petition to join the St. Raphael's Lions hockey team."

This time I threw a pair of sweatpants at him. "As if I could afford that."

"Scholarships exist," Jackson pointed out.

"Sure - for tuition. There's uniform costs, books," I listed out, and the two just stared at me. They'd grown up going to St. Raphael's Academy. Neither could really get why somebody wouldn't jump on the chance to go, and explaining to them how I wanted to stay with my friends would only lead to some smart remark, so I settled on, "Besides, blue's my color, remember?"

And - luckily - the topic dropped as Tanner snorted. "Yeah? Is it? Then why's that blue shirt in the reject pile?"

"Must've been a mistake," Jackson agreed, tossing a highlighter blue shirt over to the yes pile.

"I'll look like a sticky note," I complained, grabbing for it.

Tanner tugged the shirt out of my reach. "But blue's your color."

"Oh, screw you," I grumbled, but I let them have it. I could always get rid of the shirt when I got home. At least, I told myself that. We all knew I wouldn't, and when I finally got home, my dad gave the new sports bag stuffed with new gear a pointed look. "He was getting rid of some stuff."

Pursing his lips, he nodded, turning back to

whatever show he had been watching. As long as he didn't say it, I tried not to think about it, but staring at everything piled out on my bed, I couldn't deny it looked too new to have just been sitting in his closet for the last year. But I had gear. Maybe not gear good enough for Jackson Duke, but good, solid gear from my sticks to my skates. Honestly, besides the practice clothes, I probably wouldn't use any of the new stuff for a while. No point breaking in new skates part way through the season unless I had to do it. Anyway - it wasn't like Jackson couldn't afford it. It was just a friend looking out for another friend.

So why did that leave me disappointed?

Chapter Seventeen

Christmas came and went, taking New Year's along with it. Our first weekend after was practice only and no game, so Coach Carr had us scrimmaging to see how well we had kept up our training over the holidays. He'd also had the brilliant idea of trying to test out new combinations for lines. Nobody seemed convinced he'd actually keep them, but it was a nice change of pace.

"Come on!" Andre threw up his hands. "Seriously! Am I getting no assistance here?"

With a smile, Ryan slid back into place. "Or maybe we're just that good."

Nose wrinkling, Andre rolled his eyes. "Seaver's that good. We'd be winning twice as hard if it was the two of us on the same team."

"You think?" Ryan teased.

Sean beamed. "I'm up for switching if we want to test that out."

"You just want to be on the winning team, so you don't have to clean up," Kendall scoffed, nodding at me as he added a snide, "Beni's good, but she's not that good. No offense."

"I've scored twice. Andre's got one in. Everybody else is at zero. I think I'm good," I retorted with a smirk, earning a loud shout of 'ohh, burn' from Sean.

"Tell you what," Ryan announced, "Beni and Kendall, switch. We're up one. Let's see if we can hold the lead."

"Work for you, Coach?" Andre called.

Carr huffed as he noted the shift on his clipboard. "You heard your captain. Seaver - Colt - switch!"

Kendall and I glided in half-circles to stand on opposite sides. Slicks down, we waited. Tension building as Andre smirked, giving Ryan a feral grin as Sean cackled. Back in goal, Derek let out a long drawn-out groan, stretching his back before falling into a crouch. Prepared and ready for a break-away.

Then the puck dropped. Any doubt the defense might have had about Derek's starting position vanished as the three of us broke through the opposing offense, charging down toward goal. Clean plays - fast plays - the ones done well could take seconds. The interesting games came when two sides faced off, sending the puck back and forth with stealing and checks. A win after a hard game held me up higher than the faster ones, but a single clean play - especially against a good team where the rest of the game was rough. Those were beautiful.

Especially when the puck glided to me, and Derek's shifted - not much, but just enough that when I flicked it over to Sean, he scored, tying the scrimmage up in under twenty seconds.

Cheering broke out on our side, and Derek sighed, grumbling to himself, "I knew better. Winning beats ego every time. I knew that!"

"Lucky shot," Ryan taunted. "Bet you can't do it again."

Lining back up across from Kendall, I settled into place. We didn't manage to score again easily, but by the end of practice, we were up three, and winning meant the losing team had to clean-up. A small victory as it was just the goals, but Andre skated around Ryan with a smug smirk, speaking in a low tone.

"I'm cashing this win in tonight, Caldwell," I overheard him say as I skated past.

Before I could get off the ice, Kendall rushed to me. His eyes narrowed. "Sean says you practice mornings 'cause you work part-time for Mike. That deal open for anybody?"

"I don't think Mike's hiring," I said, and I should've stopped there, but his shoulders sagged, and it seemed like the perfect chance to make another friend on the team, so I offered, "I can see if he's cool with you coming early and joining in if you want."

His lips split into a wide grin. "Really? Yeah, that'd be great!"

"What're you guys talking about?" Ollie asked.

"Beni's gonna see about getting us a morning practice. You in?"

Ollie shook his head. "I'm not giving up my sleep to this. Graham gets up ridiculous early. Maybe he'd want to do it with you weirdos."

And it traveled around the rink, bouncing from one person to another, and by the time I was able to finally get away to the locker room, we had a solid group of five saying they'd come if Mike okayed it.

"That's the sort of leadership I like to see, Seaver. Keep it up, and you might just be captain," Coach offered, clapping me on the back as I headed toward the lockers.

Team voted captains, so odds weren't good, but I appreciated the sentiment right up until I ducked out of the locker room - hair dripping as I had rushed - to ask Mike. When I did, he shifted, sitting back as he stared at me. Squinting, he shook his head like I'd gone crazy before leaning forward to remind me that I sort of had.

"How're you gonna explain that to Jackson?" Mike asked. "Or explain Jackson to your teammates?"

My stomach sank. I had completely forgotten Jackson - the guy who I practiced with daily - was the star player on our rival team. Somehow, he had become more than the mythic all-star, but regardless of the strange friendly rivalry brewing between us - and getting friendlier every day, I forgot there was anybody else to consider. Not exactly A+ friend material.

Biting my lip, I rocked back on my heels. "Maybe I can talk to him…"

"And say what? 'Sorry, it's been great, but now people on my own team are showing an interest in me,'" Mike offered, and it was like hearing an echo as Brandon's ghost inside my head said the same thing. "Normally, I'm all for you thinking less, but this time - you're lucky I'm keeping an eye out for you."

"Thanks," I mumbled, shoulders slumping as I headed back to catch the guys coming out of the locker room.

But whatever insanity made me forget Jackson seemed to call him into being. Swaggering through the door, Jackson marched directly to me. Tanner raced after him, looking particularly frustrated. No pretending we didn't know each other. Not even letting Tanner lead in as my teammates slowly trickled out of the locker room. Right in front of everybody, Jackson Duke walked up to me with a puffed up chest and a victorious smirk.

"Thought you ought to know, they're sending a scout from Raphael's to your next game, Seaver," Jackson announced.

Immediately, a crowd gathered. A cacophony of voices demanding: "What?" "Who for?" "You're lying to psych us out."

"Why would Beni care? She's a girl. It's an all-boys school." The last came from Sean. He stood, nose wrinkled and hands on his hips after he had muscled his way to stand beside me.

Andre, who had been waiting at the tables with a hot drink, sauntered over at the commotion. "Tell them not to bother, Duke. I'm not going anywhere."

Jackson scoffed, sneering at our best player. "They aren't coming for you."

Rolling his eyes, Andre crossed his arms. "Then who? I'm the best player on this team - hands

145

down. Nobody else has ever been offered a position, and the new guys on our team are mediocre at best."

"Friendly fire, Andre. Try not to catch your team in the crossfire," Ryan warned as he ran a hand through his damp hair. "Hey, Duke. Maybe now's not the best -"

"He's coming for Beni," Jackson proclaimed, loud and proud, and even as my heart thundered in panic, the floor refused to open up and eat me.

"But she's a girl," Sean repeated. "She'd have to get into Raphael's girl-side, and they don't have an ice hockey team."

"But their bylaws state any course or academic activity not provided by one school may be supplemented by the other," Jackson informed him smugly. "We have almost identical course catalogs, but a few years back, a young man by the name of Marcus Neil decided he wanted to pursue more advanced ballet - not offered by Raphael's but included as a supplement for Mercy's dance team."

I needed to get out of there, but my team surrounded us. Any guilt I had over forgetting Jackson evaporated. How could he think this was what I wanted? We'd talked about money. Specifically, I didn't have any extra. Even if I got a scholarship to cover tuition, there were uniform costs, transport - because I sure couldn't ride my bike there, and who knew what else.

All eyes turned to me. My muscles tightened. This couldn't be happening. I had to be hallucinating. Guilt hallucination. Panic-induced images, and if I just stayed still, this would all go away. Every muscle tensed- tight and panicked and so immovable that my lungs ached. Frozen, I stared blankly at the ground.

"Beni?" Sean prompted. His hand fell on my shoulder.

"Why?" I sputtered. Too loud. Too sudden.

Jackson's brows furrowed, and Tanner sunk into his wheelchair, running his hands over his face like he couldn't bear to watch what would happen next. Glancing down at his younger brother, Jackson shifted, glancing around as if finally realizing my entire team surrounded us.

He licked his lower lip, shrugging. "Cause I want you on my team."

"Well, she doesn't want to be on your team," Andre snapped, stepping between Jackson and me. Tilting his chin up, he looked down his nose at the Duke brothers. "I know you're not used to rejection, Duke, but Beni's true blue Port Edmond. We don't waste time on snowbirds."

"Snowbirds? We were born here. We're here a full twelve months and so is our dad." At his sides, Jackson's fingers curled into fists.

"Plus, our house is closer to Beni's than yours," Tanner added, and Andre's cheeks flushed.

Everybody knew for all his bluster, Andre's parents were snowbirds. Flying south - or more rightly to Europe - and leaving their kids alone during the academic year. Nobody wanted to call him on it. He was one of us, and for all his mercuriality, people liked him, so when somebody jumped to his defense, it shocked nobody.

But Geoffrey's reply just had to be: "And how would you know?"

"Cause I've driven to both," Tanner informed the group. "I mean, somebody has to be a good human being when you jerks slash her bike's tires."

Joe reared back as if slapped, but others glared amongst each other as some - including Ryan, ducked guilty. Looking anywhere but at me. Because they had known. Known my own teammates bullied me, and they hadn't even stuck around to offer a ride, so how could they speak up now against Tanner?

But Andre didn't care about cleverness, and there was one bit of information everybody still wanted to know about - when did Tanner go over Andre's house? However, for all his impassioned fury, he couldn't retort because if he did, Tanner had an opening to reveal he and Ariadne were seeing each other, which opened a Pandora's box Ryan wasn't ready to face, and even if Andre cared about nobody else or even the basic tenets of human decency, he wasn't going to put his best friend - his boyfriend into a tight spot.

As everyone struggled - impotent rage awaiting somebody - anybody to make a move to turn things physical against a rival they'd all wanted to take down a peg, Derek shoved his way into the group. He lowered a blood-chilling glower at everyone.

"You're all going to walk away now," he told them.

Ryan, taking the chance, waved everyone off. "Derek's right. Nobody wants to go to Raphael's, but we'll sure give that scout a show, right guys?"

A murmur of begrudging agreement spread through the group, and most broke off, heading out. Those who stuck around were shoved and pushed around by Ryan and Derek - with Andre eventually growling out his own command for his little following to leave, guiding them out with a pointed look sent to Ryan.

Tanner tugged on his brother's arm. "Come on, Jacks. I told you this was a bad idea."

"Go see your girlfriend," Jackson told his brother, never taking his eyes off me.

Scoffing, Tanner waved his hands around. "What are you - why would I think it was a bright idea to leave you alone right now? Do you really want to get your face smashed?"

Shaking his head, Jackson clenched his jaw. The muscles bounced, but he stared me down, pinning me in place. "Tanner…"

His younger brother huffed, but this time, Tanner didn't bother to argue beyond a, "Don't blame me when this blows up in your face," thrown over his shoulder.

Even though most had dispersed, Sean and Geoffrey flanked me, and that should have been enough for me to move - to get the heck out of dodge. Ryan had paid for my bike to be fixed, and it was sitting out front right now - hopefully without slashed tires - so I could get home - or at least make the point of leaving. If Jackson wanted, he could drive after me. Be obnoxious and yell at me out his car window, but that seemed more Tanner's schtick than his.

"Hey," Sean whispered, nudging me with his shoulder. "Let's get out of here."

And just like that, the roots disappeared. "Can your mom give me a ride home?"

"Course," Sean replied, and he shifted, stepping between Jackson and me.

The muscles in Jackson's jaw bounced before he murmured, "Beni…"

"It's Friday. Why don't we get pizza? Sleepover like old times," Geoffrey suggested, shifting to form the other half of a blockade.

"Heck yeah! Pizza and video games! All night long!" Sean cheered.

They walled me off, getting me away from Jackson even as he rushed to round them, calling my name with increasing frustration, and I wanted to tell him he could've texted me. That I had the stupid phone he gave me. Even if it was the weekend - and we didn't practice in the mornings together on weekends, that didn't mean there weren't other ways he could've told me. Ways where I could have told him it wasn't what I wanted. That my team would freak. The possibility didn't seem to dawn on him until hours later. I had extra clothes in my sports bag, so crashing with a call to my dad - on Sean's home phone - was fine.

"You're telling me what happened when you get home," my dad said, but he didn't push.

We set up a blanket fort in the living room. Pizza on the table and even ice cream after Sean had told his mom what happened. I hadn't heard his exact words, but he pulled her aside, and then we were getting ice cream and chips and all the junk food she normally wasn't a fan of Sean having. Bowl full of cookie dough ice cream slathered in chocolate syrup and sprinkles, I sunk deep into the pillows as Sean cued the next movie.

"We gonna talk about it?" Geoffrey asked, reaching for his third slice of pizza.

I sighed, shrugging. "Maybe."

"I know I've been a jerk lately, but I seriously wanted to avoid this exact situation -" His eyes narrowed. "Well, sort of. This but with Tanner."

"I don't even know what this situation is," I confessed and shifted to bring my knees to my chest. "We've been practicing together. In the mornings."

"Okay…"

Falling into his seat on my other side, Sean sprawled with a huff. "Explains why you got so good. Wish you'd invited me."

"I didn't intend to practice with him. Tanner kind of just stuck him on me," I retorted, but Geoffrey just kept staring. "Okay, so maybe you were right. Tanner's after Ariadne, but she likes him too. But what does that have to do with me?"

Stretching, Sean rolled over, wrapping himself like a burrito, so only his face and feet showed as he wormed his way to sit up. A determined furrow to his brow.

"Well, you knocked him out once. Maybe he thinks you're a threat," he said.

Geoffrey shook his head. "I definitely was wrong. You're shit cover for Tanner and Ariadne if you aren't at our school."

"They're brothers - not the same guy. Tanner might've wanted a way to spend more time with Ariadne, but I think Jackson just got dragged along," I groaned, shoving my ice cream away on the coffee table. "He gave me a cell phone. Why didn't he just text me?"

Sean and Geoffrey both stared at me as they said in unison, "He gave you a cell phone."

A guilty churning brewed in my stomach - or maybe that was all the junk food, but I took out the cell. A single voicemail and sixty-three texts sat waiting. All from Jackson except one single text from Tanner. All three of us gawked at the thing as if it were a three-headed chicken.

Nudging me, Sean nodded at the phone. "What'd he say?"

"I don't know if I want to know," I grumbled, but I opened the first message anyway.

The tone started off frustrated. Complaints about how hard he had worked, how hard I had practiced, why I should've been over the moon. They gradually became mildly apologetic, acknowledging he could've handled telling me differently while excusing it for his excitement because this wasn't a chance most people got. Because he had pulled every string he had to make his coach even consider scouting me.

They ended with a final lashing out - not exactly vicious but strange: "They don't deserve you. Stop pretending they do."

"Well, that seals it. I'm not listening to the voicemail," I announced, switching over to Tanner's single text.

"It's not his fault he's this dumb. Give him time to cool off. He'll realize what he's done by Monday and kick himself. Sorry that doesn't help with your teammates," Sean read out over my shoulder.

Geoffrey chuckled - a small slightly hysterical sound. "Man, Beni, you don't do things half-way."

Chapter Eighteen

Staying over Sean's house meant not getting up early for the rink. Not that I did most Saturdays anyway, but with Jackson, I had started at least getting up early to go off wherever on the weekends - even if it was just over to his house. While I had once spent more nights at Sean's than in my own bed - especially after Brandon died, it had been a while. Waking up on the couch, I burrowed further beneath the blankets. Geoffrey and Sean sprawled on the air mattress on the floor. At some point in the night, Sean had stolen the covers, curling up like a burrito. Not that Geoffrey seemed to care. He spread out like a starfish with one leg thrown over our bundled friend nearly pushing Sean off the bed altogether.

The disquieting feeling remained. Honestly, it grew worse when I saw the warning from my Dad sitting on my phone that we'd talk about both my having a cell phone when he sure didn't get me one and Mercy. I already knew what he'd say, so when Geoffrey and Sean decided gaming and snacking was the best way to spend a Saturday, I put off going home until I didn't exactly have a choice.

"He can't be mad," Sean argued. "It's not like he didn't know, right?"

"Kind of. Not - not all of it," I admitted, sinking into the seat, but I didn't have a choice. I wasn't a kid. Running away wouldn't change anything. Despite the lies I wanted to tell myself, it would just make things worse, so with a quick thanks for the ride, I headed inside.

My dad sat at the kitchen table. He pointed at the seat across from him. "Sit down."

His tone said trouble, but I refused to believe it was justified. "What did I do?"

"For starters, you never told me your teammates were the ones responsible for your bike, or about that cell phone. Jackson gave that to you, didn't he?" he asked. When I nodded, he sighed and held out his hand. "Give it here."

"What? But Dad - "

He shook his head, giving me a solemn stare. "You aren't keeping it. I don't care how much money his family has, we don't take advantage of people in this house."

"How am I taking advantage of him? He's the one who offered," I retorted, but the argument fell flat even to me. Sighing, I handed him the phone. "What are you going to do with it?"

Putting the phone into his own pocket, he informed me, "I thought it was about time I spoke with Dr. Duke about what his sons are getting up to while he's working."

155

"You can't! His dad's already on his case since I bruised his ribs back in our first game."

This was ridiculous. I never intended to take advantage of Jackson, and I honestly didn't believe I did. Everything he ever gave me was convenient for him. He wanted to get in contact with me more easily, so he gave me a phone. His dad demanded he clean stuff out, so I got some new gear. Friends did that sort of thing. Maybe not with cell phones or several hundred dollars worth of hockey equipment, but that was Jackson Duke.

But I could see it in the concern etched onto my dad's tired face. This wasn't about his ego. Wasn't about what our family couldn't afford. No, this was something else. Whatever disaster he believed Jackson Duke would send our way, I couldn't argue against him. I hadn't believed Jackson would go behind my back and then announce his attempts to get me a scholarship to Mercy, so who knew what else he was capable of doing.

"Now - Mercy."

I sunk even further in the chair with a groan. "Come on, Dad. That's not even a conversation."

"A full scholarship to the best school academically in the area seems like something we should talk about. Attending a top high school, playing for the number one hockey team - national winners several years in a row - I'm not seeing a downside," my dad explained, and his no-nonsense tone made it worse. Everything he said was technically right, but he just wasn't considering all the downsides.

"I'd have no friends. My current team beat that national team. Plus, Bs at Port Edmond are better than Cs at Mercy," I argued.

He just shook his head, refusing to let it go. "You've got two years. With Mercy and the Lions, you'd be a shoe-in at any college you wanted. Scholarships to Northeastern, a place on their women's hockey team - good programs and the best chance at getting a place on a team in the National Women's Hockey League."

"I don't need Mercy to get there," I grumbled. "One way or another, I'm joining the Boston Pride."

"I believe in you, but that doesn't mean you need to make it harder for yourself. Mercy and the Lions eases the route." Frowning, he studied my face - staring me down like he could see right through to my soul. "Don't make this harder on yourself, Beni. If those morons at Port Edmond treat you like crap, leaving is a comment on them - not you. I would've sent you to Mercy in a heartbeat if I knew you'd still be able to play."

"And what about what I want?"

But I could see I had lost, and he sealed it when he told me, "Since your mom died, things have been difficult - with her hospital bills and then your brother's...I haven't been around much. We both know I can't afford to change that now any more than I could before, but I'm still your dad, and when that scout offers you a scholarship, you're taking it. You're too good to spend your life pretending to be less than you are." He let the weight of it sit on me for a moment before he said, "Get washed up. Dinner will be ready in fifteen."

Chapter Nineteen

Monday wasn't much better. Sean, Geoffrey, and I had the first three periods together - or a mix of the three of us, so I wasn't alone. Just because nobody said anything didn't mean that they weren't all aware. I could see it. The way they glared at me like I had done something unforgivable. It was exhausting. By the time fourth period rolled around - leaving me to the wolves without Sean or Geoffrey, I cared for it even less.

Joe glared at me, but if he had an opinion, he held his tongue. Ollie didn't.

"So - like - are you dating Duke?" he asked, turning around to face me in his chair as we waited for the bell to ring.

"No, we're not even friends." Especially not after what he had done.

Ollie nodded, humming. "Then he's got to just be screwing with us. Trying to get into our heads. Break up the team!"

"Bull," Joe grumbled.

The seat beside me remained empty. It was probably shocking enough to some that Ollie elected to sit near me considering I'd been branded a leper. Not like I had many friends to begin with, but even the friendly faces who I could grin and bear it with just looked right through me like I was dead to them. Which made no sense. I hadn't asked Jackson to get a scout to come, and I didn't want to go to Mercy. I was Port Edmond, through and through. Regardless, they watched me out of the corners of their eyes. To them, nothing I said mattered. I was a turncoat. Even just talking to Jackson Duke was bad enough to have me ostracized.

When Ollie opened his mouth to speak again, Joe grabbed his arm, dragging him clear across the classroom to a different lab table. The whole thing was ridiculous. As pissed as I was at Jackson for inspiring this situation, it just rubbed it in my face how taciturn my teammates were. Any reason would be good enough to hate me. No matter how well I skated - no matter how many assists or goals I had - they would just see me as this strange invading force.

Books slamming onto the desk beside me broke up my pity party. Dressed all in black, Annie McNeil glared at Joe as she sat down. "Boys are idiots," she announced. "Of course, Jackson Duke wants Beni on his team. She's the only one who stands a chance to beat him."

Joe scowled, but the dark murmuring stopped as Ollie threw up his hands as if to show his agreement with Annie.

"Thanks," I murmured right as the bell rang.

Annie scoffed. "Don't thank me. They're being ridiculous. I swear, our school is insane. Why anyone would go ga-ga for neanderthals like that is beyond me!"

We fell into an amiable silence until the bell rang once more, and as I packed up, Annie waited. I glanced between her and the door, but she stood directly in my way.

"You're having lunch with me and the girls," Annie commanded. I couldn't be sure what my expression was in response, but apparently it was disbelieving enough that she sighed. "Fine. Geoffrey and Sean can come too. Honestly, Beni, it's not like your Siamese triplets."

The crowds in the halls seemed to part for Annie, or maybe that was just the usual parting they did when they saw anybody my height lumber toward them. Either way, she glided to her locker, tossing in her books before sauntering toward mine.

"I'm dating a boy from Raphael's. Not on the hockey team. Neanderthals, like I said, but he's friends with Tanner, and honestly, I would've stepped in either way, because - really? Giving you that kind of attitude because you're a successful woman in a male-dominated sport?" Annie snorted, somehow managing to almost be stylish while doing so. "Anyway. We're going out to lunch today-"

"Sophomores can't leave school during lunch periods."

"Nobody bothers carding if they see you getting into a car since only seniors can apply for a parking place," Annie informed me. "Sarah's picking us up. She goes to Mercy - "

Dropping off my books, I shut my locker, shaking my head. "I'm not going to Mercy. I don't know what Tanner told you or told your boyfriend to tell you, but I'm staying right here. Scholarship or not."

Her eyes narrowed in suspicion, but knowing a Duke was involved, especially knowing it was Tanner, I wasn't about to let myself get pushed around. My situation was bad enough. If Andre or Joe found out I was eating off campus with a gang of Mercy girls, I'd never hear the end of it. If they knew that Annie dated a boy, well - they had names for girls who went out with boys from St. Raphael's Academy. None of them were pleasant.

"You can't give up this opportunity because it's scary," she informed me. "This isn't just about you!"

I shrugged, gesturing around. "Seems like it's my life, so…"

"And what about the other girls? Sarah's little sister Morgan plays hockey on the girl's youth

162

side. That stops at middle school at Mercy, and they have it longer than any other school. There's not even a joint team for women. If you get accepted to play with the Lions, that opens up a chance for her and any other girl interested to keep doing hockey after middle school. That could be enough to push for a team," Annie argued, storming to walk beside me as I continued toward the cafeteria, hoping Sean or Geoffrey might see her ranting at me and help me out. "Morgan's been talking non-stop about you. About Beni Seaver - the best forward on Port Edmond's team."

"If she wants to play for the Lions, she can try out."

Throwing up her hands, Annie cried out, "But she can't!"

"Why not? Nobody had done it at Port Edmond until me. I had to do that on my own. She can figure it out," I retorted.

Ducking into the cafeteria, I darted over to Sean. To my relief, Annie didn't follow, but there was a determination set in her expression which left my unnerved. Whether I liked it or not, this wasn't over, and more people than Jackson Duke were invested in me getting into Mercy.

Chapter Twenty

By the end of the day, a few people still glared at me, but most seemed to have quickly forgotten whatever they had been told, so when the coach gathered us all on the benches, my mind didn't immediately jump to it being about me. Some of the guys sat. Most stood, hanging about the lockers, glancing at each other as if someone had to know why they weren't already on the ice, but not even Ryan seemed to understand.

Couch Carr's eyes scanned our faces. "All of you know what happened after the game on Friday. I'm not going to waste practice time speculating on why Jackson Duke would be interested in scouting one of your teammates. After playing second fiddle for years, we wrecked them. They left the ice with their tails between their legs. If they weren't scouting the lot of you after that, they wouldn't be the number one team in the country."

Scoffing, Joe crossed his arms. He grumbled under his breath, "Duke's not interested in anybody but Seaver."

"And who took Duke out of the game?" Coach Carr retorted, causing Joe to startle. "Your teammate, Beni Seaver, did her part. She created an opportunity by removing their top player, and every single one of you took advantage of that. You joined together. Scored goals. Won the game."

"This is ridiculous," Andre exclaimed. "They've tried to scout me every year. Nobody made a big deal of it then. St. Raphael steals players. We all know it. This wouldn't be the first time they bought a player, and the only way Beni's going is if you idiots don't get your heads out of your - "

Geoffrey puffed up, looming by my side. "Says the jerk who wrecked her bike!"

"Quiet!" Coach Carr boomed. His face reddened like a tomato as he glowered at us as if he could set us on fire with his brain. "We are undefeated, but if you can't work together off the ice, how the hell do you expect to keep that going? We have a chance to knock St. Raphael out in State's. Anyone who wants to waste this opportunity on in-fighting, tell me now. I will be more than happy to cut you from the team." Rubbing the bridge of his nose, he ground his teeth together. "I shouldn't have to say this. You're in high school. I expect you all to be capable of keeping your house in order. Respect your teammates; respect the game; respect my time, and don't be idiots. Got it?"

"Yes, Coach!" we called in unison.

Crossing his arms over his chest, he glowered at us as if we'd just insulted his mother. "Defense and offense, split for warm-ups! Derek - Ryan, step up."

Geoffrey elbowed me. Rolling his eyes, he pulled a face. Odds were Coach Carr wouldn't notice anything just as he hadn't realized the wreck made of my bike repeatedly. Speeches like his covered nothing but his own backside. Winning mattered most. Mattered more to him than anything else. As long as I didn't throw a fit, he had no intention of cutting anybody. Not at this point in the season.

"Don't poke the bear," Sean hissed, glancing toward Andre.

Scoffing, Geoffrey headed off after Derek. "Accountability!"

We shuffled out onto the ice, separating into warm-up drills. I didn't expect anybody to pull anything. For all Coach had said, conflict had never usually followed me onto the ice. Not since the first week or two of the season. Focusing on hockey, I let the world outside the rink fade away. While on the ice, I was a Port Edmond Mariner. Silver, white, and blue - seafarer through and through. Born and bred.

So when Coach called the end of practice, my brain floated somewhere between the frustrated indignation of my day and the calm of practice. Showering, I dressed, and with something like resigned exhaustion, I headed out, expecting to either see my bike a wreck or some other disaster. I didn't expect Andre to be standing outside with Sean and Geoffrey.

The older player had his arms crossed. Each pale curl on his head was perfectly coiffed like something out of a magazine. Him and Duke. Pretty boy models the both. Both ridiculously stubborn and edging on narcissistic. Not that either of them would like the comparison. Or that it was true. Jackson wasn't as much of a jerk as Andre. Andre went out of his way to be a complete tool, ensuring if he was miserable everybody else was too. Even if Jackson had pulled the rug out from under me with his little announcement, for some stupid reason, he had thought he was doing the right thing.

And just thinking that left me uncomfortable. Uncomfortable and tired. "Am I going to need a ride home?"

With a scoff, Andre gestured at my bike. "I never screwed with your bike."

"Sure…" I mumbled, undoing the lock.

"I'm serious, Beni. I didn't mess with your bike. I didn't tell Joe or Donovan to do it either," he announced, and when Geoffrey shifted, looming as best he could with the few inches difference

167

between them, Andre growled, "Despite what everybody wants to think, I'm not the bad guy here!"

"You're only saying it wasn't you because Ryan's pissed at you," Sean pointed out.

Running a hand through his hair, Andre glared at the ground, "Because Ryan's being an idiot. I might not like you - but I don't play with fire."

"What?" Geoffrey sneered.

But understanding settled in my stomach. "It wasn't playing with fire until after it stopped."

"It was always playing with fire," Andre retorted. His gaze darted here and there, but whatever he sought, he didn't seem to find it. "You're Brandon's little sister. If Scott found out I messed with you, he'd make my life a living hell."

If he wanted to lie, I didn't have the energy to care. Scott hadn't been around for a while. Hadn't ever even come to the hospital for more than dropping off Brandon's homework. After Brandon died, he vanished. Off to college. Even before that, he never talked to me. Never came to the funeral. There was no way Scott cared about me. Ryan - maybe. Maybe Ryan cared because Ryan was Ryan. He cared about everybody, but that sure hadn't gotten him to go against his boyfriend.

Which left me drained. Thinking about how much pressure Andre dealt with between Ryan's family and his own. Dealing with hiding who he was with - probably minimizing who he was to not bring too much attention to Ryan - all this with his fate in the hands of his sister, and while he had chosen to trust her with the information, he never intended for me to know. Never wanted to bring in somebody he barely knew.

It was so much easier to just hate him. To look at Andre and see a snowbird's son. A guy who had the money to get out of Port Edmond even if he spent his life not caring enough to do anything. Silver spoon in the mouth sort of kid. Andre could be a complete slacker. But he wasn't. He cared. A lot. About how people saw him. About whether his teammates looked up to him. Whether he scored the most goals. Proved himself the best player - because he wanted to be. For reasons I didn't know. Reasons I wanted to pretend were empty and selfish and hollow, but standing out in the cold, that seemed less and less likely.

"Okay." Shifting my bags, I sighed. "I believe you."

Rolling his eyes, Geoffrey set his hands on his hips. "She believes you, so what now?"

"So if anybody messes with her, they're messing with me," Andre announced, and the moment the words left his lips, the awkward shuffle was entirely gone. He stood tall, staring me down. If he wanted to say something else, he held his tongue - storming off toward his car without even so much as a goodbye.

"Well...that was weird," Sean muttered.

I shrugged, climbing onto my bike. "No point living in the past."

"Bull," Geoffrey grumbled. He glared as Andre sped away. "He's just covering himself. I heard St. Raphael's isn't the only scout that'll be around at our next game."

Blinking, Sean leaned back. "Seriously? Who else?"

"Boston College's sending somebody out. Heard Coach talking with Andre and Derek about it," Geoffrey informed us, rocking back and forth on his heels.

"What about Ryan?" I asked.

When Geoffrey snorted, Sean huffed. "Just 'cause he's not as good as Andre doesn't mean he's not getting a scholarship somewhere."

Geoffrey rolled his eyes. "Well, Boston College isn't interested."

"Hope you're that nice about it when you and Beni get scholarships, and I'm stuck somewhere that probably won't even have a team," Sean said, punching Geoffrey in the arm. "Poor little ol' me! Best enjoy hockey while I can before you talented folks run off without me."

"Night, Sean," I replied.

Placing a hand over his heart, he dramatically sauntered off to his mother's car. Trailing not too far behind, Geoffrey followed with a last: "See ya tomorrow, Beni."

Before I could head out, a voice called my name. Mike leaned against the open door, frowning. "You didn't show up this morning."

"I left a voicemail."

He nodded. "You showing up tomorrow?"

"Yeah."

"You realize Jackson's going to be here."

Right - because I couldn't spend the rest of my life avoiding him. "I know."

"Great." Mike held out his hand, offering me a phone. "Your dad dropped this here with me. Thought you might want to listen to your voicemails."

Shaking my head, I kept my hands on my handlebars. "He's got practice after mine, right? You can just give it to him or Tanner."

"Yeah, that's what your dad said, but - ya know - I'm really not gonna play middle man to whatever mess is going on here." Crossing to me, he held up the phone. "You can give this to him

171

yourself, or I can chuck it in the trash. Either way, far as I'm concerned, I've never seen it."

Grabbing the phone, I shoved it into my practice bag. "Fine, I'll do it tomorrow."

"Good. And listen to the voicemails. If you're going to argue, might as well figure out how deep he dug the stupid hole, right?" Mike gestured dismissively. "Off you get, mini-Seaver. Don't want to run into Duke Two before you've dealt with Duke One. I hear the second version is better at arguing on the fly."

Both brothers could probably outrace me in a one-on-one fight. Talking wasn't exactly my strong suit. The moment Jackson and I talked - or worse Tanner and I - they would somehow make this all some big misunderstanding. A completely innocent mistake. Which maybe it was. Jackson probably hadn't meant any harm, and after everything he knew I went through, it wasn't exactly a big leap for him to think I might want to get out of Port Edmond, but he had asked. He had asked me, and I told him I didn't want that - even though I thought it was a joke. Because it was supposed to be a joke.

If I intended to argue, I had to find something I could justify being angry about. Something beyond my feelings. I needed to have facts. Reasons and data and more than just how I felt. Which left me miserable as I biked home. Why couldn't my feelings be enough? Because they couldn't be counted? Because no amount of apologies would take that away?

But a day had already calmed the weirdness - even with my teammates. Coach Carr - even if he wouldn't follow through - made a point of at least saying he would step in if anyone bullied anyone else. Sure, having a girl just randomly come up to me - probably because of Tanner - to push the whole Mercy issue helped. It was another moment to point to, but just thinking like that left me exhausted, groaning in frustration. Arguing never helped. I got all emotional, and everything I wanted to say flew right out of my mind.

I didn't want to be mad. People died. They got sick, and then one day, they were there, next - gone. Being angry never ended well. Life was short. Too short to spend with someone who would inevitably create tension. Make things even worse between my teammates and I. Keep giving me things and saying we were friends and making my dad think he liked me - because guys can't give women anything without it being for one thing - even though there was no way that Jackson Duke liked me like that. I was a beast. Too tall. Too big. Muscled and too quiet - not saying the right words.

Oh yeah, no way this could go wrong.

Chapter Twenty-One

Seeing Jackson shouldn't have been hard. We saw each other Friday morning. If I forgot about the post-game mess, it had only been three days. A couple weeks ago, we weren't meeting on weekends, so the gap between us shouldn't have seemed so big, but it did.

Sitting out in his car, Jackson bowed his head, resting it against the wheel. Like he'd been waiting a while. My hands shook as I adjusted my bags, wishing he had just shown up at the rink. It would've been easier. Easier than getting into his car. Sitting beside him and pretending that I wasn't fighting the urge to bolt. Trying to argue when I didn't know exactly how to tell him what he did wrong. Not in a way he'd understand. If there was a way to bring us back to before, I didn't know it. Couldn't find the words to ask.

"Hey…"

His head snapped up so fast, I thought it might break. Biting his lip, he shifted forward, leaning back with a sudden jerk as he glanced away. "Hey."

"We need to talk." Yeah - of course, we needed to talk. He already knew that. Idiot. This did not bode well. By the time we got to the rink, he'd have me all spun around, and I'd be apologizing and hating myself for it.

His gaze dropped. "I didn't think you wanted to talk to me."

I didn't. Not like I could say that, but his eyes studied my face, and his shoulders slumped. Until then, I hadn't realized he had begun to look hopeful.

Shrugging, I sighed. "Still need to do it."

"You can put your bike on the back - if you want…"

I nodded, falling into the familiar pattern. Hooking my bike to the rack and tossing my bags into the back before I climbed into the seat beside him. With the passenger side window open, it was freezing, but as we headed out, the heater hummed to life, and as the glass rolled up, there was nothing to do but talk. If I wanted a chance at this not going belly up, I had to talk first and fast. Neither of which was a strength of mine.

"I didn't think you and Tanner were serious when you asked me if I wanted to go to Mercy. I'm happy at Port Edmond. Even if I could afford to go elsewhere, I wouldn't want to," I told him, hoping he wouldn't ask for more. Hoping just my wanting it would be enough.

I never got lucky.

Jackson wrung his hands around the steering wheel. "Why would you want to stay there? They treat you like crap."

"A couple of them screwed with my bike. Everything was already calming down," I argued, but he set his jaw, gritting his teeth and glaring at the road ahead of him.

As he glided into the parking lot, he inhaled - taking a deep breath before he set the car into park and faced me. "And what about the rest? Why didn't they stop them?" When I didn't immediately answer, he pressed a hand against his chest. "I want you on my team. All the Lions agree. Having you on the team would make us unbeatable. Come on, Beni. Think about it. A team that supports you. Appreciates you. You could have that. We could play together. Not just practices."

"And when scouts come to the games, who are they going to be looking at? Me? Or Jackson Duke?"

He sneered. "You want to play for a women's team in college. We wouldn't even have the same scouts."

Everything about him screamed he was right. From the way he stared down his nose at me to the lopsided curl of his lips, Jackson looked down on me like the man standing on top of the hill and not the friend I had become used to seeing in him. It made it easier to fight back, but easier came out swinging blindly. No buffer against friendly fire. Not that there was anything friendly between us anymore. If he didn't respect my choices, how could we be friends? I never expected him to understand. I just wanted him to realize this choice was mine, and I wasn't going to let him bully me into anything I didn't want. Maybe if I thought that enough, I would be able to hold my ground.

"And my friends? You going to get Geoffrey and Sean scouted too?" I retorted, and Jackson scoffed.

"Why would I do that?"

I shrugged. "Why would I want to go to some weird school with people I don't know?"

"You know me!"

Shaking my head, I leaned back, pulling away as he leaned forward. Retreating because running away seemed a better chance than staying here, listening to him act like he had thought everything through. Like I had no right to argue.

"You'd be at St. Raphael's," I reminded him, forcing my eyes to remain on him. Refusing to cower as he stared me down. "We'd see each other at practice, sure, but I could count my female friends on one hand."

Not that that was a good thing. I had Sean and Geoffrey growing up, so I hadn't tried to spread to other circles, and by the time I realized how strange that was, there was my mom and then Brandon, and all the friends on the periphery only stuck around so long, and I didn't grieve prettily. Spending months pushing everyone away left me with excuses and twisted reasonings because if they couldn't stick by me when I chased them away with silence, why would I want to be friends with them anyway? Knowing I made a mistake didn't make it easier to undo.

And I could see it. His struggle not to tell me to just make new friends. If nothing else, Jackson had the same struggle. The desire to push people away when he struggled. To hide away. To pretend it didn't hurt when they finally left, realizing no amount of patience would 'fix' him, and in his eyes, I could see the epiphany. That moment when he recognized I wasn't backing down.

Sinking back, he swallowed. His eyes flicked away, jumping from the dark rink to me and back again. "Tanner has friends at Mercy. They'd adopt you in an instant."

"I'm not your charity case."

"How does that make you a charity case? You're Tanner's friend. Why wouldn't he want to introduce you to his other friends? If that's the first time anybody has done that for you, then the friends you have are crap," Jackson growled, gesturing wildly.

"And you're such a great friend? You aren't even listening to me!"

"I've heard every word you said, and you know what I'm not hearing? A decent reason why you'd give up the chance to be on the number one team in the nation at a top-rated school with courses that would make you a shoe-in at any college you wanted to go to!" Jackson spat.

And that was it, wasn't it? He saw this as me giving up an opportunity. Objectively, he wasn't wrong. We were set to have our best year yet, but that didn't change history. The Lions were known even outside of America, but nobody talked about their hometown rivalry with the Port Edmond Mariners. Going to Mercy opened doors. The same sort of network won doors that St. Raphael's students got. Hands shaking hands with money in-between. If I denied those opportunities existed, I'd be lying.

179

"Because I earned this." I just wanted him to understand. To get this wasn't about him or opportunities. "I worked hard. Practiced every day. Fought to get onto varsity. This is mine, Jackson. I made this for myself."

"How is this any different?" Jackson's voice cracked, and his eyes shimmered, leaving my stomach churning at the sight of tears in his eyes. "When the coaches offer you a scholarship to join us, it'll be because you worked hard. Because you practiced like mad. That'll all still be you."

"They're only coming because you told them to."

Rearing back as if I slapped him, Jackson set his jaw, squaring his shoulders and staring me down like a stranger sat in front of him instead of me. "So - I'm the problem?"

"What?"

"You don't want to be on the Lions because it's my team. You don't want it because I'm involved." With each word, Jackson's voice dropped lower and lower.

"Jackson, that's not - "

"No," he cut me off. A haughty cold distance stretched between us. "I get it. What's the point of practicing with me if you can't take me straight on, right? Prove how much better you are than breakable Jackson Duke. Money can only buy off the coaches for so long, right? Maybe I'll manage to get into college and get on a team, but eventually, the money won't be enough. Not like I'm professional material, right? Nobody wants a hockey player who might die if he's checked into the boards at the wrong angle."

The more he talked, the more he riled himself. Somehow, we flipped. Him, furious with me while I struggled to figure out where everything had gone so wrong. Once again, he had only heard what he wanted to hear. My opinion meant nothing. Obviously, I either had to fold and go to Mercy, or I became the enemy. Just another person looking down on him.

Fury roiled up inside me. Clawing until I wanted to vomit. "None of this is about you!"

"Isn't it?" Jackson sneered.

"Would you leave St. Raphael's?" I asked.

His brows furrowed. "Why would I do that?"

"Because I'm asking you too. Because I'm your friend, and I want you on my team," I parroted back, pleased to finally have some traction. To have figured out a way to let him know. He had to see this way, right? If I used his own words, he had to get it. "If you went to Port Edmond, we could eat lunch together. Drive to school together. Play hockey together. We'd spend more time together than if I went to Mercy."

He blinked, sinking back into his seat as if stunned. I did it. Relief swelled over me, and the warmth of hope growing left my cheeks flushed as I waited, tense and desperate for him to say something. Anything at all to show I had done the right thing. To confirm he heard me. That I finally got him to understand. It wasn't about him. Wasn't about the opportunities. That for all the jerks there were at school, I loved my friends. Loved what I had, and I didn't want change. Didn't want to face all those new people who would ask the questions and stare like people did when they first saw me.

I spent years in Port Edmond, and as much grief as some of the guys gave me, they knew me. Knew I was tall and muscular and didn't question when I lifted more than the footballers could. The gym teachers let me shift classes to be with my friends. Some people made fun of me. For being too tall or weirdly strong or too much like a guy. But my friends had my back, and I knew those people. The ones who had been making snide remarks since I started school.

The thought of going to a completely new place - a new school with all new people who could make the same assumptions those people did when we were in kindergarten hurt in an entirely different way. At least, the people who continued to point out how that stuff at Port Edmond were only the small-minded immature jerks. It might not be so contained at Mercy. They might see me, and it could be middle school all over again. High School wasn't perfect, but it was going so much better. I never wanted to go back. Not to the growth spurts and the laughing behind my back in the locker rooms. The fear about boys - because back then I didn't know about Ryan. Back when crushing on Ryan hung as another impossible. A reminder that some guys were nice to me - but that I wasn't that sort of girl. The kind of girl that guys like in that way.

And without guys around, maybe it would be easier because nobody would care that I was on the guy's team, or they could care all that much more, and I would be trapped passing messages for girls to their boyfriends at practice. Or they might be angry that some weird giant girl spent so much time with their boyfriends, and rather than looking at me like one of the guys, they'd see me as some kind of wannabe.

"Okay," Jackson exclaimed, drawing me out of my thoughts. He smiled at me. "It's midseason, so I'd have to talk with your coach, but he'd be mad to not let me on the team. I mean, I'm Jackson Duke."

I made a mistake. "You'll do it?"

Nodding, he swooned back into his chair with a sigh. "Course! You're right. I'm a star. Together - Lions, Mariners, whatever, we're going to be the top team, so scouts will show up wherever I am. If I go to Port Edmond, I can match up our schedules. Sure, I'm a year ahead of you, but that'll still be more than if you went to Mercy."

"But you like St. Raphael's...and Tanner goes to St. Raphael's," I reminded him, but he shrugged.

"I see him at home plenty. Anyway, it's not like we're in any of the same classes. Tanner's a genius," Jackson informed me.

Scrambling, I asked, "But your teammates know about your condition? What if they target you?"

"Like every other team does anyway? I'm faster than them, more skilled than them - I'm honestly the best player in the division."

Andre would be pissed. Half the team would be too, but the other half would be excited to have the best high school player on our team. Coach Carr would love it. Even though our schools rivaled each other, a number of the girls adored Jackson - swooning over how good-looking he was. If he came to Port Edmond, all the attention I feared at Mercy would be there anyway. The people I grew up with would ask questions and make assumptions about why Jackson Duke decided to 'slum it' at Port Edmond when his dad could totally afford St. Raphael's.

"What about your dad?" Thank god. His dad would never let him switch. "He'd have to okay the switch. Do you think he'd do it?"

Pouting, Jackson frowned. "Yeah, you're right. Well, guess you have to go to Mercy after all."

"What?"

"Well, if I can't switch schools to play on your team, you'll just have to switch," he informed me with the same imperialistic upturn of his chin where the conversation had started to go downhill from in the first place. "Mercy has connections to Northeastern. A few of the staff even attended, so you'd have a leg up getting in, and that's where you wanted to go, right?"

Like nothing had happened. One second he was angry. The next he's making plans as if I've already said yes. As if my deciding to switch to Mercy was written in the stupid stars. Some fated change. The scout hadn't even offered a scholarship or anything yet.

If we kept this up, we'd just keep going round and round. This whole mess had to be stressing him out just as much as me, right? Unless…

"You're manipulating me." Of course. While my stomach squirmed like a snake with the level of anxiety building inside me, he was fine. This was all just a trick.

Jackson gaped. "What are you talking about?"

I was so stupid. Throwing the door open, I grabbed my bags, not caring if they hit him as I tugged them over the seat. Tearing my bike from the rack, I swallowed the fury and anger, but they just kept coming back. How could I be so stupid? He would've gotten me to do whatever he wanted. I didn't want to go to Mercy. Hockey with him was fun. Practicing in the mornings with him helped me improve, and I liked practicing with him better than going it alone, but being friends didn't mean I wanted to change schools. Why did anything have to change?

"Beni! Come on! What's the big deal?" Jackson yelled, stepping out of the car. "Mercy

185

would be better for you anyway. You're too good for Port Edmond."

And Mike was nowhere in sight. Of course not. Because Jackson probably asked for time to talk to me because he thought ahead. Planned this whole thing out. Ripping the phone from my bag, I shoved it into his hands as I jumped onto my bike.

"What the - ? Beni, I gave this to you. Come on, Beni, this is stupid!"

His hand wrapped around my arm, and I couldn't get away fast enough. "I'm not going to Mercy. I'm a Port Edmond Mariner, and if you've got a problem with that, you can go back to your stupid gold lion school because I'm not leaving mine."

"Fine. I'll back off. If that's what you want to - "

"Stop it!" I yelled, shoving him back. "Stop trying to act like you're the victim here. You aren't listening to me! I thought we were friends, but you've made it clear that you don't care what I think at all. I don't want to go to Mercy. I don't want to play for the St. Raphael Lions."

Jackson's fingers curled into fists. "As your friend, I'm telling you that this is your best chance of going professional."

"Switching schools midseason is stupid! My teammates and I know each other. We can read each other, and that doesn't happen overnight!" This was ridiculous. We weren't getting anywhere. Just another circle for him to try to spin his way.

"I can read you better than any of them! I know you!"

"But it's not just you!"

Jackson paled. Blinking, he scoffed, "I get more ice time than any of your teammates."

"Great - so scouts would see how well we work together, but we can't go professional on the same teams. They'd see me working well with one person. They'd see an entire team built around one person!" Why couldn't this just be over? Why did this ever have to happen at all? I just wanted to go home. Get back into bed and pretend today never happened. That this whole stupid week hadn't ever happened. "I'm not some tool you can buy because it's inconvenient to have actual competition!"

"Do you honestly think I want you on my team because I'm intimidated by you?" Jackson spat as if the idea was ridiculous.

This was pointless. I gave him the stupid phone, so mounting my bike, I pushed off, but he ran out, blocking me as he grabbed my handlebars. All around us, the wind howled. No Mike. No sun. Just gray and icy wind. A Port Edmond January - dreariness that soaked into everyone's bones.

"You only made friends with me after I took you out of the game."

"Tanner was the one who approached you. I didn't ask him to do that!"

Rolling my eyes, I scoffed. "Then why aren't you listening when I say no?"

"Because you're only saying no because you're scared of change! Nobody's going to die if you switch schools. Your stupid friends will still be your friends. Change isn't always bad," Jackson informed me with that same superior upward tilt to his chin.

"And people don't have to do what you tell them. If you had backed off, we would have still been friends," I retorted.

His eyes narrowed, and as we struggled with the handlebar, he growled, "I don't want to be your stupid friend!"

"Good! Because you're not!"

Releasing his grip on my bike, he tugged me toward him by the collar of my jacket, slamming his lips into mine. Mouths closed, our teeths still clacked together. I'd never been kissed before, but they couldn't have all been that painful. The smash of our faces together rippled through my skull, ringing like bells until he pulled back, panting and red with rage.

"I love you, you giant beast!"

After holding back for so long, the tears came, but I wasn't about to let him see me cry. Shoving him back toward his car, I glared as best as I could through the fog of water threatening to pour from my eyes. "You're such a jerk."

Even faced with him lying to me - using the crush on him I had desperately tried to push down against me, I couldn't tell him I hated him. Couldn't tell him to take a long walk off a short pier. None of the spiteful anger would come out. Just stupid me, running away again as he stood back, shocked that the last trick up his sleeve hadn't worked. I should have never trusted a guy like Jackson Duke. He was a Lion; I was a Mariner. We could never be friends.

Chapter Twenty-Two

Distance didn't help. No matter how fast I
pedaled, Jackson stuck around. Sitting in the back
of my head. Hiding behind my eyelids whenever I
blinked. Cold wind swept around me. In the gray of
November, the cold coast churned - salt filling the
air, but the briny sea offered me no comfort. The
hole in my stomach just kept getting bigger and
bigger as if it could swallow me whole, and to be
honest, I kind of wanted it to.

More than an hour ahead of schedule, Port
Edmond High School stood open, but the parking
lot held only a handful of cars. All the better. I
probably looked absolutely mad. Locking up my
bike, I ran inside, shoving my backpack in my
locker before running toward the gym, hoping
Coach Doug had gotten in early. I didn't want to
hang around. Didn't want to be stuck inside my
head, and without anything else to do, tearing
myself apart in the weight room - pushing my limits
there - seemed safer than any of the alternatives
crawling around my head.

Instead, the P.E. teachers' room was dark.
All the doors locked, I couldn't even run laps in the
main gym. Like wires inside my chest, anxiety
curled.

Jackson hadn't said what I thought. It was
windy. I probably misheard. That was it. I misheard,
and I ran away for nothing because there was no
way Jackson Duke liked me. As more than a friend.
Probably not even that much. Friends listened. They

might screw up like Geoffrey and get caught up wanting what they wanted so much they forgot about what I wanted. Which maybe Jackson had done. If I could forgive Geoffrey, why was I having such a hard time with Jackson?

Because Jackson threw his selfishness all around. Dumped it at my feet in front of my team - undid what felt like all the work I had done, but it hadn't, right? Sure, some of the guys had their tantrums on Monday, but Coach shut them down. Andre shut them down. Even if neither backed up what they said during practice and after, the pressure just from the beginning to the end of the day showed how quickly people forgot. Not everybody cared, so it wasn't the end of the world.

Just the end of our friendship.

Because when pressed, he hadn't apologized. He kept digging. Tried to manipulate me. Everything he said - every word seemed aimed to turn me around until I couldn't tell up from down, so how was I supposed to trust him? Believe him? Especially when he used my feelings against me.

While I would never blame Ryan for being who he was - for not liking me or even being capable of liking me in the way, Ryan never used my crush against. Considering Ariadne's comments, he had to have known. If she recognized the way I got flustered enough to risk her brother's happiness - as much as Andre seemed to think she had been dismissive of the risks, Ryan had to know. Had to realize I had been crushing on him for years, but

Ariadne tried to use that. Ryan hadn't. Which made me like him more, but I couldn't lie to save my life. Omitting my practices with Jackson were as far as I could go, so dating - fake dating - Ryan never would have worked. My heart would've shattered.

But Jackson? Until he said…I hadn't thought about it. Pushed it down as impossible when somebody else suggested it, recognizing the futility of getting my hopes up, but I wanted to be his friend. Wanted to keep spending time with him. It was more than I ever managed to do with Ryan. So-called growth, but the second he could, he used it against him. Jackson Duke - perfect model best in the nation Jackson Duke couldn't like somebody like me. Didn't like me. Crushes weren't weapons. People who liked other people didn't use that against the person they liked. That wasn't - that could be anything but a trick.

Flimsy thoughts shattered into sharp barbs turning quickly against me. Unable to find the right words even in my own mind, I leaned against the wall, sinking down onto the cold floor as I brought my knees to my chest.

"Beni? Are you okay?" A voice called, and my heart dropped as I looked up at perfect Ariadne. Not the last person I wanted to see right now but pretty close.

"Nah, I'm fine," I lied. "Just got here early. Kinda tired."

Her pink lips twisted into a mix between a frown and a pout, but before she could say anything, Andre stormed up behind her. His usually pristine hair in a curly disarray.

Nudging her up toward the English hall, he huffed, "Don't you have some stupid student council meeting?"

"And what? You're going to take care of this?" she demanded, gesturing at me like I was some kind of spill in a grocery aisle.

Brows furrowing, Andre growled, "My teammate. Back off."

Ariadne rolled her eyes, but running a hand over her skirt as if there was a flaw anywhere on it, she sauntered away with a small wave. "Come find me if he makes things worse. Student council is meeting in room one-ninety."

"Jesus Christ, Ari, I've got this," Andre grumbled, but when he turned the full weight of his attention on me, I really hoped he'd just give up and go away; instead, he threw down his backpack and sat down beside me. "Talk."

"I'm fine."

When Andre rolled his eyes, he looked just like his sister. The same tilt of the chin as if he was so far above the insignificant problems of normal teens. Like he didn't have a secret boyfriend or the issues that came from dating his best friend - who was his hockey captain - who pretended to date his sister. If anyone had regular drama between the two of us, Andre owned ridiculously and unnecessarily complex personal issues.

Somehow, that made it okay for me to finally deflate, curling around my knees. "Just the whole Ja-Duke situation."

"Jackson?" Andre perked up. "Great - what's that prick done now?"

Of course. Why wouldn't he be eager to dig into that? Considering Jackson and Andre clashed regularly on the ice - with Jackson always winning, he probably pined for a leg up, but it wasn't like it would help him. Not like Andre cared. Not really. Odds were Ryan pushed this whole new leaf business, so this was just another way for him to gain brownie points with his boyfriend. The one who he was terrified of losing. Despite Ryan being a pushover. Because he was a pushover in a family of homophobes.

Maybe I should've just taken a vow of silence. I couldn't put enough words together to argue well, and sitting beside Andre, I didn't trust myself to phrase any sort of explanation. Not without hurting Jackson, and for some stupid reason, I still cared.

Ruffling his curls, Andre sighed. "Come on, Seaver. Out with it."

"Nothing. He just…pushed," I retorted. "It's fine."

Andre snorted. Digging through his bag, he pulled out a small mirror. "Obviously, it isn't." Fixing his hair to its usual obsessive perfect, he explained, "You brood with the best of them, but you're two seconds away from completely panicking, and if I can tell that, whatever happened isn't fine."

"I'm not panicking."

"Sure." He snapped the mirror closed and turned to face me. "Look, I'm not here to be your gay sage. I've got enough problems on my own, but if your head gets messed up, I'm on my own against St. Raphael's. Stop acting like you're being a bother," Andre commanded, imperious and condescending. "If someone is messing with you, I said I'd take care of it."

Set small goals. Brandon used to say that. When my mind wrapped me up in everything that could go wrong, he made me count out the actual steps. Rephrase. Rethink. What was my goal? If I wanted to become a professional, I needed to go to a top school, making a women's team straight away. The closest school with the best women's team that offered full tuition scholarships was Northeastern. Grades remained where I needed them. Working at the rink and assisting in charity drives padded my application, but beating out St. Raphael's - especially in my first varsity year on a men's team - in State's would be noteworthy. Get me on the map.

All the drama with Jackson, I had allowed my focus to waver. None of that mattered. Get the grades. Practice. Be a team player. Win. I had the grades, and so far, we hadn't lost a game. Sitting and hating myself because a guy wanted me on his team wasted valuable time. So I was a threat. Whether Jackson ever saw me as a friend, he distracted me. Thinking about him left butterflies in my stomach. Nauseous and too big for my own body. Like a snake getting ready to shed, but for some reason, the skin stuck.

No more. "St. Raphael's is undefeated too."

"You're avoiding the question, but yes," Andre drawled.

Nodding, I sighed. "I'm not - not good at things outside hockey. All my friends played, and when the girls' team ended, Brandon died, and getting onto the guy's team was all I could handle." I tugged on the end of my braid. "I think I forgot that."

"Forgot what?"

"That I'm not good at things outside hockey," I repeated, meeting his furrowed gaze. "At first, we were just practicing together. That's when it worked, but I wanted it to be more than hockey. I wanted to be friends." Expecting his derision, I barreled on, "Which was stupid. Blew up in my face. I get that is what I'm saying. This is me - getting it."

The immediate insult I expected didn't come when I forced myself to stop. Instead, Andre stared at me. My heart thudded against my ribs, counting down the seconds as the silence dragged on until he finally said - softer than I imagined him capable of being to anyone - even Ryan, "It's okay to want more than hockey."

"Hockey's enough for me."

Shifting away, he swallowed with a slight huff. "Fine. Whatever. Let's wreck the Lions and take nationals."

"How about we start with taking the league first?"

Chapter Twenty-Three

In only a month, Jackson somehow invaded every corner of my life, and just as quickly, Andre forced himself into Jackson's place with a slightly terrifying determination.

"What time did Duke pick you up?" Andre demanded, catching me at the bike rack after practice. Then he proceeded to show up fifteen minutes earlier and honk, bothering my dad and sending me tumbling over my own feet to get out fast enough to tell him to shut up.

Mike never asked questions. Didn't even cock a brow, but he let me keep coming. Let me take care of the majority of the lights and setting up the women's locker room. Andre complained the entire time, but he managed to prep the guy's side without trouble. Running me ragged, he demanded perfection like Jackson, but for all that Andre invited me to trust him, the friendship I had thought between Jackson and me couldn't be matched. Besides our love for hockey, Andre and I had little in common.

"Faster, Seaver," he demanded, skating sprints until we both nearly puked.

But he meant well, and each night, I collapsed into bed, not even having the time or energy to think about Jackson Duke and how quickly another person had slipped right out of my life. However, as the end of the week loomed, so did the game, and while skating used to calm me, nerves turned my stomach.

"If they offer, you take it," my dad said.

Sean and Geoffrey both scoffed when I told them. "He can't make you switch schools," Sean announced over lunch on Thursday.

Geoffrey rolled his eyes. "Yeah, he can. He's her dad."

"I'm not switching. They probably won't even want me anyway."

When neither argued, my heart sunk. Regardless of Andre's change of heart, there were others - Joe and Graham and Ollie - they watched me, waiting for me to accept a scholarship I didn't have to a place I didn't want to go. If the scout never offered me a scholarship, the uncertainty would remain. A rejected offer would be the only way to settle the growing distrust, and even Coach Carr seemed to recognize it, pushing me harder and harder as if wanting to be sure I would be at my best on game day.

For all my nerves, I slept like a log on Friday and woke to my dad cooking. The smoky smell of sizzling bacon wafted up the stairs. Not for the first time, I wished there was a tree outside my window, so I could skip the stairs and the kitchen and the inevitable lecture. Getting my gear ready for the game - and a quick exit, I squared myself off, prepared to face the music.

In a blue flannel and worn jeans, my dad puttered about the kitchen. When I dropped my bag at the door, he half-turned. "Grab a plate. Today's an important game."

"Yeah - about that…"

He shuffled his spatula through the scrambled eggs. "Do you want to become a professional hockey player?"

"Yeah, but - "

"Do you still want a full scholarship?" he said, cutting me off.

My fingers curled, pressing my short nails into my palm. "I can get a scholarship playing for Port Edmond."

Pulling the pan from the heat, my dad focused all his attention on me. Leaning forward, he studied me. His eyes as dark as the sea before a storm as the silver in his beard glinted in the early morning light as he said, "Brandon wouldn't want you to give up this opportunity."

"I don't care about what Brandon would want," I confessed, and for the first time in a long time, I actually meant it. "This is what I want."

We stared each other down. Stubborn and stoic - that's how I always thought of my dad, and we were more alike than different, which meant when we both decided on something, our heels would dig in, but we hadn't been on the opposite side since Brandon's funeral. Of all the places to plant my flag, I never believed hockey would be one. My dad always supported me. When the girl's side ended, he stood beside me every step of the way to getting onto the guy's team. Maybe I should have expected it. St. Raphael's would've been the easier path.

Their coach - and Jackson - had an iron grip on the whole team. They focused their entire game play around him and his skills, and while I recognized how I might fit in - the way we worked well together and how our strengths played off each other, Jackson always would be their star. I rather deal with being one on an all around good team than the supporter on a team focused on a single star. At least then I could have a moment. Times when I stood out. On Jackson's team, anything about me would always be about him.

Crossing his arms over his chest, he sighed. "I can't support this, Beni."

"It's my career, and this is how I want to do it." Hold my ground. "I'll play the game. We'll win. If they offer me a spot, I'll say no."

Not because it meant finishing out at the same school where Brandon had died before graduating. Definitely not out of some masochistic want to deal with the jerks. While the desire to prove myself simmered beneath the surface, my reasons came from St. Raphael's. The knowledge that the team wouldn't get better. That I'd only have Jackson, who I couldn't trust to be honest with me, and I would lose Geoffrey and Sean. I grew up with them. Spent every year of school with them. Odds were the rest of the team would be as split as my current team, and I had the background with Port Edmond. They knew me. Respected my abilities. Even if they were jerks off the ice, we played well on the ice. If the Lions saw me ditch my team, would they trust me?

"And as your father, it's my job to stop you from screwing yourself over. Change can be good," he told me. "Going to Mercy could be the difference between you getting on a team or not."

"If I don't make it on a team, it's not going to be because I went to Port Edmond."

"No, it's going to be because you weren't challenged -"

"We beat them!" I exclaimed. My dad leaned back, blinking at my sudden outburst, so I took the chance and barrelled on, "I knocked their top player out of the game. Odds are we'll face them in States. Which means I have a chance to be part of the team that takes down the biggest high school ice hockey player in the United States. If that doesn't get their attention, then being part of the Lions sure won't."

Running a hand through his hair, he huffed. The lines about his eyes seemed to deepen as he shook his head. "And if you don't? What happens then? You're on a team that hasn't won States in the past couple years. Dealing with crap from guys who can't skate half as well as you - at a school that doesn't exactly win awards - they aren't going to give you a second chance on this one, Beni. People - people like that - they're proud. You turn them down once, and they'll pretend they never wanted you to begin with."

"Why would I want to be around them then?"

"Because they can get you where you want to go."

"For a price."

His lips twitched, and he scratched at his graying beard. "Sit down and eat. We'll talk about this after the game."

Which was as close as he came to waving the white flag. However, this wasn't a clean win, but this was a retreat - and I could live with that. If I refused before we could have our post-game talk, well, I owed him some teenage rebellion.

Chapter Twenty-Four

Maybe it was the drama of the week, but the whole school seemed crammed into the stands. They stared down. Pom-poms and painted faces cheered down, chanting in unison as they stomped their feet and glowered down at the Woburn Wolves like they could set them on fire with their fury. If the scouts sat mixed in that mess, I couldn't tell, and I refused to even look.

Ollie, however, had no problem. "Do you think it'll be their coach? He's got a red beard, right?"

"Somebody from Mercy has to show up too," Geoffrey grumbled.

Rolling his eyes, Andre carefully retaped his stick. "Don't let them get in your head. We're undefeated, and if we keep this up, we'll set a record."

"Andre's right. This is a huge deal," Ryan agreed, and Andre preened a bit, smirking even as our captain continued. "We have a good chance of taking States! Just think about it - going to Nationals for the first time in over a decade."

"Do you ever wonder if we're the only ones who think we're rivals with St. Raphael's? I mean, sure we were the last group to beat them at States, and we had an even score through the seasons in between then and now - but...come on, even before Duke got in, nobody else really stood a chance, right?" Sean pondered, earning an elbow from both Geoffrey and me.

Andre stood, shoving himself off the bench. "If we weren't before, we will be once we knock them out of the running for Nationals."

"That's the kind of talk I like to hear!" Coach Carr bellowed, storming in for whatever his pre-game spiel would be. Normally, I met the guys heading for the ice, but he had swept me into the locker room before muttering to someone on his phone. "Now, Boston College is out there tonight, and we all heard about Mercy and St. Raphael's sending their cronies, but tonight, I want you to focus on a good clean game. The Woburn Wolves have a strong defense. They've kept their losses to low scores, so if we give them an inch, they'll take us by a mile. Starting line-up on defense as usual. Seaver, Page, and Caldwell - you're taking the first swing at them. Pasternak, Galliger, and Teague - I want you ready to go."

His eyes scanned our faces. A gleeful madness sparked in him, and I didn't honestly want to know why. Maybe he had money riding on the game. More likely, he wanted us to go out there and make any scout watching realize that whoever they came to get was only one of a team full of players worth taking. I hoped for the latter. Probably stupid, but I knew how much Ryan loved playing, and if there was a chance of him getting recruited to Boston College, his life - and Andre's - would be so much easier.

It was better if I didn't think about myself. If I just focused on Ryan and Andre and Derek. They wanted to do this professional just like me. Living for the feeling of the ice beneath their blades. The chill of the rink. More scouts would come if we did well today. Reps from Wisconsin and Harvard - maybe even some international schools if we made it to Nationals. I just had to think about it. Think about how brilliant it would be to hear the news that one of our own - a Port Edmond Mariner - would be another step closer to going professional. If Andre had his way, he'd skip school and go straight into tryouts. Maybe the Bruins would hear about us and come out. That would be the dream.

But if Jackson 'Model Perfect' Duke wasn't getting professional recruiters, they wouldn't send somebody to a Port Edmond game. Not until we took home the National trophy.

Settling into position, I focused on my opponent. Their black against our blue. A bruise-like blur as the puck dropped. Ryan swept it to Andre, and up we went. Swirling around, charging across the ice, I caught the pass, spinning around the opposing forward, breaking into their defense.

An elbow slammed into my ribs, but the puck already slid across the ice back to Andre. Two players surrounded him, and before he could escape, one slammed him into the boards as the other cleared the puck. Back to their forward - who Geoffrey intercepted, and with a resounding slap, I had the puck again.

Up to their side. Passed to Ryan, blocking a check from hitting as he sent the puck forward to Andre. Back and forth - the defenders walled us out, but we kept coming. A minute in, and the tension tightened. Any moment, and the coach would tug one of us, substituting, and we would have lost our first chance. Growling, I slammed forward. If I was a beast, I'd be the one who ensured her teammates scored.

An elbow to my ribs. I'd taken worse, and my hips were bigger. Big enough to send them backward and out of our way. Buzzers sounded as Andre scored.

"Come on, Ref!" one of their defensemen screamed. "Are you blind? That was clearly interference!"

Andre sneered. "And you clearly elbowed. That's instigation!"

"We scored, Page. Keep your comments to yourself," Ryan commanded, gesturing for Andre to get back to center.

Either way, the referees weren't interested in what either side had to say, and the same stayed true throughout the game. Not that that was a change from usual. Best we could expect was for them to punish us down the line if they actually felt like they had missed something, but my best hope was being the sort of beast that won games but wasn't worth recruiting. My dad couldn't be angry for not getting an offer if I won. That couldn't count as throwing anything.

Despite myself, however, I wasn't the first one in the penalty box. For as much as Woburn's defense held tight, they played dirtier than I would ever dare. Elbows flew throughout, but while I got as good as they gave, Sean was half my size, so from the bench, we all roared when what looked like an elbow turned into a nasty slash, and Sean slammed down onto the ice.

The whistle blew, and a cheer broke out behind us as their defenseman growled, skating into the penalty box; however, any joy was short-lived. We scored the next charge, putting us up by two, but Andre had a vendetta, and when the defenseman got out of the box while he was on the ice, Andre hooked his stick. Another whistle, but the charge on

209

that round was already lost, and Derek blocked the one attempt they managed.

"What?" Andre grinned at Ryan's scolding glare. "Derek needs a chance to show off."

Coach Carr scoffed. "We play clean, Page."

The words beneath the words rang clear - seniors play clean. Nobody needed to risk their chances of being recruited, and while it might not have been what Coach wanted, nobody intended to let a hit go unanswered, but we could answer a dirty hit with another goal, so when our line slid in, I didn't hesitate.

When Andre lost the puck, I was there, slamming into the defenseman with a clean check as Ryan came by and swept the puck. Andre followed close behind. Ryan took a shot on goal as the other defenseman had gotten cocky, heading forward for a pass that never came, but their goalie dropped back, blocking off the goal. The puck rebounded, right to Andre, and with a slapshot, he sent it in the gap on the opposite side, and right into the net. Screaming, Andre rounded, and we knocked gloves as he crowed.

"So much for low-scoring," Ryan laughed as he and Andre knocked helmets.

Slapping Andre on the back, I laughed. "Three in the first period isn't exactly high-scoring."

"Shut up, Seaver," Andre growled, but as we fell back into line, he was beaming from ear to ear. His eyes glistened, a fire lit inside them, but the buzzer sounded, marking the end of the first period. As we skated back toward our bench, Andre bumped Ryan's shoulder. "Bet I can get another goal before you get one." When I laughed, he smirked. "You too, Beni."

Climbing into the bench, I grinned back at him. "Losers buy winner's dinner."

"What are we betting?" Sean demanded, but Coach pulled us, plotting out the next period as we started to settle, prepping to switch sides.

Sitting beside him, I grabbed my water bottle when Sean handed it over. "Whoever scores next gets a free dinner."

Scoffing, Victor rolled his eyes. "Like that's a challenge."

"Depends on which line starts the second period," I noted.

And Coach Carr wasn't about to waste time. "Tracey, Teague, Cody - you're on first. McCoy, keep it clean this go around."

"Well, guess that's none of us," Victor muttered.

Andre shrugged, slamming his bottle's cap. "Highest scorer gets free dinner."

Reaching across me to fist bump Andre, Ollie called, "You're on!"

Chapter Twenty-Five

Sometimes, a game seemed won, and teams would get cocky. They'd ease up. That often resulted in the almost miraculous victories. Half the game was mental, right? That's what coaches used to say. Two teams evenly matched - whoever won had the better headset. Psych out displays - the New Zealand All Black rugby team's haka before every game played to unify the team as much as their movements and chant tore at the opposing team's psyche, so sometimes the games - treating it lightly - went too far. Sometimes it helped.

Andre and I were too competitive to let anything ruin our game play. Worse still - for Woburn - as much as I didn't want to get offered a place at Mercy, I wanted that free meal. Not because of the food. But because of what it represented. A joke with Ollie and Victor - where I was part of the team. Because I was. They accepted it. Joe could be a jerk, but he was only one person, and despite everything that my dad or Jackson said, the majority of the team appreciated me. They understood what I could do, but this was my chance to hammer it home.

And I did. When the final buzzer screamed out - over the cheers of the ground and the lamentous roar of the Woburn Wolves, I stood with four goals to Andre's three. Covered in sweat. My face red and my hair sticking to my neck. Every muscle in my body was singing and ready for a deep shower and the soft warmth of my bed. At the same time, I wanted to run a marathon. Conquer the world. Do anything.

The team gathered round, cheering, and a euphoric high came over me - lasting all the way off the ice, and I thought I'd be able to at least get shower or something before the scouts came around. Honestly, I had completely forgotten they were there. Nobody mentioned it when we came together on the ice. With my mind focused on the game, hockey did what it always did for me - helped me forget my troubles.

As Coach Carr focused on bringing Derek and Andre over to the Boston College scout for a chat, I headed toward the women's locker room, but a middle aged man with a full black beard walked up with a woman with her hair pulled into a bun. She reminded me of a movie librarian. Glasses a bit too far down on her nose.

"Beni Seaver?" the man said as if my name was on the back of my jersey. "Hi, I'm Coach Raymond Steele; I work with the varsity ice hockey team over at St. Raphael's Academy. This is the Headmistress of Mercy, our sister school, Dr. Alejandra Cortez."

The woman held out her hand with a small smile. "It's lovely to meet you, Beni."

Frowning, I tugged off my glove to shake her hand. Even if I planned to reject any offer sent my way, I didn't want to be rude. This whole mess wasn't their fault. Though I couldn't help but think she had no common sense. My hands weren't that great at the moment. Clammy and too warm - touching anything before a shower should have been avoided, but what else could I have done?

"Now, I'm sure Jackson has already mentioned our interest," she informed me with a big smile. "We'd love to offer you a spot at Mercy."

Coach Steele nodded, smiling. "We're always looking for the best players in the league for our team."

"I appreciate your offer, but -"

And out came one of those large manilla envelopes. Yellow and rectangular. Presented like a trophy - received like a curse as Dr. Cortez pressed, "We understand you have some reservations, but I think when you have a chance to see exactly what we're offering - and everything Mercy and the Lions can do for your future, you'll make the right choice."

"We love to have you come by. We practice right here, so if you wanted to view one of our practices - maybe meet the rest of the team - I'd be happy to schedule something," Coach Steele suggested.

They had to have practiced this. Talking in the same condescending we-know-better-than-you tone. On one hand, their salesmanship impressed me. They hadn't accidentally been hired at the best schools - or the richest - in the area without good reason. Everybody knew Raymond Steele had played professionally until he'd gotten injured. Wisconsin had offered him a coaching position, but he'd turned down a university for St. Raphael's. Probably because it was his alma mater. So many professionals - short-lived or not - came from the Lions. All the arguments my dad and Jackson threw my way made sense. If this was just about the easiest path to success, I might've done it, but sometimes the easy way wasn't the right way, and there was no telling for sure that their success could be repeated. They had never had a girl on the Lions. Their interest wouldn't guarantee a professional career.

Boston College, Harvard, and Northeastern - those were the three top schools the Boston Pride recruited from. My best chance to get to them. Not a high school change - a college, and Boston College had been there that night. Scouts had seen me outscore a guy they aimed to recruit, and that might have been for the guy's side, but they had to understand - had to see and know, and I could be seen just as readily by them with Port Edmond as I would have been with the Lions. Better probably - because my coach wanted me to compete with Andre. He wanted to see what I could do, and every time I thought about the Lions, I struggled to name a single other player. I should've known more. Not a single one stood out.

Everybody played support to Jackson's star, and I wouldn't do that. Spend the rest of my high school career propping somebody else up - even if they could skate circles around me, and he couldn't. Day in and out - I had proved that, and the only reason he wanted me on his team came from those mornings when I ran just as many plays around him as he did around me. Maybe Jackson feared competition. He understood, probably better than any of the guys on my team, what it meant to need to be ten times as good as everybody around in order to get half the credit. His brittle bones - no matter how mild he argued his condition, and me - because I was a girl.

"I appreciate your offer, but I'm happy with my school and with my team," I repeated, keeping my back straight and shoulders squared. Again and again - my mantra repeated: *I am a beast. Too tall and too strong - and I get to make choices about my life.*

Not the most creative, but it kept me from backing down when Steele crossed his arms and said, "You know, I hear you want to join the Boston Pride. I happen to be a good friend of Tessa Grant, their head coach."

A voice - like Brandon's - whispered in the back of my mind, "Make him say it, Beni. There's cameras everywhere in this joint. If he's going to make threats, make him own them."

So I stared him straight in the eyes and asked, "Are you planning on stonewalling me if I say no?"

Low blow. Strike the pride. Brandon never backed down, and he never cared who he insulted when it came to the important stuff. Probably why Scott liked him. They were both ice cold when they didn't like people. Scott just hated more people.

However, Steele's face closed off the second I asked my question. Dr. Cortez's brows jumped like they might leap off of her face, and I could see it. That pride inside them - just like my dad said. I said no. When they pushed, I did not move, so now they had to say they didn't want me. Just like the snowbirds. Here when here was good. Flying anywhere else when things got the slightest bit tough.

Eyes narrowing, Dr. Cortez stepped closer to me, holding out the envelope between us. "I understand this is sudden, and it likely feels as if we are coming on strong. We were already considering recruiting you before you and Jackson started to practice together. You are a determined and capable young woman, Beni, and that's exactly what we're looking for at Our Lady of Mercy." Her lips twitched into a small smile. "There are quite a few young girls who found your pre-season thrashing of the Lions to be inspiring. Like your own personal fan club."

Because talent had an ego.

Taking the envelope would be bad. My dad would know. For all I knew, he was somewhere watching this all unfold, and the moment I had that envelope in hand, he'd have a thousand new arguments that all sounded almost identical to the ones we'd already fought over. Worse still - my teammates might see. The guys would think I was accepting the offer, and those who had backed me would feel betrayed. Those who hadn't would seem vindicated.

"Thanks, but I'm good where I am." Ducking to the side, I headed around them. "Have a good night."

Nothing could describe the relief of the women's locker room door closing behind me. Everything inside me screamed sanctuary - probably because nobody could normally follow me inside. Showering, I dressed, determined to get my victory meal, but when I went to the locker to grab my bag, the manilla envelope had been taped to the door with a handwritten note on the front: *Nobody on the Port Edmond team needs to know you're thinking about it.* Well played, Cortez. Tearing the envelope into pieces, I dumped it into the trash.

"Beni!" Sean cheered when I joined the mass of teammates waiting in the rink's lobby. "Did you see their faces? I swear they were gonna cry when we hit the double-digits, and they still hadn't gotten a goal!"

Geoffrey snorted. "Pretty sure Matthieu almost committed seppuku when they got that first one through."

He still seemed pretty upset. Lincoln patted Matthieu's back as our second goalie groaned. His hands covered his face, but from the slump of his shoulders, his self-flagellation screamed loud and clear.

"They were bound to get a couple through," I argued, but Matthieu glanced up with watery eyes.

"But I let in three!"

Sighing, Lincoln patted his friend's back. "They lured you out of goal, man. Classic move. You'll spot it next time."

"What if I cost Derek a scholarship?" he retorted.

Scoffs and rolled eyes abounded. As guilty as Matthieu obviously felt, there was no way he could cost Derek a scholarship to Boston College if they had any plans of giving him one. If anything got in the way, it would've been the limited action the defense had seen all game. Sure, they had scored half the time they got it through to our side with Matthieu, but even though Derek saw more play time against Woburn, he hardly saw them down his end any more often.

Bopping out of the locker room, Ollie danced his way over to us with Victor and Graham not far behind. "I'd just like to say - I'm incredibly proud of my two goals."

"Yeah - yeah, rub that ego," Victor snarked with a friendly smirk. "Who wants to bet Andre's gonna argue we should pay for his meal too?"

"If he does, I'll pay for that idiot," Ryan volunteered with a shake of his head.

Slapping me on the back, Ollie grinned. "But he lost! This is gonna be the best week ever!" As he sang the last bit, his eyes fell on Matthieu. "Ah, come on, Mattie. Don't beat yourself up. It would've been embarrassing if we hit fourteen against one of the best defenses without them getting something through."

Matthieu's lip wobbled, but he nodded. "Yeah - fourteen to three isn't bad."

"Isn't next week Manchester? That should be a high scoring game." Victor crossed his arms; eyes narrowing, he added, "We should do a rematch then. Most of us only got one."

"Four, Beni. Three, Andre, and two for Ollie and Ryan. One each Sean, Victor, and Donovan," Geoffrey counted out. Cocking a brow, he turned to Andrew. "What happened? Were you not playing?"

"Ha ha, Statham. Peter and Kendall didn't score either. Get off my back," Andrew retorted, crossing his arms over his chest as Andre swaggered over.

The tension swelled as everybody faced him. Ryan practically vibrated with excitement. Tilting up his chin, Andre smirked. "Charlie's?"

Scoffing, Ryan punched his boyfriend's arm. "Come on, you jerk. What'd they say?"

"You better get into a college in Boston if we're going to get that apartment with Derek after graduation - cause barring injury, we're in." Andre beamed. His hands reached out toward our captain, and their eyes met. A glimmer of something passed between them before everyone cheered, and Andre pulled Ryan close to his side, keeping an arm around the brunette's shoulders.

Matthieu leapt to his feet. "Wait, Derek too? I didn't screw it up for him?"

Clucking his tongue, Andre shook his head. "Ego much? There was no way you were screwing this up for him. Derek's top tier." Glancing back toward the locker room, he suggested, "Maybe you chumps should buy us both dinner to celebrate."

Ryan snorted as the rest of the team laughed. "Sure, I'll spot you, and you can spot Derek."

"Rude." Andre's face contorted into a scowl, but he struggled to keep it. His eyes smiled the entire time. "I accept."

When Derek wandered out of the locker room not long after - dark hair damp and his bag over his shoulder, we all cheered once more. "Come on, Andre. You couldn't wait like two minutes to tell them."

"Shower more efficiently," Andre replied.

Derek rolled his eyes. "Whatever. I'm starving. Charlie's?"

"Charlie's - Charlie's," Ollie cheered, bounding off with his friends close behind him.

Sean, Geoffrey, and I headed out, getting a ride from Derek. Our gear piled into the trunk as we climbed in. Wyatt grabbed the front seat, so the three of us were left in the back as we headed off toward our traditional after game Charlie's.

"So?" Sean whispered, leaning in close to me after they had stuck me in the middle.

I frowned. "So what?"

223

"Did the scouts show up? Or was he full of crap?" Geoffrey demanded.

"They were there. They offered, I said no. Simple as that."

"And they just gave up?" Sean's nose wrinkled. "That doesn't seem right."

With a shrug, I hoped the conversation was over, but Derek had ears like a wolf. Glancing at us in the rear view mirror, he let out a soft, "Huh."

Wyatt turned around in the passenger's seat. "Last year, they went after Andre hard. Spent like a month sending him and his parents these offers. Started off with tuition stuff. Not like Andre needs it. I mean, his parents are loaded, but they just kept coming. Throwing money at him."

"Which should get them pushed into prep rather than varsity, but somehow they're still considered varsity, which is just stuipid," Geoffrey grumbled, leaning back in his seat. "Don't they board?"

"They recruit locals. If their players just happen to get an apartment in their area…" Derek trailed off with a shrug.

Another reason not to join them. For all their connections, it would be just my luck if I switched teams the year the USA Hockey decided to kick the Lions from varsity into prep. Not that they weren't recruited just as heavily, but people had opinions about players who went after the payouts that early. I couldn't name a single women's league player who had come up in a prep team. Not that there were many women's prep teams. The girl's side was cleanly separated from the guy's so less tournaments and less teams overall made a prep side kind of unnecessary.

"Didn't they try to recruit you too?" Sean asked Derek.

Derek shrugged turning into Charlie's parking lot. "Took weeks to get them off my back my freshman year when I made varsity. I still hear from them at the start of every single season. They don't know the meaning of no. Especially if you're local."

Derek pulled into an open spot right next to Andre's car. Ryan and Andre sat inside, talking with their heads close together. Jumping out, Wyatt banged on the window, startling the pair. Neither looked particularly happy, but Ryan forced a smile.

"Food time!" Wyatt cheered. Spinning to face us, he gestured vaguely between all of us. "No more Lions talk. Beni's not trading blue for red. We're celebrating another tally on our perfect season."

"Hey, no jinxing it. Seasons not over yet," Andre called after him.

Ryan shook his head. "As long as we keep focus, we'll make it to the play-offs. Odds are we'll hit States."

"Nothing new there," Derek grumbled.

Inside the restaurant, Ollie and Graham pushed together tables. "I don't care if Batman has kryptonite, he's not beating a sun-charged Golden Age Superman," Graham said.

Ollie slumped into a chair after they got the last set in a line of tables together. "Batman's got a counterplan for everything. Plus, he's Batman."

"Are you honestly still arguing about that?" Andre sneered, sliding into a seat beside Derek as Ryan came to sit on his other side. "Martian Manhunter beats both of them, hands down."

When eyes turned to Ryan, he held up his hands. "I have no dog in this race."

"Nobody's going to mention Wonder Woman?"

In a single sentence, Jackson sucked the excitement right out of the room. Like pod people, the team rounded on him. Dementers couldn't have torn the happiness away as fast. His bright eyes honed in on me. From the designer knit hat to his kicks, he owned the model elitist image he had been given, and sitting in his wheelchair resignedly beside him, Tanner kept his head down. His expression screamed embarrassed, but the Duke

226

brothers - if nothing else - were ride-or-die with each other. That being said, Tanner didn't hesitate to throw his brother under that bus if it could protect him.

"Please ignore my brother. He's a very passionate Wonder Woman fan," Tanner announced. Smiling like someone might pull a knife out on him, he shifted his chair, almost running over Jackson's toes. "Congrats on the win."

Shoving his hands in his pockets, Jackson glared at me down his stupid perfect nose. "You got a minute Seaver, or you want to do this in front of these idiots?"

"Seriously?" Andre swiveled in his seat. "Get a life, Duke. She said no. Obviously, Beni said no, or you wouldn't be here, and Beni wouldn't be here, so how about you get off that stupid high horse of yours and get lost?"

Tanner nodded placatingly. "Of course. Just picking up an order, and we'll be right out of here."

Jackson's hands clenched into fists at his side. The muscles along his jaw twitched, but he said nothing. Letting his younger brother herd him toward the counter, he stared me down. His eyes screaming that we needed to talk. Not a conversation I planned to have any time soon. Luckily, when the host handed over a brown bag, everyone shifted back together.

227

Slouching in his chair, Joe huffed, "I swear that guy gets more annoying every time I see him."

"Forget about him," Andre commanded.

"We're here to celebrate."

Ryan smiled. His eyes sparkled, shifting to me. "And Beni's the high scorer."

"Free food! Free food!" Sean chanted.

"You're not the one getting free anything, idiot," Geoffrey scoffed.

His lips pulled into a bright smile. "I'm just happy for Beni - and the fries that I will steal."

"Get your own fries, Galliger."

The same high of the game returned, and when Derek dropped me off back at my house afterwards, I almost cheered in relief. My dad's car wasn't there, which wasn't that unusual on a Saturday. Sometimes he worked on his boat or others for some extra cash. Either that or he went somewhere to deal with his disappointment in me. Or maybe errands. There was no reason to suspect his absence had anything to do with me. No matter what - a little extra time to myself had me almost skipping until I got to the end of the driveway. Jackson sat on the stairs of my front porch.

Frowning, I shifted my bag. "Jackson."

"Well, at least you're not calling me Duke," he grumbled, furrowing his brows. His eyes rose to meet mine. "Coach Steele told me you turned them down flat."

"I told you I would."

He nodded solemnly. "And you asked if he was going to stonewall you?"

"He didn't say no," I retorted.

Another nod, and he reached up, adjusting his knit hat. "You realize you're too good for that to be it, right? They saw you. You're - you're - shit," he muttered, ducking his head into his hands. "You're a force of nature, Beni. You've got to see that. How could they see you skate and not want you?"

"That isn't going to change my mind. I'm happy with my team."

If Jackson nodded anymore, he'd become a bobblehead. "Okay. I get it, and I-I wanted to tell you I'm sorry. I manipulated you - I can't pretend I didn't mean to, but it wasn't what you think."

"Jackson…"

His cheeks pinked, but his eyes rose to meet mine. "I know it's too late. I know I screwed this up, but I meant what I said, Beni. I'm head over heels for you." Pushing himself off the porch, he stood in front of me, and my mouth went dry. My heart raced. "I don't expect you to believe me. You're incredible, and it's crazy that you don't know that. If you think we could ever be friends again, I can figure out how to keep that to myself. If not, I get it. I still think you deserve better than Port Edmond...but maybe you deserve better than me too."

Heat rose to my own cheeks at his earnest expression. My heart pounded, roaring in my ears as I tried to process what he had said. He couldn't be telling the truth. Riding high from the game, I actually sort of believed him - believed that Jackson Duke could like me as more than friends, and I wanted it. I wanted to play for the Port Edmond Mariners and be Jackson's friend. I wanted to not have to keep it a secret. But I also couldn't forget how small he had made me feel. The certainty and horror when I realized how easily he had manipulated me. How he hadn't even thought about it. Just did it on instinct.

I shifted my weight from one foot to the other. "How am I supposed to trust you?"

Most people would've taken that as a bad response, but his entire face lit up. "Then I guess I'll have to show you I'm worth trusting." With a smile, he swaggered off, pulling out his cell phone as he headed toward the road. "Tanner? Yeah, you can come pick me up." Glancing over his shoulder, he smiled. "Better than expected."

What have I done? I can't afford a distraction - can't afford to get dragged into the mess of him again. But I couldn't find anything within me strong enough to silence the wanting, so I ignored the fear. It's not like I could put it all to rest. Jackson Duke would do what he wanted. No use wasting my time obsessing over it.

Chapter Twenty-Six

Normally, I slept like a log; instead, the night after the game, I paced. Back and forth, I crossed from one side of my room to the other. I ran on Sundays. I'd spend the day doing maintenance training - cleaning up and getting ahead on schoolwork, but come Monday, I'd be back at the rink, and after talking with Jackson, I had no idea if he would expect us to go back to how we were before. Would he show up to drive me? Would he expect me to act like nothing had happened?

Did he actually like me?

My entire face heated up. Glancing over to my mirror, I flushed harder, groaning at the sight of my face as red as a tomato. This was ridiculous. He couldn't like me like that. We were just friends. Guys always thought of me as that friend - not a girl. I wasn't pretty or feminine. Unlike the other girls, I couldn't conquer the field and come off with that triumphant athletic sheen. No, I smelled like unwashed socks after a hard game, and my hair clung to my face no matter how well I tied it back or how short I cut it.

Collapsing back onto my bed, I covered my face with my hands. There was no way I could do this on my own. Maybe I should have invited Sean and Geoffrey. They both lived on the other side of town, so they'd probably say no - but what about Andre? He practiced with me all last week. Odds were he'd be there Monday morning. Worse case scenario - Andre and Jackson. Together. It'd be like a monster truck rally. Which sports car would win?

A knock rattled the door. "Beni? You still up?"

"Yeah, Dad. You can come in," I called from the bed.

Opening the door, he stepped into the room - a familiar manilla envelope in his hand. "Dr. Cortez mentioned you rejected their offer."

"So she tried to go over my head? I told you I'm not going to - "

He shook his head, waving the envelope back in forth in the negative. "You're as stubborn as your mother - " and my brother, but that went unsaid. The pain was still too raw. "I get you're not planning on going, and life's too short for me to fight you on this. Just...give it a read, Beni. Make sure you know what you're giving up," he said and set the envelope upon my desk.

Keeping my mouth shut - letting him walk out that door - that would've been the usual. To not say a single thing. To buckle down and find my own way. I had done the same again and again since Brandon died. Before then, I turned to Brandon, and we found a way together. Or more honestly,

Brandon went whatever way he wanted, and having to either follow or wallow in the emptiness left behind by my mother's death and the silence in my father's heart, I followed Brandon.

My father's heart bled too easily. He loved in absolutes. When my mother died, a piece of him broke off, shattering and cracking all that remained. As he worked to put himself together, he could barely do more than go out to sea, cast his cages and nets, and raise them up again. If there was money for food and clothes and the house, how could I ask him for more when her death halved him? With Brandon, his remaining arm or leg fell right off. Either he could only stand or he could only drag himself, reaching out without any stability - especially considering how Brandon went - so how could I lean on him when he could barely hold himself up?

But I couldn't go to Sean and Geoffrey with this. Mike would laugh. Or take sides. They all took sides, and I needed somebody on my side. If he wanted to be in my life now, maybe I could offer him this. This strange sentiment which I could understand and didn't actually want while starving for it. The sort of reckless emotions which made Romeo and Juliet seem romantic.

"Jackson kissed me."

His brows leapt, wrinkling his forehead as he looked back at me over his shoulder. Shifting to face me, he blinked. "Oh."

"But it was while we were fighting, and I thought - I think - I don't know if he meant it. Really meant it. Not kind of meant it but also thought it might get me to do what he wanted," I explained, but every word that came out twisted round, making less sense the more I spoke. Running my hands over my face, I sat on the edge of my bed. "Now he's trying to 'go back' to what we were before, and I want to be his friend, but I also like him, and I'm not sure I can be his friend and not end up hating him for trying to screw with me."

Like a fish, his mouth opened and closed. I could see he had something in mind, so I waited, yearning for him to make sense of the jumble in my head, or at least say something that contradicted enough with what I actually wanted that I'd be able to recognize the truth of it inside the mess, but he didn't. Instead, my father sat down beside me.

"That's tough." Groaning, I fell back against the bed. He held up his hands in a placating gesture. "Okay, okay - not helpful, I get it."

"I don't know what to do, Dad."

Patting my leg, he stared up at the ceiling. Probably talking to Mom. We used to stumble upon him doing it out loud - but since Brandon...a lot changed after Brandon died. No matter how much the after became the norm, I never seemed to get used to the way my mind looped around to before - even in the most stupid moments. Why did he always pop into my head when I already felt like shit? If Brandon were here...but he's not. I woke up on my own - nobody kicked me out of bed or decided to wake me up with a flashlight and the opening song from the *Lion King* - with the completely wrong lyrics. On the rare days when both Dad and I were home, he didn't start doing the robot rather than scooting to the side to let me pass him in the narrow hallways.

Maybe Brandon took one of my limbs with him too. Maybe Mom talked to Dad, forgetting her son was right there and wanted a response. Wanted to know she was really there and understood. Maybe Brandon hated that she didn't try to braid his hair when they watched TV, or that Mom never did the worm when he said the floor was lava, claiming to be a balrog going for a swim.

Or maybe she did. I didn't really remember her well.

Crap. Tears streamed down my face. My brain looped from one bad feeling to the next, meshing everything frustrating and depressing and unfair into one gigantic mass, and my chest hurt. The weight built and built.

Falling back beside me, Dad pulled me to lay with my head against his chest. "If thinking about him makes you miserable, he's not the one for you."

"But it hurt you," I whispered before I could control myself.

"No - oh, sweetheart, thinking about your mom never hurts me." He sighed, his chest falling beneath my ear. "I'm happy when I think about her. What hurts is knowing that all I can do is think about her."

I brushed away my tears. "Thinking about Jackson is confusing."

"Confusing exciting or confusing anxious?"

"Like seeing something in the water - like it might be a dolphin, but it could also be a shark."

He chuckled. "You've been around the water all your life, Beni. You know how to tell them apart."

"But I can't tell with him," I confessed. "All I know is that I like being with him, but I don't like what he did or how everything goes when he's around and my teammates are around. I don't like having to pick sides. Or keep secrets! It was easier to like Ryan."

"Course it was. You never had a chance with that boy."

"Hey!"

He hugged me tighter for a moment. "Beni, that kid mooned over your brother. I'd've been blind not to notice."

Sitting up, I tried to put my thoughts in order. "You knew?"

"Well, yeah. Your brother never seemed to realize - you two both got that from your mother. Took forever to..." he trailed off, shaking his head. Rising to sit beside me, he frowned. "I always paid attention. I'm always here for you, Beni, and I know I had moments when you and Brandon didn't think you could rely on me, but I was always watching over you too - even when I didn't do nearly as good as you deserved."

My vision blurred. Tears poured down my face again, and I couldn't find the words to say anything at all. All I could do was hug him back when he dragged me back into a tight embrace. Maybe I didn't have an answer for Jackson, but I wasn't on my own.

Chapter Twenty-Seven

Surprising Andre with Jackson - and vice versa - seemed like more drama than I could handle. For all they had in common, they seemed to hate those pieces of themselves the most in each other. Idealistically, I might have hoped they could find common ground, but I've never been an optimist. Which meant I had to think like someone better at controlling conversations than me. Someone who knew how to shape people's thoughts. Ariadne and Tanner both came to mind, but I couldn't go to either to help me deal with their brothers. Even if Ariadne didn't want to pretend to date Ryan anymore, she still cared about Andre. Probably more than he wanted to admit when he griped about her decision.

Tanner might've felt he owed me. Which meant I would be forcing his hand, and my head got all twisted at that. My stomach churning as if calling him on his part in the crap-storm of this season somehow wasn't fair because he was still recovering. Wasn't that just as bad? Trying to soften the blow as if being in a wheelchair made him emotionally weaker. With one thought line wanting to protect him and the other to not offend him - I didn't want to deal with his talent for uncovering exactly what I didn't want him to know and get the whole mess somehow turned back on me.

So like usual, I turned to my only sensible resource: Ryan. After all, I didn't have Andre's cell number. We'd only been practicing a week, and I had his house line. Coach Carr gave out the list on the first day of practice, but Andre spent almost no time there if rumors were true. Plus, I kind of wanted Ryan to realize the situation and jump into fit it like he used to do when I was little. Back when he probably just wanted to impress Brandon. Knowing about his crush put a lot of reasons I had a crush on him into a new perspective. Which made no longer crushing on him easier. He probably loved the way Brandon would ruffle his hair when he thanked him for looking out for me. The same lovesick anxious glee I used to feel when he clapped me on the back when I learned a new shot.

The phone rang. One trill extended note followed by a drop in tone hum before bouncing back to the original trill. It wasn't late, but Ryan's family were pretty formal about dinners. They always ate them at their big, long dining table. Graces said. No dressing down or slouching allowed. Definitely no phones at the table.

Pacing the length of my room, I practiced the question over and over again in my head, mouthing the words until the familiar click and slightly out of breath - "Hey?" came down the line followed by a muffled string of curses and a different voice saying, "Hello, this is Ryan."

All thoughts fled my head, and the practiced question escaped. "Do you have Andre's cell number?" Which was a stupid question now. Andre had answered the phone, and obviously, Ryan had no idea who was on the other end of the line, so I really should have said who it was, but my brain just kept questioning what they'd been doing and pushing back with equal measuring knowing the answer and not wanting to think too much about my friends in that context.

Dead silence buzzed down the line. Then, hysterical laughter echoed as Ryan groaned. "Hey, Beni. The idiot's right here..." his voice grew softer as he probably held the phone to Andre, but I could still hear him say, "That could've been anybody. What if -"

"Calm down, sweet cheeks, I saw the ID." A smacking sound and more cursing followed before Andre asked me, "What's up, Seaver?"

"Jackson asked me to practice with him, and he promised to drop the Mercy thing, so I said yes," and there went any hope I had of a plan.

I had interrupted them - though Andre didn't seem put out about it, and I'd word-vomited all the main parts, but they weren't great. Heck, even hearing myself say that made me want to hang up and dive under the covers, pretending the world didn't exist. But I came this far, so holding my breath, I waited.

Andre sputtered, "What were - ? How did...why would you?" In the background, Ryan said something too muffled to hear, and Andre growled, "Not the time, Caldwell. Seaver's gone off the deep end."

"I know it's stupid, but we were friends, and he didn't mean -"

Andre cut me off, "You're being naive. He's gonna pull the same stunt again - *no, I'm right, and you know it, Ry* - and stupid Joe'll act like you're some boy-crazy girl."

"I am!" I admitted. "Which is why I want you there. He's - Andre, I like him. We work as friends sort of, but I want more, and he says he does too, and I've got nobody who'd be better able to see through his bullshit than you."

That, at least, seemed to bring him up short. "What?"

"Come practice with us - with me. Worst case - you're right, and you can help me accept he's just using me. Best case…" I trailed off, unsure what exactly I was hoping for. Well, mostly what part of it might appeal to Andre who got absolutely nothing out of the deal.

Inhaling, Andre released a long, put-upon sigh. "You realize how sad this is, right? You're asking me to cockblock you."

"Emotionally. Yes."

"This is a horrible idea!" He fell silent, and for a moment, I was sure he'd say no, but a shuffle sounded, and something like cloth rubbed against the mic. Despite his attempts, Andre hadn't muted me, so I could still hear him ask Ryan, "*How many brownie points do I get for babysitting Beni and Duke Jackass?*"

"*So many.*"

"*But...if you had to put a number on it?*"

"*Less the more you ask.*"

With a huff, Andre brought the phone back to his ear. "Fine. But I'm driving you. No private car time. I don't care who lives closer to you!"

Relief swept through me. "Thank you, Andre. You're seriously a life-saver."

"Yeah-yeah, I'm the best. Now, I'm emailing you my number. Let's not have this call happen again." Without so much as a goodbye, he hung up.

Maybe some foolhardy belief in universal balance had me hesitating when everything went so well with Andre, I couldn't help suspecting Jackson would be a mess, but delaying only made the stress grow. Both guys showing up in the morning horrified me, so I stared down the home phone and dialed Jackson's cell.

"Hello?"

"Hi, Jackson. It's Beni."

"Beni!" Jackson cheered. "I forgot you don't have the cell phone anymore. I still have it if you want it back."

Swallowing, I pushed down my nerves. "I'm good, thanks. Just wanted to let you know Andre and I have been practicing in the mornings, so -"

"Yeah. I saw."

How did I reply to that? Was it a statement? Or was it an attempt to make me feel bad? Not that that was hard. I guilted myself over way too much. This wasn't on him. Pushing it down, I forced myself to keep going. "One-on-one practice is great, but I think having a third person there would be best."

"Tanner could come," he offered.

I shook my head until I realized he couldn't see. "Andre said he's open to practicing with us."

"Why?" The question came abruptly. Too loud and sudden, but after a silent beat, Jackson inhaled and exhaled in almost the same way Andre had. "Sorry. I get why you'd want someone else there - especially someone like Andre, but why not one of your other teammates? One of the ones that doesn't go out of his way to make my life miserable?"

"Andre's the one I've been practicing with. Sean and Geoffrey can't do mornings, and Ryan can't either. He's in student council with Ariadne, so they meet before school," I explained. If Jackson could take a breath and stay calm, I could answer whatever questions he had.

Another huffy sigh. "Fine. Tanner's back with Ariadne anyway. I guess I'll have to deal with him eventually anyway."

"That's the spirit."

Chapter Twenty-Eight

Leaning against the side of the rink, Jackson huffed when we walked in after changing. His eyes slid from me to Andre. "You know - if I picked -"

"Shut it," Andre growled.

Running his fingers through his hair, Jackson tugged on his helmet. "Whatever - warm-ups first? Or are you two ready for rotating two against one?"

"I'm warmed up. You good, Beni?"

Both stared at me, and I nodded. "Why don't you two - "

"I've got Beni. You can get the puck first. Starting at Center," Andre commanded, glowering down his nose at Jackson with the most frustratingly pretentious expression.

The muscles in Jackson's jaw twitched. His lips shifted, but with a forced grin, he shrugged. "Sure. Why not?"

Practicing with Jackson had helped. My teammates commented on how much I had improved, and I recognized new weaknesses - areas I had been able to work through with him, but Jackson kept one bit of himself in tighter check than I knew. From the middle of the ice, he flew at us. Andre charged, and I shifted to back him up in the attack, yet with a twirl, the star of the Lions whizzed by Andre, coming straight at me. I could have stayed on course. If I checked him, I could have taken the puck, but I altered the angle, planning a less direct hit - like I had been doing to minimize his chance of injury - and he spun wide, just outside my reach after I moved to dodge.

"Head in the game, Seaver." Andre thundered by, pursuing Jackson with the fury of a man who rarely had his ego challenged. All the more stunning the more I learned how often that wasn't the case.

Splitting wide, I covered the wide side, allowing Andre to straight charge, guiding Jackson's route to goal. As much as Jackson knew my moves, I knew his, and when he prepped for a tight turn for a trickshot into goal, I checked him, grabbing the puck and passing it to Andre. He headed toward goal, and I glided back, watching Jackson recover. His eyes narrowed - slits of green as he breathed out through his nose, taking off after Andre.

"On your five!" I called.

Andre shifted, aiming for the shortest curve to goal. "Get up here then!"

Jackson avoided checking, but he wove around Andre, stealing the puck and dodging the elbow which followed. Sweeping by, I took the puck. Jackson swiveled on a dime. Andre followed wide. Right before he caught up, I sent the puck to Andre who slapped it toward goal. As the puck slid across the ice, Jackson lunged forward; his stick stabbed out, but the black circle flew right out of reach of his blade. The moment it passed the line into the goal, Andre released a cheer, which only grew in volume when he heard the frustrated growl coming from between Jackson's clenched teeth.

Looping the crowd, Andre swept his blade into the goal, dragging out the puck. "Why don't you help him, Beni?"

Jackson sneered. "I don't need help."

"You lost, Duke." Andre glided toward the midline. "Appreciate my generosity. I'm not a fan of sharing."

"Come on. We can take him down," I cheered, bumping our shoulders together, hoping to stop the comeback I could see building on the tip of his tongue.

Shrugging, Jackson spun. His eyes narrowed, and tilting back his head, he bared his teeth in a mocking grin. "Guess you've got to take what you get with Pages. Your sister isn't much of a fan of sharing either. Tanner can't go five minutes without her calling or texting."

"Honeymoon phase, am I right?" I tried, but from their expressions, it fell flat.

248

Andre scoffed. "She's not used to dealing with players. I mean, Ryan's a gentleman."

"Never knew gentleman meant 'guy who screws -'"

Slapping my stick against Jackson's, I slid between the two. "If you want to be a jerk, there's a whole other rink that way."

His nostrils flared. When his tongue dragged over his teeth, I couldn't help but wonder if we should've put mouthguards in. Jackson and I didn't. I never hit him hard enough to knock him down - not now that I knew that a wrong move could take him out for the season, but Andre never held back. In the last week, he hadn't knocked my mask or put me on my back on the ice, but he had left bruises on both of us.

"Whatever," Jackson grumbled.

Racing back, Andre rounded - not waiting for us to get into position before he drove back. His brows furrowed. This wasn't a game anymore. Bringing Ryan into their already contentious feud, Jackson did more than put a target on his back.

I skated as fast as I could, and on a sprint, I matched Jackson, so the small advantage I had was enough though I could feel him almost breathing down my neck as I forced Andre to head to the outside. However, Andre - on his best days - beat me in a sprint, so he managed to outmaneuver me long enough for Jackson to overtake me. He swept past, chasing while he worked to box him in. If Andre only wanted to take him down a peg, a race to goal would've worked. He had enough of a lead to take a clean shot. But this wasn't just ego anymore. Rounding the goal, Andre gave Jackson the time he needed to catch - to excuse a hit.

I pushed myself faster, struggling to keep ahead, but Jackson cut tight, gaining on Andre as he crossed the goal to intercept him on the other side. Andre didn't back shot into goal; instead, he charged at Jackson as if the Lion had the puck rather than him.

Like a panicking idiot, I screamed, "Time out!"

But they, of course, weren't listening, so I threw my stick forward, half-diving as I hooked Andre's - shoving Jackson aside with my extended elbow which did less than I hoped but more than Jackson probably expected. We smashed together, with me taking the brunt of the force - falling backwards and aside. Thankfully, nobody's skates cut anybody else, but my relief didn't last, and it certainly wasn't shared.

"What the hell was that?" Andre roared, pushing himself up.

Jackson growled, slamming his stick against the ice. "I don't need your protection!"

"You would have broken your arm! You would have been out the rest of the season, and we're finally on track to Nationals without some cheap win in State's because you got hurt! What were you - "

"As if Port Edmond will get anywhere close! You'll crap out at State's against us like always," Jackson interrupted. The two glared at each other for only a moment before turning back to me.

"If you guys can't handle practicing without attacking each other, then I don't need this. I practiced just fine on my own," I informed them, pushing myself to my feet. "Your siblings are dating. Both of them are generally okay people. You both have secrets, and honestly, Jackson if you don't want me to try to help you when I see you're in trouble - I'm not gonna do that."

"But I'm supposed to?" Jackson demanded, throwing off his helmet as he got in my face.

I shook my head. "I didn't say that!"

"That's exactly what you said with Mercy!"

"Hey! That's not the same," Andre cut in. "I was gonna knock you down - "

"Ha! I knew it!"

Jackson rolled his eyes. "I can take a hit!"

"Can you? Because my sister might have loose lips on my dating life, but your brother worries about your delicate bones," Andre jeared, sneering as he crossed his arms over his chest. "My sister cried after he told her he couldn't complain about P.T. because if you'd been in the car, you would have been dead."

All blood drained from Jackson's face. His fingers curled and uncurled at his side. "He said that?"

"Kid's stuck in a wheelchair trying to be Captain Positivity, so you don't kill yourself with guilt for not getting killed like you apparently think you were meant to." Andre's tone dropped lower and softer than I had heard him with anyone outside of Ryan and - at rare times - Ariadne.

Jackson skated backward. Scooping his helmet, he retreated. "I don't need this. I don't - I don't need to be interrogated."

"Who's interrogating you?" I shifted closer, but he held up his hands.

Grinding his teeth, Jackson slid further and further away. "I don't need this crap from a-a closeted - "

"You don't want to continue," Andre warned. Jackson's lips twisted in a strange expression, but he stopped in his tracks, holding his tongue for once.

"The accident wasn't your fault." I told him.

A thousand different expressions danced across Jackson's face, and for a terrifying moment, I couldn't breathe - couldn't think of anything but how much I wanted to hug him. The same sort of helpless need to be sure he was there that I had the first time I heard about the accident. My stomach churned. Anxiety built, itching at my nerves the longer Jackson just stared, like he couldn't process everything. I shifted to move forward, but Andre reached out, not enough to break whatever trance Jackson fell into but enough to keep me in place.

After a moment, his face scrunched up then fell apart completely. "Older brothers are supposed to protect their siblings. I'm supposed to protect him, and no matter how strong I get, I can't - he's always - always the one who - who..." Shaking his head, Jackson swallowed. He rubbed the heels of palms over his eyes. "You don't get to talk to me about my brother. I don't care what kind of craptastic Romeo and Julio bull-crap you've got going on - it's not - it's not even close. You don't get to -"

"My boyfriend's father will beat him to death if we get caught. Nobody talks about it, but when his elder brother, Scott, had a breakdown and got caught walking to the hospital in a blizzard to try to say goodbye to his dying best friend after his parents refused to let him take the car, they did everything they could to stop him, but he climbed out the goddamn window, telling my boyfriend to cover for him. Fever of a hundred and three - ended up with a bad case of pneumonia turned bronchitis turned extended hospital stay. Funnily enough, same hospital where the friend was - just - you know, a couple days after the friend died," Andre explained, glancing at me as if I didn't recognize what he meant. "Almost joined his friend. All because his dad decided cutting him off from his dying friend was the 'healthier alternative.'"

"You don't get to take my story and use it, and you sure as hell don't have any right to take Beni's," Jackson hissed. Tears gathered in his eyes.

Taking off my helmet, I shrugged. "I'm not the only one who lost Brandon."

"And I'm not saying I know what it's like to be in either of your shoes. What I'm saying is I know what it's like to want to be responsible for someone else's happiness - and thinking you failed. I don't want to be like Scott - always feeling guilty 'cause I didn't say what felt when I felt it. He's got a head full of what-ifs. Like somehow if he could have gotten to the hospital that night, his best friend wouldn't have died." Andre's voice pitched, and wiping his hand over his mouth as if he could brush his emotions away, he gestured widely at the rink. "I'm dating the most amazing guy, and I can't tell the world - can't even really fully come out myself because if his family finds out his friend is gay, he'll get shit for staying anywhere near me. Like I'm a disease."

Running a hand through his hair, Jackson released a hollow laugh. "So what? We're a bunch of tragic stories?"

Andre rolled his eyes. "Ryan and I are coming out once we're in college. Getting an apartment - thanks to my parents, and if his parents disown him, that's their problem. When does your tragedy end? When's the light at the end of the tunnel?"

"That doesn't work for -"

"Not for your mom," I added, and Andre nodded. "When do you stop blaming yourself for what happened to Tanner?"

"When does Tanner get to be his own person?" Andre asked.

Blinking, Jackson furrowed his brow. "When he can walk again."

"Is that possible?" Andre pressed, glancing between the two of us as if I might know the answer. When Jackson nodded, he continued, "Okay, is that in your control?" Jackson shrugged. "Figure that out. What can you do to get there faster? How do you need to support Tanner to get to that goal? Every day, I remind myself that I'm not just that guy stuck in the closet because of his boyfriend. I'm the boyfriend helping the closeted, certain he's going to lose his parents when he comes out guy realize how much happier he could be - how many people he won't lose. I'm - "

"Going to be late for first period - seriously, what's wrong with you kids? Do you need this many heart-to-hearts? Should I be worried for you?" Mike called from the side of the rink.

Andre slapped Jackson on the shoulder. "Same time tomorrow, Duke."

Skating forward, I hugged Jackson. Maybe it was weird. Both of us were padded up and sweaty, but he hugged me back, so it couldn't have been too bad of an idea. "Tanner doesn't blame you, and it'll be easier for him to talk to you about things getting hard when he knows that you aren't blaming yourself. It was the drunk driver's fault. Not yours."

"You don't have to share everything. Brandon was your brother - only yours," Jackson whispered back, holding me tightly. "He's not so bad. I guess you can bring him again."

Parting, I raced off after Andre, sliding into his car right before he peeled out toward the school. "Thank you - for today."

He smirked. "Didn't think I could pull of the wise gay best friend, did ya?"

Chuckling, I shook my head. "Three out of four don't apply, but you faked it pretty well. Think it'll earn you extra brownie points with Ryan?"

"Ouch, Seaver."

"Too cool, kind of a jerk friend?"

"Rude." Andre smiled, glancing over to me as we paused, waiting to turn into the school's parking lot. "I'll take it."

Chapter Twenty-Nine

"Does anyone else feel like having a perfect season is screwing with their brains?" Sean asked from where he had collapsed in the booth. His burger sat half-eaten in its wrapper on his chest.

Hunched over his own meal, Geoffrey groaned. "I blame Coach."

"Who is going hard on us because we've had a perfect season." Sean's hand snaked up, patting around to grab a fry. Unfortunately, he found none. "Man - give me some of your fries."

Taking a handful of mine, I tossed them down on his tray. "Next time, maybe just order a bunch of large fries."

He tucked his chin into his neck. His eyes lit up as he saw the burger sitting on his chest even as he stuffed my fries into his mouth. "Burger!"

"You're such an idiot." Geoffrey shoved his meal aside to rest his face in his arms.

Sean didn't even bother arguing, already shoving as much of his burger into his mouth as he could manage without choking. Coming off our latest victory should have felt great. Like the heroic home team, but for all the cheering, Coach seemed to get more and more tense each time we won. With State's looming - and St. Raphael's only loss being in the traditional pre-season game to us, we looked on the road to a dramatic loss if history suggested anything. At least, Coach Carr seemed to believe that.

Ryan, however, buzzed around from table to table, handing out milkshakes with a heart-shattering grin. The girls who came to the game swooned from their corner booth, but Andre held half the shakes in his arms, herding his boyfriend as far away from them as possible, blocking any who wanted to come up with sudden empty flirtation and excuses about team bonding. Though the Ariadne and Ryan break-up hadn't been dramatic or even loud, word got around quicker than anyone could have imagined that Ryan - the sweetest and one of the cutest guys in our school - was now without a girlfriend.

Needless to say, Andre had taken it better than anyone expected. Which was still worse than any normal best friend, but Andre and drama went hand in hand, so everybody sort of assumed he would be a bit weird about it.

"Seaver!" he roared, dropping his armful on our table. "Three weeks until State's - either we cancel morning practices, or we're kicking your bestie to the other rink."

Despite knowing the answer, I couldn't stop myself from asking, "Why?"

"Trick plays. No cats allowed."

Sean moaned, sitting up with his burger hanging from his mouth. Taking a bite, he stuffed it into his cheek like a chipmunk. "He's been practicing with you for over a week. You think you got any moves left to hide?"

"Practicing with Beni longer than that," Geoffrey mumbled into his arms.

Andre shoved shakes at both of them. "Which is why we're mixing up the front line. Ryan's coming, and we're dragging Kendall and Ollie into the mix."

"What about me!" Sean demanded, one hand against his chest as the other took Geoffrey's milkshake. "Ollie lives on my street. He can give me a ride!"

Swiveling, Ollie searched for who had said his name. "I can do what now?"

"Give me a ride to early morning practice!" Sean yelled back.

With a huff, Andre collected the rest of the milkshakes, half throwing them at the guys in the booth beside us. "Whatever! Either way, text your friend to stick to his own rink."

"I don't have a cell phone," I reminded him.

I could almost see his fuse burning low as his eyes narrowed. "Then call your boy toy. I don't care how you do it, but no cats - players or brothers or whatever. Mariners only. Got it?"

"Loud and clear."

And off he went, throwing an arm around Ryan's shoulders as he joined him where he stood surrounded by a group of players from the junior league. At the sight of Andre, the young boys lit up - a look of admiration and wonder filling their eyes. They'd probably all heard he had a scholarship lined up from Boston College. Unless the Bruins approached someone, there wasn't really a better way to impress the younger crew than being recruited by one of the top collegiate hockey teams around.

Well, any professional hockey team might've done it if it weren't Boston College, but there was a keen leveling of loyal - Massachusetts teams, New England teams, and then everybody else. Same reason I wanted to be part of the Pride. Sure, I'd be more than happy - beyond thrilled frankly - to get onto any professional women's team. There were only five after all, but the Boston Pride associated with the Bruins, and that made their victories personal even to those in Port Edmond who barely paid attention to a women's league existing.

Releasing the two straws from his mouth, Sean placed a hand to his forehead. "Stupid brain freeze."

"Serves you right for stealing my milkshake," Geoffrey announced, but he made no move to try and reclaim his drink.

"Not like you were going to drink it."

Not even bothering to argue the point further, Geoffrey turned his head to glower toward where Ryan and Andre stood. "Any recruiters come through for Ryan yet?"

"Couple from lower tier schools, but he's already accepted at Boston University and Boston College, so he could just go to open tryouts, can't he? Don't they have those there?" Sean posited, stealing more of my fries.

"I guess." I sighed and set my milkshake down.

Sitting up, Geoffrey shoved the mess of his finished meal onto Sean's tray. "Caldwells go to Harvard, don't they?"

"They are legacies. He's probably a shoe-in there too." Sean reached toward my milkshake. "Not like he planned to go professional anyway."

Humming, I smacked his hand back. "Still sucks."

"Don't know - he seems happy."

Sean wasn't wrong. Even with the break-up and whatever drama that likely caused at home, Ryan smiled more in the last few days than he had in a while. He probably had a countdown going to freedom. Or to his entire life turning upside down. I couldn't even begin to imagine how nervous he must have been. The light at the end of the tunnel for Andre may have been the train for Ryan.

Comparison stole joy, but it eased the sour uncertainty inside me. How could I be so certain of my end goal - certain of where I needed to go to get there - and yet so horrified of anything outside those points? A stupid question. I didn't like surprises. Jackson Duke wasn't exactly a surprise anymore. He existed as chaos. Or maybe, more a force of nature. He had some reasoning behind his choices, but whatever it was escaped me - which seemed to confuse him as much as my choices seemed to do.

"Want to borrow my phone to deal with Duke?" Geoffrey asked, fumbling with his coat to pull out his phone.

I shook my head. "I'll tell him tomorrow."

"He's gonna love getting ditched so soon after you two started hanging out again," the defenseman mumbled.

Popping the top off his milkshakes, Sean dumped one into the other. "If he's a friend, he'll hang out without practicing."

"We're going to the movies."

Both guys froze, glancing at each other and then to me. Setting down the empty cup, Sean leaned back, slurping his new concoction with raised brows. "Whatcha gonna see?"

When I shrugged, Geoffrey huffed. "He's planning it?"

"He's always the one planning it."

"You know you're going to have the same problem if you take a passive role in your relationship. Forcing one partner to be actively in charge of decisions for both doesn't generally work long term," Sean commented, drawing confusion from both Geoffrey and myself. "What? My parents went to couple's counseling for a while back in fourth grade. Not big on babysitters, so I read the pamphlets."

Geoffrey's brows furrowed. "You can read?"

Snorting, Sean slurped on his straw. "Mock me all you want. I'm right."

"I know, but it's just...it's weird," I tugged at the end of my braid, struggling to find the words. Explanations helped. If I could figure out enough to tell them, I might be able to wrap my own head around it. "Half the time I'm not sure spending more time with him is a good idea, and we can't go to most places without risking somebody seeing us together. Even the movie theater sort of feels like a risk."

"More of a risk if he's bringing you there for a makeout session in the back row," Sean conceded, and my entire face heated up. "Aw, tomato Beni."

"Shut up," I hissed.

"You want to kiss him. You want to date him," Sean chanted, punctuating his sing-song teasing with slurps of his milkshake.

With a groan, Geoffrey sunk back into his arms. "If Beni gets a boyfriend before either of us get girlfriends, I quit."

"Quit what?"

"Life."

Wrinkling his nose, Sean scoffed. "Lame."

"It's not gonna happen," I informed them. "We're just friends."

Geoffrey snorted. "Does Jackie know that?"

"Tanner's coming to the movies, so I think we're on the same page." If Ariadne showed up, then I could panic. Until then, I firmly set myself in the belief that we were on the same page.

With a shrug, Geoffrey returned to his post-game half-nap, and Sean slurped his milkshake, stealing my fries with a roll of his eyes.

Chapter Thirty

Shoving my wallet into my pocket, I raced down the stairs. "I'm headed to Jackson's - bye!"

"But you aren't dating?"

I shook my head. "I swear - you'll be the first to know."

With a hum, he returned to the net he'd been mending, and I headed out into the cold winter morning. Between Andre and Jackson, I rarely biked to school anymore, so it was nice to take out my bike and head up along the coast. The ocean roared as the tide rushed toward the shore. A crisp frost spread across the grass. Most of the snow had melted during the week, but here and there, piles of refreezing slush gathered like tiny ramps. Wind swept through my hair. As the sun cascaded across the waves, the only interruption to the peace existed in my mind.

Which was ridiculous. Jackson would understand. Honestly, he was more protective of his winning streak - the legacy of the St. Raphael Lions - than Andre was of whatever secret plays he planned, so he probably wanted to ask the same thing.

Turning down the driveway, I pedaled up the long curve which separated the Duke's house from the rest of Port Edmond. Jackson's car sat in the drive. Right next to it, Tanner rolled out down the front porch ramp toward his own car parked parallel to his brother.

"Hey, Beni!" he waved, tugging his door open.

Sliding to a stop, I frowned. "You're driving?"

His eyes widened, and he froze. "Uhh…"

"He's ditching us," Jackson informed me, locking the door behind him. "Apparently, Ariadne volunteers at an animal shelter downtown on weekends, and her partner for today never showed up."

Dismounting my bike, I guided it over toward their porch. "So…they're back together?"

"Hey! Hey-hey-hey, nobody's dating anybody, alright?" Tanner lifted himself into the driver's seat of his car. "Enjoy your movie! I'm going to play with some kittens!"

Jackson smirked. Winking at me, he leaned against the hood of his car. "Hmm - sounds kind of fun. We could come along if she really needs more help."

Faster than I'd ever seen him go, Tanner collapsed his chair and threw it into the passenger's seat. He didn't respond verbally, but he slammed the door and flew out of the driveaway. His hand popped out of the window. A middle finger aimed back at his elder brother as he flew down the road toward his 'not girlfriend.'

He hadn't been around much anyway, so I didn't actually mind Tanner ditching us. With both brothers around, odds varied pretty much like a coin flip whether they'd force each other to be better or drag each other into some weird side bar I couldn't follow. I appreciated their bond. Part of me envied it, but one-on-one with Jackson eased the anxiety about State's.

"Shit, it's cold," Jackson complained, jumping into his car. "Hurry up!" Sliding into the passenger's seat, I buckled as Jackson turned on the seat warmers and shifted into gear. "I can't believe you biked here. You know I could've picked you up."

"I like biking."

He snorted. "You're ridiculous."

Combing my fingers through my hair, I undid my braid, sticking the elastic around my wrist as I redid it. "Movie theater is in the opposite direction. No point in you zig-zagging."

"You just wanted the wind-swept Elizabeth Bennett look." Ruffling my hair and forcing me to redo it, he laughed. "Not bad. Honestly."

I smacked his hand, starting the process of braiding all over again. Though I wanted to make a joke about Mr. Darcy, the implications kept my tongue tied, so like a jerk, I rained on the parade. "Since we're only a few weeks from State's, do you mind if we split off our morning practices? Andre has some kind of secret plays he wants to practice."

"Secret plays? I don't know - now I'm interested."

"And now Andre's going to be paranoid and probably drag Ariadne to practice to distract Tanner," I retorted.

Jackson laughed and rolled his eyes. "Please don't encourage that. Andre's growing on me, but the idea of being related to him, even by marriage, is still not great. I'm fine with splitting practice until after we wreck you in State's."

"As if."

Pulling into the parking lot, he jumped out of the car, sliding across the hood like something out of *Grease* before almost completely falling on his face when I opened my door. He threw an arm around my shoulders and kicked the door shut behind me.

"Are you a before the movie popcorn person? During?" he asked. "There is a right answer."

The weight of his arm across my shoulders made my stomach itch with a strange anxious excitement. "Preview popcorn. It's an alliteration for a reason."

"Exactly! No box shuffling or crunching during the cinematic experience - and bottled water over soda every time." Jackson tugged the door open and held it for me before spinning around to beat me to the counter. Before I could blink, he had paid for the tickets and dragged me toward the concession counter. "Just popcorn and bottled water? Or do you want nachos? Candy?"

"I'm good with popcorn." Thankfully, for the matinee, the line was short, so we only waited for a minute in line, and he whipped out his wallet. Reaching out as he ordered for both of us, I pulled out my own wallet. "Seriously, Jackson, I brought money. You don't need to pay for everything."

His lips pressed together. Not exactly a frown, but a sort of contemplative look, but he stepped aside, letting me pay. Once my wallet returned to my pocket, he took my hand in his, swinging them slightly as we headed into the theater and to our seats. Though Jackson talked about the movie, I couldn't help but fall into a bit of a panic. This was a date. Geoffrey and Sean were right. Jackson wanted this to be a date. Did I want this to be a date?

The warmth of his hand radiated up my arm. My whole body flushed. In my chest, my heart raced faster than it did even during games, but there were so many variables. What if things went weird between us again? I liked him. Really really liked him even though he did things that drove me insane, I understood his intentions, and I wasn't the best at that. I didn't have great intuition - it was something I always envied in Brandon, but Jackson kind of didn't either. We were both so stubborn, and while he was loud and assertive, I dug my heels in just as much. We both took longer than most people to click in those moments when we disagreed, but we didn't actually disagree a lot. Mercy had been the big one.

Maybe Mercy should've been a deciding factor. The worst part of his personality. A warning sign or red flag or whatever, but if that was his worst, I knew he could recover from it. That he cared enough about me to learn and to fix his mistakes. Or maybe that was an excuse because I really really wanted to date him.

When we sat down, our tickets were in one of those couples chairs. There was an armrest. We could pull it down, but it was already up, so when we sat down, he released my hand to throw an arm over my shoulder. It wasn't the cliche yawn move. He did it without even blinking, but when I curled up against him, his own heartbeat thundered almost as loud as my own.

Biting his lip, he blushed. Even in the dim light of the theater, I could see the pink painted over his cheeks. The knots unwound within me. Somehow, his nervousness made everything easier.

Cuddled up together through the previews, I could almost hear a running commentary from Andre on how stiff we were, but I rather we both were kind of awkward. I had no experience. Nobody ever asked me out, so dates weren't a skill I mastered, but so many girls liked Jackson. All kinds of women who were smart and pretty and strong.

Before I could overthink, I shifted and took his face in my hands. It wasn't an important scene. Just some cinematic shot, and who knew if there were too many more, so I took his face in my hands and pressed a quick kiss to his lips. The flush across his face brightened once more.

"Beni," he whispered, sputtering and smiling so brightly I thought my heart would explode. I couldn't contain the not appropriate to the scene laugh, and he pulled me closer to him. I pressed my lips against his shoulder, trying to stifle the giggles bubbling out of me. Arms wrapped around me, he kissed the top of my head. "Stop being cute!"

With his arms around me, we settled down to watch the movie. If, in our awkward excitement, he dropped me off at my house with a kiss and my bike left at his, it didn't matter. Tomorrow was Sunday, and we'd already made plans to hit the rink and see which of us was worse in figure skates during the free skating hour. Even my dad's knowing look couldn't dim the serotonin high.

Chapter Thirty-One

When had I ever panicked about clothes? Maybe middle school - but I had believed I gave up on being pretty before then. Always at least a head taller than the next girl, I outgrew clothes like a weed, taking my brother's shirts and even his old jeans because the thought of him or my dad taking me shopping terrified me.

They didn't like it much either. The discomfort always showed on their faces. At least, on my dad's. Stuck in pinks, crop tops, and skirts, he turned from his usual calm self into someone else entirely. Everything became too short or impractical. Pockets were never deep enough - which I agreed with, but somehow, his voice carried, and all the other shoppers would start watching and whispering like it was some strange show.

Brandon was worse. If I showed any sign of embarrassment, he veered into it. Throwing sequence-covered skirts at me until I grabbed the nearest graphic T-shirt in my size. Neither protested my decision to wear guy's jeans. More pockets - deeper too. Though I had muscular thighs, my hips weren't as wide as women's jeans or any pants expected. With my waist being not significantly smaller than my hips, I didn't have the curves expected by my thighs or the thin legs expected by everything else. My height just made matters worse.

Dresses skipped the whole mess, but seeing myself in them left me uncomfortable. Pulling at the hems already plenty long enough and putting shorts on top of leggings - my face never seemed to match the outfit. I felt bulky. Too big and too muscular for anything stereotypically feminine. I never seemed to be able to make them look casual. Either formal in dresses or casual in sweatpants.

And formal might've been fine. Any time I imagined a date, dresses seemed the safest choice. Plus, skater's wore dresses - or skirts, right? But falling on the ice hurt. I admired how fearlessly figure skaters could throw themselves around with no padding, and I wasn't afraid of getting hurt. Between checks and just practice in general, I spent my life with bruises, but I liked a bit more between me and the ice. Not to mention the cold. Odds had Jackson definitely being more graceful, and now that I knew that this was dating, I wanted to wear something else. Something not the usual. Something that said - date.

So - a dress. Fit and flare to even out the hips - that's what the internet said would work, and it looked okay. Thermal tights and a sweater. My boots and a coat - that made sense, right? Sounded easy; however, I couldn't figure out if I needed to change my hair. Normally, I kept it up in a ponytail or bun or braided. But people dressed up on dates. I didn't yesterday. I hadn't realized it was a date, and if Tanner went with us as planned; maybe it wouldn't have been one.

Racing down the stairs, I slid into the kitchen. "Hair down? Hair up?"

"Whatever's most comfortable," he suggested. "Guys generally don't care."

"This isn't about that," I huffed.

Though I wanted Jackson to think of me like he would any other girl in the beginning, I understood what I really wanted was for him to like me better than other girls. Not because I was different. Not different in the ways I had always felt. I wanted him to like me in the way movies showed guys liking pretty girls. The girls who only seemed different until they took off their glasses. Girls who weren't actually different - not really, not from the other girls, but who had been made to feel just not like anybody else because people decided to ostracize them for not wanting to or not pretending to fit what other people wanted from them. Not the rebels. The ones who had a dream and didn't let somebody else take it away. Didn't want to or weren't good at playing the game. Whatever that meant.

Normally, I only wished I understood how to do that stuff when I felt like I was missing something. I admired women with perfect make-up. Those who expressed themselves with clothes - knowing how to use something which made me feel so insecure to make themselves feel brave. Women who knew how to say the right thing at the right time to play people or to diffuse situations, but appreciation only turned to envy when I thought I lost something by failing - failing to learn, failing to inherit some sort of girl sense or not allowing myself to learn because I thought learning would somehow stop me from mastering a new shot or play.

I wanted other people to see us. See handsome, stylish model Jackson Duke with a girl who they wouldn't blink twice at him holding hands with. Playing hockey, I fit those who might think of hockey star Jackson Duke, but nobody probably would be there who knew me in that way. My teammates didn't go to the free skate. Not during the season. People recognized Jackson from his modeling - from interviews. Even as the only girl in the local league, nobody would see me and put my name to my face. I wanted to be the girl who fit with Jackson.

Because I had no confidence. The skates would have toe-picks. I'd be okay with them, but anything fancy threatened my stability, so I needed to look the part. Or at least not look like a mess. Because this was a date. He kissed me goodbye yesterday. We cuddled! He liked me for who I was, so I shouldn't panic about what I wore, but I wanted to be better.

"What about that braid thing you did for your school picture last year?" my dad said, gesturing about his hairline to get the style he meant across.

"A crown braid! You're a genius!"

I raced back upstairs, searching for a smaller elastic and bobby pins. Though the first time wasn't perfect, I heard the doorbell rang, and any further fretting failed before it could take off. Rushing down the stairs, I wasn't prepared for the way my heart raced when I opened the door.

Jackson smiled, and it was so strange after so long to see him standing on my porch. His cheeks flushed with the winter's chill. "You ready to go?"

"Yeah, I'm good." Tugging on my jacket, I waved goodbye to my dad, shutting the door tightly behind us.

His hand slipped into mine. "Promise not to laugh when I faceplant the first time I hit the picks?"

"I'll be flat on the ice beside you, so not much of a promise," I replied, trying to ignore the way my cheeks heated when he opened the door for me to climb into the passenger's seat.

As high as my nerves were, forgetting this was anything but hanging out with Jackson proved surprisingly easy. Mike made no comment on the dress. We both posed, laughing at how delicate the figure skates were in comparison to our usual blades. Both were white. Laced up, they walked the line between the familiar sensation of my usual skates and something entirely new. Neither of us fell on our faces. We held hands, skating in wide slow loops around the rink.

"If you let go, I'm slamming into the boards," Jackson warned as we turned the corner. A complete lie - he was the only thing keeping me from falling flat when I accidentally hit the picks.

Squeezing his hand, I hummed. "So you're saying I should let go?"

"Sadist," he gasped.

"I would've thought your dad might've pushed you toward figure skating at some point." When he sent me a questioning look, I added, "Fewer injuries."

"Mom did. I started off on figure skates when I was little, but Doctor Dad tried to push archery and fencing. Fencing wasn't bad. I liked sabre," Jackson explained.

I nodded, considering. "What about archery?"

"My aim is good, but it was way too calm for me."

"But more people do watch the summer Olympics..." I trailed off, and we glanced at each other. His side-eye game was strong. "I'm just saying - better sponsors."

"They watch for the gymnastics and soccer. People watch winter for figure skating and snowboarding. Either way - any sponsors are after my gorgeous face and bod, not my athletic prowess...if I made the US Olympic team for whatever," he said before spinning, dragging me with him as he started to skate backwards to grab both my hands. "You've got a better chance at the Olympics than I do."

"Well, we did just beat Canada."

He huffed, but his lips twisted up into a smile. "And men's didn't even medal. Don't remind me."

When the free skate time ran down, we headed off the ice, dropping off our skates before we went to grab food. As the sun went down, Jackson brought me home. He parked in my driveway, and we chatted a bit - both recognizing that we wouldn't be together tomorrow, and between school and practice, we weren't going to see each other until Saturday.

"You sure I can't convince you to get a cell phone?" Jackson asked.

I shook my head. "You could always call the landline."

"Sheesh - ok, grandma."

Rolling my eyes, I pulled him into a kiss. "See you Saturday."

"Bye."

Slipping out of the car, I fought the urge to run inside as if walking would increase the chance of me doing something to ruin it, but I made it through the door, locking it safely behind me. If my dad gave me a pointed look, I didn't care. My lips tingled from where I had kissed Jackson again. Warmth swelled in my chest just at the thought of him. We weren't perfect, but somehow, today felt pretty impossibly wonderful.

Chapter Thirty-Two

For years, I worked alone in the mornings. Skated and trained until I fought my way onto the varsity team, and in this season, I had gone from one partner to being part of a trio, and now, half of the forwards on our team gathered. Groggily, they stumbled inside, following Andre's bright command. When he'd suggested he had a plan for our pre-State's training, I wasn't sure what to think. Maybe I underestimated him. Coming out of the lockers with a binder in hand - and Ryan nowhere in sight to save any of us, he got to work. Within ten minutes of getting on the ice, we were ragged.

"Is that all you've got?" Andre bellowed.

Sean groaned, gliding in a hunch. "Give us a break, man."

"Come on, whiners! The Lions aren't taking it easy. Get your butts back into position!" Andre raced across the ice, herding Sean back into place across from Ollie as he yelled.

Already in position, Kendall scoffed. "You mean Duke isn't taking it easy. We're kinda screwed. Beni spent half the season practicing with him, so - " he shrugged, "there goes that advantage."

Ollie's nose wrinkled. "Pretty sure he just needs to, ya know, not get hit by her."

"Great strategy. Don't get hit. Revolutionary," Graham grumbled as he settled into position across from me.

"Hey!" Andre waved his binder, skating down the line between the two sides. "Get your heads in the game! We beat St. Raphael's in the traditional pre-season game. We're undefeated. If there was a year to take this all the way, this is it. Take us to Nationals! Which means going to Ohio, so that's not too exciting, but that's the sort of legacy which'll get recruiters in those stands for the lot of you next year. Look around! I'm the only senior here. I've got a position. Ryan's set. Victor, Donovan, Peter - all know where they're going."

He wasn't wrong. Some of us were sophomores, so college stood a bit further off, but it wasn't like we suddenly realized we had to figure that out in senior year. Despite being the least serious of our friend group, Sean worried about college more than any of us. Probably because he didn't have any trust in his ability on the ice. That said, not everyone wanted to play professionally - or even in college. I did. Sean and Graham joked about how much better their friends were, but they still wanted to play. It seemed safe in those moments to assume we'd all aim at going professional. Even if someone didn't want that, they wouldn't say it. Not any place where Coach Carr could overhear. Not to Andre. So, head's down, we ran the play again.

Tuesday came and went the same way. Beginning with Andre drilling his new plays - cleaning up our weak shots, and each day ended with Coach Carr doing the same. By Thursday, the new morning crew seemed exhausted. Sean collapsed into the seat beside me at lunch. His head immediately falling into the crux of one elbow as he groaned.

"I'm not cut out for this," Sean moaned.

With a hum, Geoffrey leaned back in his seat. "Well, you lasted longer than I thought you would."

"Come on." I nudged his arm. "It's just an extra forty minutes."

Flopping up to poke at his food, Sean pouted. "You're a mad woman. How are you not wrecked doing this all season?"

"I'm used to it," I reminded him.

Though he glowered, he didn't bother to argue. Instead, he shoveled his lunch into his mouth, barely chewing as Geoffrey and I winced in disgust. After so many years, we should have been used to it, but Sean's half-dead with exhaustion eating edged on disaster sort of gore. Forcing myself to look away, I refocused on my notes.

"Derek has us getting up early for a run tomorrow," Geoffrey offered even as he continued to watch Sean with morbid fascination and disgust warring on his face. "We're just meeting at the school to use the paved section around the football field."

"Isn't that icy?" Sean asked around bites.

Nose wrinkling, Geoffrey nodded. "Yeah, but they salt it. Shouldn't be too bad."

"Why don't you guys just join us?" I asked, flipping through the plays. "I don't get why we're splitting offense and defense off in the morning practices."

Geoffrey shrugged. "Andre is Andre. I'm sure it makes sense in his head."

"Can we not talk about hockey? I never thought I'd say it, but I'm hockeyed out. I'm this close to hanging up my stick." Sean set his thumb and finger nearly touching for only a split second before he downed his milk and shoved his empty tray aside.

Cocking a brow, Geoffrey rolled his eyes. "I thought your mom required all you guys to do a sport each season."

"Yeah - I mean, I could totally become a figure skater or something. Sparkles, low number of guys, ice - that's kind of my daily life with my sisters already. Plus, anything Sadie can do, I could totally do better," Sean announced.

"Isn't Sadie nationally placed?"

Sean gasped. Pressing a hand to his chest, he leaned away from me, sputtering. "How dare you!"

"Too far, Seaver," Geoffrey sardonically agreed.

"Hey, hey-hey-hey, Sadie's not just 'nationally placed,'" he corrected, putting air quotes around my words. "She's doing tryouts for the Olympics, which means - like, I'm a shoe-in."

"Your sister's a potential Olympian, who you think you can beat, but you get all mopey thinking you won't get a hockey scholarship. That's some kind of cosmic dissonance going on there," Geoffrey informed him.

With a pointed glower, Sean shifted back in the seat beside me. "More important - Sadie stopped by the rink on Sunday. Her training starts right after free skate nowadays…" Oh no. My cheeks heated, and I pointedly kept my eyes trained on the notebook, but the weight of their gaze left me nowhere to hide especially when Sean crowed in delight. "Beni's a cherry!"

"Shut up," I hissed, smacking his arm.

"Hey, come on, it's good, right?"

Geoffrey's brows furrowed. "What's good?"

"Beni went on a little ol' date with a certain Jackson Duke," Sean announced. At least he had the decency to keep his voice low, but my heart still raced, wondering if someone might hear over the usual roar of the cafeteria.

"Oh god, is it official?" Geoffrey looked to me then groaned. "Ah, really, Beni? You could do so much better than Duke."

I glared, trying to calm the blush. "I like him."

"Apparently, Sadie says you were super cute together," Sean informed us, and the blush returned full force. "When did that happen?"

Why did I even hang out with Sean? He knew exactly when it had happened. While we didn't hang out every weekend, our Saturday camp outs in his living room or over Geoffrey's house dropped significantly since I started spending more time with Jackson. But I grew up with Sean. I knew how he thought. I recognized the little cocky smirk.

"Saturday."

And there it was. The smirk shifted into another level of smug. "Huh? So that movie was a date?"

"It became a date," I corrected. "Ariadne asked Tanner to help her volunteer - and things just...happened."

"Things happened? Hmm...." he leaned forward, sharing a pointed look with Geoffrey who just rolled his eyes.

"Drop it, Sean."

Geoffrey scoffed. "The idiot's got a point. He called it."

"I called it!" Sean cheered.

"You got lucky! How was I to know it was a date?"

"How did you not know it was a date?" Geoffrey retorted, shaking his head. "Don't make me feel bad for Duke, Beni. He pretty much screamed he was into you."

"I thought we were friends." Which we were. We just happened to be friends that were a bit more than that too. I didn't have to explain myself to these two. Even if Sean had said something to that effect last week, I was not going to admit he was right.

Snickering, Sean gestured between himself and Geoffrey. "We're your friends. Best friends even - and there is no way I'd do morning practices with you if Andre wasn't making me."

"Jackson did an extra practice session anyways. He just moved it up. It's easy to practice with another person," I argued.

But Sean wasn't having it. "He gave you thousands of dollars worth of gear."

"He gets free stuff when modeling." Not the best argument. My dad had pointed out the same thing, and the more I thought about it, the more awkward it made me feel. I didn't want Jackson thinking he had to give me stuff for me to like him. Still, I hadn't exactly given him back the new skates. Or the bag or any of the gear. Pretty much kept it all except the cell phone. Did that make me a horrible person? He also didn't let me pay on our dates. But he did make more money modeling than I did in a month or even several months at the gym. Sean wound up for probably another on his list of signs. I couldn't take it. "Okay, okay, I get it. New topic!!"

Sean snorted, but he had the decency to actually listen. "Anybody want to talk about how Ryan and Andre have been avoiding each other lately."

"Can't we talk about something besides other people's dating lives?" Geoffrey groaned, grabbing his empty tray to dump it on Sean's.

"This could affect how well the team works together! Plus, it's just weird."

A second too late - it clicked into my brain. "Wait, what?"

Both froze. Their eyes wide as they glanced at each other then at me before Geoffrey leaned back. In one drawn out hiss, he mumbled, "Crap."

"I hate you both - so so much."

"It wasn't our place to tell you! You were crushing on Ryan, and I mean, that's like half the reason Andre hated you, so it just was weird, and it's like an open secret to the guys on the team." Sean glanced at Geoffrey and then sighed. "Most of us."

Geoffrey nodded. "It's not like Ariadne's the only one they've ever roped into covering for them. They aren't exactly the most subtle."

"Back when the whole Tanner-Ariadne thing happened, she told me and asked me to take her place covering for them! I thought I couldn't talk to you about it!" I buried my face in my hands. "Do you have any idea how stressed I've been about that?"

The two just shrugged. "We thought you realized we knew after the whole Mercy Jackson being an idiot thing," Sean told me.

"Plus, not exactly our place to tell you if you didn't know," Geoffrey added.

I couldn't argue with that. The whole reason I hadn't brought it up, confessing how much Ariadne's question - request really - bothered me, came from the knowledge that this wasn't my secret. "Weirdest season ever."

"Good weird, right?" Sean stood, grabbing the trays to throw them out.

Following him and Geoffrey out of the cafeteria, I shrugged. "Not entirely sure. Ask me after State's."

Chapter Thirty-Three

A sea of red faced a sea of blue. Feet stomped in time, and the Lions' section sang their ridiculous song about being 'lion proud,' which had the Port Edmond side taunting them. Rarely were we so divided, but we'd beaten St. Raphael in the traditional pre-season for the first time since Jackson came up. We'd marched all the way through the season - undefeated - to State's, and now, in TD Garden, we faced off.

Settling across the ice from Ryan, Jackson winked at me - not even trying to hide how cocky he was. The puck dropped. Racing across the ice, Jackson, took the puck. Ryan stayed close, and I curved around, stealing the puck away. Back and forth, we moved from one side to the other. A few minutes in, our lines switched. We had a low scoring game pegged from the start. Even at their best, we usually could keep the Lion back for a while - most if not all of the first period, but Jackson bounced back in the second like nobody's business. His endurance horrified me some days.

Then the buzzer sounded - first period over. Coach lectured, but I couldn't pay attention. Adrenaline thrummed in my veins. Second period passed - no score. Drained and ragged, Graham and

Peter took the ice with Ollie. Within two minutes, Coach Carr pulled them, and we were back on the ice again. As if he could sense the Lions' coach prepping to send Jackson back in, Andre sent the puck across the ice to me. Diving forward, he outpaced the forward. Andre's forward raced toward the boards. I sent the puck to Ryan. Like some innate sense, I could hear the sound of Jackson jumping the boards above the roar before Ryan sent the puck to Andrew, and the sweet sound of a slap shot sent the puck across the ice.

Jackson rushed, but he couldn't stop it. The goalie missed the block, and the entire blue side of the rink shrieked, screaming and clapping as Andre rounded the goal with a crow call of his own.

"See that, Duke!" Andre yelled, sweeping up beside me. "That's teamwork!"

Jackson scoffed. Rolling his eyes, he shrugged, skating backward. "Yeah, yeah - celebrate while you can."

Back to center. This time, Ryan took the puck. He cleared to the outside, sending it toward Andre, but Jackson stole it away. Andre chased him down. His eyes glinted with a determination which seemed the edge of frenzy. He came up on Jackson, forcing him to look for a pass, but I intercepted his closest teammate, and Ryan shifted ahead, predicting how Jackson would clear us.

One minute, Jackson dodged Andre's reaching blade. In the next, Joe slammed him against the boards, jabbing with the top of his stick. Only the referee's whistle got him back, and even an immediate penalty didn't destroy the smirk as he stared down when Jackson crumbled onto the ice, struggling to breathe.

"Jackson!?" I dove forward, sliding down beside him. He wheezed, struggling to breath. Then his eyes rolled up in his head, and he collapsed, but his breathing didn't get better. "He's unconscious! We need a medic - "

"He needs an ambulance," one of his teammate's retorted, shoving me out of the way. "Danny, grab the board!"

A sharp tug dragged me back. Ryan pulled me away from Jackson - and from Joe who continued to watch the panic with that stupid smirk, but he shouldn't have worried about me.

Coming up behind him, Andre punched Joe, sending him to the ice. "What the hell was that?"

"I just took out their stupid progedy. You were all for it when Beni did it in the pre-season," Joe yelled back. His cheek already started to swell.

They attached Jackson to the board, lifting him and heading off the ice as sirens sounded. Tanner screamed from the side. Tears streamed down his face, and if he could get his chair over the

lip and onto the ice, he would've been by his
brother's side, but he bounced back and forth,
wheeling in inches as if he could do something by
those little movements. Better than me. I froze.
Panicked. I should have been able to do something.
Why couldn't I think of what I should do?

"Dad…" I raced across the ice, leaping the
boards. "Dad! Tanner shouldn't - "

But my dad was already moving. He
side-stepped his way through the crowd to Tanner,
who looked up at him in a mix of relief and panic.
Where was Dr. Duke? Where was Ariadne? I didn't
have either of their numbers, but Andre -

Two hands landed on my shoulders, forcing
me to face Ryan. "Beni, sit down."

"I have to - "

Pushing me to sit down on the bench I had
been standing on, he crouched to keep his eyes level
with mine. "Coach subbed us out. Joe's in the
penalty box -"

Andre scoffed, throwing his stick down. "He
should be off the f-"

With a glare, Ryan forced Andre to cut
himself off. "The ref's going to start the game back
up. There's only six minutes left. Six minutes,
handshakes at the end, and I will drive you to the
hospital, okay?"

"Or I could go right now. I don't need to be here," I replied. Coach Carr paced again. His bellowing followed once the puck dropped. "Coach -?"

"Beni! Six minutes."

"What if he doesn't have six minutes?"

"He took a hard hit, but he'll be fine," Ryan reassured.

"What if he's not?" My pulse rushed in my ears. What was I doing? How could I stay at the game when Jackson had been literally knocked unconscious? His lungs sounded weird. What if he'd broken a rib? He could've broken a rib - or multiple ribs - puncturing a lung and bleeding internally. They brought out a board. Boards meant spinal injuries which meant paralysis, right? "I've got to -"

Ryan pushed me back onto the bench when I stood. "You've got to stay here. Stay calm. Your dad's taking Tanner to the hospital. Mike said Dr. Duke's headed back from some conference in Boston, but he'll be here shortly. It's fine. There's nothing you could do."

"I could be there!"

Wrapping an arm around me, Andre slid into the seat beside me. "Jackson would probably be pissed if you went running off from your first State's game because of him. Win the game. Shake hands - tell the Lions they did a good job, shower, and then we head to the hospital."

"But -"

Geoffrey jumped the boards and stumbled close. "We going?"

"Dear god, shut up!" Andre hissed at him. Raising his hands, Geoffrey backed away. "Game's almost over. Be professional!"

"Quiet! All of you!" Coach Carr commanded.

I glanced at the clock and regretted it almost immediately. Still two minutes. Two minutes, handshakes, and then the hospital - waiting would be best. Why didn't that feel right?

Chapter Thirty-Four

When the final buzzer sounded, I jolted toward the locker rooms, but Geoffrey grabbed my shoulders, spinning me back toward the ice. Nobody liked this part. My eyes darted to the scoreboard.

"When did we get a second point?"

Geoffrey huffed, pushing toward the ice. "Victor did like a minute ago. Pay attention."

I couldn't hold back a grumbled, "This is stupid."

"Suck it up, buttercup," he hissed, and there we skated - lackluster 'good games' with slapped hands that passed as high fives. A rote routine of faux sportsmanship made all the worse with Jackson gone.

My stomach churned. All the sweat on my body chilled quicker than normal, leaving me too cold and too hot and all mixed up all over. I wanted to claw at my skin. Throw my gear aside. Run all the way to the hospital - as if that would get me there faster. As long as I remained at the rink, Jackson seemed in flux. Both dead and alive. Injured severely - lung pierced, internal bleed, everything horrible I'd ever seen in a television show or read about. Or maybe just the wind knocked out of him and a concussion. His wheezing breathing - that could be just bruised ribs, right?

The moment we looped, I raced off, jumping the boards and rushed through the routine, leaving my gear in the locker. Pulling on my sweater, I tugged on my jacket as I raced out the door - my boots untied.

"Beni!" Ariadne called, running up to me with a banner in her hands. "Congratulations!"

Blinking, I frowned. "What? Whatever, can you take me to the hospital?"

Her eyes traced up and down me. "Are you okay? What -"

"Jackson got hurt!" I informed her, already heading toward the door. "My dad went with Tanner. They probably went to Port Edmond General, right? That's the closest, isn't it?"

"Wait - Beni, what happened? Why did they -?"

Rounding on her, I yelled, "I can answer on the way, or I can get another ride. Do I need to get another ride?"

When she froze, I growled, glaring out onto the floor, searching for Sean's mom as I stormed toward the front of the rink. Somebody had to be here. It was the State's. Everybody should have had family here. Why wasn't Jackson's dad here? Then my dad wouldn't have gone with Tanner, and I could've gone with my dad and not been looking to bum a ride off somebody.

A hand landed on my shoulder, and I rounded ready to start a fight, but Ariadne gestured at me to follow her. "Come on. My car's in the side lot."

My shoulders sagged. "Thank you."

"Please - just explain what's going on," she requested as we ran out the door toward her car.

"Joe pinned him to the boards." That much I could explain. I had seen it, so it should have been easy, but the rest of the words tumbled over each other. "Jackson fell. He wasn't - his lungs - it didn't sound right, and then he blacked out. Eyes rolled up and everything, and his team - his teammates…" I tried to swallow, but my throat clenched too thick to do more than leave me struggling all the more. My hand reached out, but the door stayed firm as Ariadne fumbled with the keys. When the lights flashed, I tugged it open, sliding in as she rushed to do the same. "They had to use a board." Why was everything so blurry? I couldn't be crying. I needed to not be crying. Crying didn't help. Why did everything hurt? "Their dad's not there. He - he had a conference or meeting or something."

"He's probably fine," Ariadne assured.

But how could she know? She hadn't been there. Hadn't seen the way he crumpled to the ice after Joe let go. Like a rag doll. Just crumbled right down - no cutting comment, nothing. We'd scored. We'd scored, and he needed to get a goal, so he hadn't been as careful as he should have been, and I pressured him. Sean and I had him nearly cornered. He couldn't have dodged Joe even if he hadn't been out for blood.

Swallowing, I ran my hands through my damp hair, trying to find some way to stop the shivers that not even Ariadne's heated seats or the vents on full blast could stop.

Ariadne sighed. "Look, I wanted to apologize, so now that you're stuck in a car with me…I'm sorry. I shouldn't have pressured you. It wasn't my place to tell you about Ryan and Andre, and I shouldn't have tried to make you fake date Ryan."

"You wanted to protect them. I get why you did it."

"Doesn't make it okay," she retorted, and I couldn't argue even though this was among the conversations I least wanted to have. "Honestly, though, I thought you knew. With everything with Ryan and your brother. God, I don't know if I've ever seen Andre as jealous as he was over Ryan liking Brandon."

Shrugging, I shook my head. "My dad knew. I guess I never really paid attention. Brandon never really cared about that stuff."

"Yeah…" Accelerating as she got onto the highway, she gave a half-hearted laugh. "He turned down all the girls, didn't he? Ryan used to hope it meant he had a chance, but I always thought Brandon didn't feel that way toward anyone. Like - he was ace aro or something."

I'd never thought about it. Brandon was just Brandon. He laughed when Romeo killed himself and rolled his eyes at most of the couples on screen and how illogical their decision-making was, but we never talked about it. He mocked a lot of stuff. Sappy and romantic and anything selfless somebody else did. His friends generally could be sorted by location, and he rarely socialized with anybody besides Scott outside of those places - school

301

friends, swim meet friends, rink friends. Even with all that, he always looked out for me.

I struggled to find something to say. "I don't know."

There was so much I never asked. So much hadn't mattered. Because he was my brother, and I'd find out eventually, and then because he was dying, and what did any of that matter when I spend more of my life without him around than with him. Not like he'd know about Jackson.

"I thought it was a Seaver trait, honestly, but I guess you guys are a bit more romantic than that, huh? I mean, it's not like your dad dates, and you pretty much weren't interested until Jackson." Before I could protest, she added, "I mean, interested in somebody who could actually like you back."

"It wasn't like there were a lot of guys around who liked me." Which made Jackson seem like less than he was. I wouldn't have gone for any other guy outside of Ryan probably, and honestly, as much as he frustrated me - as much as he made no sense at times, I had cared about him from the moment I checked him, and maybe it started out as guilt. A squirming worm of responsibility in my gut - but it grew, and now... "His dad hates him playing. What if he can't now? What if he's paralyzed?"

Another sigh. Ariadne reached over the gear stick, resting a hand on my arm. "He'll be okay. Look at Tanner. He's got a spinal injury. Everybody said he wouldn't be able to ever walk unaided again, and last week in physical therapy, he managed the whole parallel bar platform. This week, Pete said we'd try a go around the room with the walker."

My stomach clenched, twisting within my abdomen like it could force its way up and out of me. Tanner hated his wheelchair. Loathed people who tried to contain him, and if his father hadn't let him get a chair regardless - bought one specifically for people who couldn't use their legs, Tanner would've come up with some contraption to work his brother's car, but Tanner wasn't Jackson. Jackson fought. He refused to stop even as he smashed himself to pieces over and over again, but he couldn't bounce back like Tanner.

But he didn't give up either. He bounced back from my hit, and while Joe had gone after him with the desire to hurt him, I couldn't lie and say I hadn't checked him with the hole of getting him out of the way. He recovered.

Pulling into the hospital, Ariadne lucked out finding a parking spot, and as we rushed across the parking lot, she texted Tanner.

"They're in the waiting room." Grabbing my sleeve, Ariadne tugged me. "I volunteered here last summer. It's easiest if we go through that door."

Maybe it was because she volunteered, and the nurses recognized Ariadne, or maybe she just had that assertive charm, but nobody glanced twice as she dragged me toward a large room filled with chairs. People hung all around.They milled about in small clusters, murmuring to each other in groups of chairs. An old man in the corner sat with his legs crossed. He had the newspaper up in front of him, but his toe flicked up and down in the air. His eyes jumped to the door.

In my chest, my heart stuttered. "He's in surgery."

"That's a good thing," Ariadne assured me.

Which was stupid. How could surgery be a good thing? I didn't need her to placate me. Kid gloves never helped. Everything with Mom came with kid gloves, and it hadn't made it any easier - not that the lack helped with Brandon, but the whole mess choked me. Strangled and stuck in my throat. Left me swallowing nothingness as my nose and eyes tingled. Biting my lip, I blinked, trying to push back the tears. They came anyway.

"Come on, Beni. They're right over there." Ariadne pointed ahead.

Tanner and my dad were near the doors and the nurses station. My dad had a hand around Tanner's shoulders. Head ducked forward, Tanner held his hands to his mouth. His whole body shook, trembling as he nodded along to something my dad said.

Ariadne didn't even hesitate. One second, she stood beside me. In the next, she crouched before Tanner, hugging him tightly. I just wanted to hide. To run and skate and do something - anything until I couldn't think anymore. I got here. I was in the hospital. Everything I'd told myself up until this moment suggested I should be calm now. That I should know what was going on and that Jackson would be okay. I needed answers, but Tanner held tightly to Ariadne, sobbing into her shoulder.

My feet wouldn't move. Tears poured down my face, and everything blurred, so when arms wrapped around me, pulling me against a warm chest and a Port Edmond hockey hoodie, I stiffened before melting into my dad's embrace.

"It's going to be okay," he whispered, pressing a kiss on the top of my head.

I held tight. "What if he's not?"

Chapter Thirty-Five

Waiting. What sucked worse than waiting? Not knowing whether Jackson would be okay. Whether they'd given him anything for the pain. If his ribs pierced his lung or his heart. Sitting in a hospital - in a chair listening to the droning alerts and muttering between nurses, and everyone sat. Waiting. Wondering what exactly would come out of those doors. Would he be okay?

Curling up in the chair, I leaned into my dad, trying not to cry. Tanner paced back and forth. Ariadne followed, reassuring that his dad would be there soon. That the doctors would inform us about Jackson soon. Waiting and soon - and then the background noise of dress shoes clicking stopped being background. Dr. Duke stormed in with his coat still on and furious expression as his eyes surveyed the room, spotting first Tanner - a small sigh of relief - and then me.

"You!" Dr. Duke hissed, turning on me with a venomous glower. "Of course, it was you."

Tanner waved his hands. "Wait - Dad! It wasn't - "

"Have you proven yourself yet? Brutalized my son enough to justify your position in a male league?" he sneered at me. His lip curled into a snarl. Crossing his arms over his chest, he shifted

306

his hateful glare onto my father. "Three injuries in the last four years - and two of them were caused by your daughter. To think, I threw the considerable weight of my reputation - "

"Beni didn't do it!" Tanner yelled.

Everyone in the waiting room reared back as if struck except Dr. Duke. He froze, blinking with the same squeezed expression of disgust.

Inching closer to me, Andre said, "Joe Dale slammed him into the boards and rammed him with his stick. He's gonna get kicked off the team."

"And that's supposed to comfort me?"

My dad sighed, squeezing my shoulder as he stood. Even though he had a head on Dr. Duke, Jackson's father seemed to tower out of pure spite. "No. Nothing will change anything until you know your son is going to be okay."

Whatever biting comeback he had planned, the other man quickly shut his mouth. His teeth clacked together. This was it. At least, he had the decency not to avoid eye contact immediately. People acted so strangely when they remembered what happened to Brandon. They connected us as his family, and suddenly, pity overwhelmed everything else. We ceased to exist as people. Instead, we became mourners. It was always terribly sad. Brandon always died too young, so much life left to live.

"Tanner." And there it was. Jackson's dad looked away, refocusing on his younger son. "Is the hospital stay kit still in your car?"

Eyes widening, Tanner paled. "Beni's dad drove me."

"I can run back to the rink," my dad offered.

Running a hand through his hair, Dr. Duke inhaled slowly and sighed. "Thank you. Tanner…"

"Here." Tanner held out his keys. "It's in a red St. Raphael's bag in the trunk."

With a quick kiss to the top of my head, my dad headed off, and Dr. Duke stormed toward the nurses with Tanner wheeling right behind him.

With a loud exhale, Andre fanned himself, falling back into the chair where my dad had been sitting. "Man, you're going to have one crazy father-in-law, Seaver. Hope you're ready to get a graded report on your parenting skills."

"Bit early for kids."

Andre just hummed before jumping to his feet as Ariadne raced back. "Dr. Duke interrogated the nurses - Jackson has internal bleeding, multiple rib fractures, and a ruptured spleen, but he's in stable condition."

I sunk deeper into my chair, deflating like a tire. "He's going to be okay?"

"He's going to be okay," she reassured.

Collapsing forward, I buried my face in my hands, choking back the sob which wretched its way from my throat. All tension drained. My body ached with a bone-dead tiredness as Ariadne patted my shoulder reassuringly. Exhausted. Emotionally. Physically. Every part of me just wanted to curl into a ball. Jackson was going to be okay. The season ended with our win, so he had no reason not to let himself recover.

It snapped through me like lightning. He'd recovered from rib fractures before. Internal bleeding and a ruptured spleen - those sounded severe. Were they related? I couldn't even place the spleen on a body. Abdomen somewhere? If a ruptured spleen didn't cause the internal bleeding, there had to be damage elsewhere, which meant a longer recovery.

Wiping away the tears, I shifted to look at Ariadne. "What does it mean that he had a ruptured spleen?"

With a small shrug, Ariadne pulled out her phone. "I wish Ryan were here. He'd know -" her eyes widened, "Oh shit."

"What? Is it really bad?"

Her wide blue eyes jumped to my face then back to her phone. "No - it's...umm…" Biting my lip, I waited, watching her uncertainty before she showed me the screen of her phone. "Ryan came out to his dad."

My brain buzzed like a TV between stations. I needed answers, not distractions. The first instinctual thought flashing through my mind raged at Ryan deciding now was the best time to come out. Which wasn't fair. If he wanted to come out now, his choice mattered. He didn't have to wait. Ryan's life didn't have to stop because Jackson got hospitalized.

Taking a breath to center myself, I sighed. "Is he okay?"

"Scott and him are grabbing his stuff. His dad gave him an hour to get his 'shit and get out,'" Ariadne informed me - dropping her voice into a gruff growl to imitate Mr. Caldwell's voice. "Andre's prepping one of our guestrooms, so at least, he'll be able to finish out the year." Her fingers flew across her phone, and she shook her head. "Sorry - everything's just hitting all at once."

"It's a lot."

Nodding, I wrapped my arms around myself, glancing over to where Tanner and his dad stood. Both looked wrecked. Dark shadows cradled their eyes, and every so often, Tanner sniffed, blinking rapidly as if to hold back tears. Hearing Jackson would make it - hearing he was stable, that must've been a relief, but a rigid tension remained in Dr.

Duke's spine. His shoulders stretched, pushed consciously down as he rubbed his hands over his face. Better than any of us, he knew how sudden bad turns could be.

"Huh, well, it sounds like the ruptured spleen was probably the reason behind the internal bleeding," Ariadne informed me. "They said he had gone into surgery to fix it, and the nurse mentioned them closing him, so it must've gone well."

"Will it stop him from playing?" I asked, tearing my gaze away from the Dukes.

Ariadne's brows pulled together as she frowned at me. "Beni…"

"If it doesn't automatically knock him off the team, he's going to argue his way right back on." And get hurt again. Joe hadn't seemed repentant or even surprised to see the way Jackson went down, and anyone watching had to know he fell hard. Everyone would go after him. Not that they hadn't before, but it would get worse and worse because I had hit him that one stupid time. "He's going to get injured again."

"He will." Both of us jumped at Dr. Duke's voice. He loomed like some kind of monstrous giant with a dour scowl. "That boy will never be happy watching someone close to him live the life he's wanted. Jackson would rather chew off his own arm."

Tanner huffed, wiping the tears staining his face. "Dad, he's not a dog."

"A clean break would be best," Dr. Duke announced, completely ignoring his younger son. "It'd be an unnecessary temptation."

I could read between the lines. I was an unnecessary temptation. As long as Jackson and I dated, he wouldn't be far enough away from the ice to forget the feel of it - to forget how much he wanted it. Our relationship grew out of a love for hockey. Sure, we spent time together outside the rink nowadays, but how much? Without hockey, we'd just fall apart.

Someone like Ariadne would probably have a response. Something poignant that would show Dr. Duke was wrong, but I couldn't find a way to get my tongue to move at all. No words. Not a single one, and then his pager went off, and the man cursed, storming away as he pulled his cell phone out of his pocket to snap at some man named Abraham.

"Ignore him. He's just pissed he had to come back early." Tanner gave me a tense smile. "Jackson knew he had an end date. It's earlier than any of us expected, but…" he offered only a slight shrug. "He's stubborn, but he's not stupid. Don't let the old man get in your head."

"Tanner!" Dr. Duke called. Another doctor in scrubs stood beside him.

Backing up, Tanner glanced over at Ariadne. "You don't have to stay. My dad's probably not going to let anyone see him."

"Do you want me to leave?" Ariadne retorted.Tanner shook his head. "Then I'll stay."

With a small smile, he looked at me. "When your dad comes back, you should bring the bag through; otherwise, I'm not sure you'll get to see him."

"I will...thanks."

And off he went.

Chapter Thirty-Six

The second my dad returned, I took the bag from him, racing down the hall toward where Tanner and his dad had gone. Every door looked the same, but the number Tanner gave me repeated over and over in my head. It was easy enough to find.

Tanner's voice carried down the hall. "You're going to be so pissed when you find out they lost. Would've been something, huh? Star player got injured, and the rest of the team rises to the occasion, right?"

I raced into the room, trying to disguise the disappointment when I saw Jackson wasn't awake.

"You've got impeccable timing," Tanner told me. "My dad decided to interrogate the surgeon. Chuck the bag wherever."

Biting back my relief, I could only offer him a half-smile as I set down the bag on the chair closest to the door. Any sense remaining focused on Jackson. He laid in the hospital bed. White surrounded him from the walls to the blankets. Everything made to bleach. His pulse spiked and dipped - lines on a machine I couldn't understand, but they meant he was alive when everything else looked anything but. Pale - everything about him was too pale. Except the dark circles under his eyes or the exaggerated hollows beneath his cheekbones.

An I.V. hung beside him, dripping liquids down the tube into his arm.

Tanner wheeled closer, gesturing for me to come into the room, but I couldn't move. "Weird, right? He goes all snazzy corpse when he gets sick too. Almost expected him to sparkle when he got the flu last year."

"You don't have to joke," I murmured, frozen at the door.

He shrugged. "Don't know what I'd do if I stopped. I kind of can't process all this. I mean, last time Dad made him come to a hospital, he wouldn't shut up about finally having some competition. The smitten idiot - I swear our dad wanted to smack him." Reaching onto the bed, he squeezed Jackson's hand. "Time before that - I didn't have to be the one waiting for someone to wake up."

And he woke up needing a wheelchair. His mother had died too. Jackson remained stable. Stable meant he'd be okay. That was what the doctors always said, but just seeing him in the bed - the place with the white sheets and the monitor and everything inside me screamed to run as if not seeing him there would erase the whole situation.

"You planning on standing there all day?" Tanner joked.

Biting my lip, I shook my head and forced myself to take a step. One I got one leg to move, the second came easier, but then I couldn't stop. Opposite Tanner, I stopped from throwing myself onto the bed, but touching him didn't seem right. What if I hurt him? They pumped meds into him, but if I jostled him, he could still be hurt. I'd never broken a bone before. Bigger than all the girls, they never managed more than some bruises, and I towered over most of the guys still, so even when they hit, I knew how to take it. Or maybe I was just lucky. Strong bones maybe.

"Your dad's right." Watching Jackson breathe, I couldn't fight back the tears anymore.

"What are - "

I shook my head, furious at myself for unloading on him. His brother was in the hospital, and here I was whining. What a jerk. "I should go."

"Beni…" Tanner's shoulders slumped.

Patting him on the back, I forced a smile. "He's going to be great. I'll come back tomorrow during visiting hours. Don't want to screw with his beauty sleep."

Tanner forced a laugh. His half-smile tilted to one side from the half-hearted effort. "If you need a ride, you can always text me."

I didn't have the heart to remind him I didn't have a phone. Ducking out of the room, I sighed in relief when my eyes landed on my dad. He leaned against the wall beside the door with a frown to match the wrinkles in his furrowed brow.

"Let's go," I muttered.

He stood with a glance back at the room. "That was quick. You sure? I could wait if you want to stay longer. I don't mind."

"He's resting. I just needed to see him."

"What about Tanner?"

I swallowed, shrugging. I wasn't in the place to offer anybody comfort. "Ariadne's still in the waiting area. I can - I'll just tell her to go through for him."

If he worried for me, he never said; instead, he wrapped an arm around me, shifting topics completely. "Guess I've got to save up to see you in the National game. Is it in Ohio this year?"

"Yeah. Cleveland."

Nodding, he guided me back through the halls. "Not too bad a drive then."

"Might be able to get a deal on a hotel room if you talk about it with Coach Carr," I suggested, but before he could respond, Ariadne popped up, heading over to us.

"Is he awake?" she asked, wringing her hands. "Is everything okay?"

"He's still unconscious. You should go through. I think Tanner needs someone right now," I offered, leaning into my dad.

Nodding rapidly, Ariadne said, "Okay. Are you going?"

"Yeah, um…"

She meant it nicely. I knew she asked because she wanted to make sure everyone was okay, but somehow, her question beat me down. Someone better would stay. Would comfort Tanner and wait by Jackson's bedside. The idea left me nauseous. Hospitals helped so many people. They terrified me.

Ariadne launched forward, hugging me as I froze at the quick contact. "Call if you need anything! Okay?"

And she raced off, leaving me unmoored.

Squeezing my shoulder, my dad guided me along. "Cheryl's probably already planning some group deal. For the hotels. Sure she'll include me if I let her know I'm interested. I swear - that woman has her hands in everything." He glanced at me, but quickly focused on navigating to where he'd parked. "Good thing you and Sean hit it off back in kindergarten. I don't know what I would've done if she hadn't driven you to and from hockey when everything happened with your mom."

Arriving at the car, I shifted, hugging him in full. "Thanks, Dad."

He ruffled my hair and kissed the top of my

head, announcing, "I'm ordering food tonight. Any preference? Pizza? Chinese?"

"We haven't had pizza in a while."

Starting the engine, he agreed, "Pizza it is."

"Dad...do you think Coach Steele and Dr. Cortez would still be open to me joining the Lions?"

His brows jumped as if trying to escape into his hairline. "I thought you wanted to stay with Port Edmond."

"I did, but now that Joe knows, the whole league will know about Jackson's condition. Everybody will be out for him," I explained. Wrapping my arms around me, I sunk as far back in the seat as I could, yearning to just curl up into a ball and not think at all, but my mind whirled. "If I were on the Lions - "

"There'd still be plenty of time when Jackson would take the ice without you. You shouldn't make your life about him. I wasn't a fan of you staying with Port Edmond, but if it meant you weren't forced to play second fiddle, I supported it." Sighing, he rubbed a hand over his face.

"What if he doesn't make it next time?"

Reaching over the console, he squeezed my knee. "From the way his dad was acting, I'm pretty sure there's not going to be a next time."

"After I took Jackson out, he probably acted the same way." Tanner had looked so terrified. With a life spent watching his dad say no and Jackson go ahead anyway, he recognized the pattern. The moment Jackson could. He'd be back on the ice. "Jackson doesn't listen, and he'd probably emancipate himself if he thought it meant he'd get to keep playing."

"That's still not on you."

Not on me. As if responsibility mattered right now. "He's my boyfriend."

"You're fifteen," he retorted.

"Sixteen in May!"

Snorting, my dad shook his head. "You're fifteen. This is your first relationship. I might not have planned on being the one to give you these kinds of talks, Beni, but never throw yourself away for somebody else."

"Even if I spend next year watching Jackson's back, he wouldn't be there my senior year," I argued.

Though his eyes remained on the road, my dad tilted his head, and the weight of his attention hovered over me. "And how do you think Jackson will feel?"

"About getting his way?" I shook my head, turning up the heater as I shifted all the vents to concentrate on me. My hair still dripped. Water trailed down my spine, leaving me cold inside and out. "I'm pretty sure he'll be thrilled."

His fingers drummed across the steering wheel. "Some boys wouldn't be too happy if their girlfriends tried to protect them."

"Well, he's definitely not like most guys."

Most guys would have looked at all six feet of me and walked away. Too tall - too broad. Nobody liked me before. Not like Jackson. A good friend. Decent teammate if they didn't get upset that I skated circles around them - if I could make myself smaller when they paid too much attention or if their want to win outweighed their ego.

Goosebumps rose beneath my clothes. Shivers and purple nail beds - everything too cold. Too big in an all new way.

Like some kind of sorcerer, my dad's words barreled right through everything else. Being with me meant he'd have to deal with hockey. That he couldn't pretend he never wanted to play professional or pretend the sport didn't exist at all. I loved the game. Loved playing it, based most of my life around it, and my stomach rolled, churning at the thought of pretending it didn't matter to me. I couldn't quit. Not for him or anyone, but I wanted to somehow make it alright. Somehow erase the guilt boiling. Up inside me. If switching teams and being another wall between him and broken bones - puncture organs, paralysis, and all other sorts of horrible complications of a hit going wrong, then should I do it? Even if it only gave him one more year?

"Beni, there's a difference between taking care of someone and enabling them. Tanner explained Jackson's situation on the drive. He shouldn't be playing hockey," my dad announced, and when I opened my mouth to argue, he gestured at me to keep quiet. "I don't care if he's gone around his father's back in the past. This time, Dr. Duke isn't going to take chances, and no judge is going to enable Jackson. Emancipation isn't happening. He's lucky he's alive."

"it's Jackson. He'll find a way."

Rolling his eyes, my dad sighed as he turned onto our street. "No decent coach will let that kid get back on the ice."

"He's a prodigy!"

"I don't care if he's the second coming of Wayne Gretzky, if Coach Steele lets him back on the team, he's doing a disservice to Jackson and to the whole team, and that's not a coach I'm to let my daughter play for." His tone left no room for argument.

Athletes expected injury. No matter how hard you trained or what you did as preventive measures, the risk remained. I'd had bruised ribs before and a couple concussions. Once, Geoffrey broke an arm in middle school, and Sean chipped a tooth and broke his nose the first time when he landed face first on the ice last year. Coaches expected their players to get hurt, to recover, and to get back out there.

Not that my dad cared. Of course, the second I have a boyfriend, he got involved. Years of fending for myself meant nothing. My dad said no, so I just had to deal. No matter how wrong he was.

Grinding my teeth, I glared out the window, barely waiting for him to put the car into park before I jumped out and ran to my room, slamming the door in frustration. Back and forth, I paced. From too cold to too hot, I wretched off my coat, throwing it onto my desk.

I hated feeling helpless. Not knowing what to do. Brandon always used to know exactly what needed to be done, and I just followed along. Outside of hockey, it wasn't that I didn't care, but everyone seemed to care so much more, and they knew things. Things I didn't think about - keeping track of things better than I could, and I tried. I tried so hard because I promised Brandon I would, but Brandon never dated. Every lesson I learned from him - this relationship wasn't one of them. Nothing prepared me for romance. Until Jackson, I never thought anybody would be interested, and besides Ryan, I hadn't thought I'd be interested in anybody too.

Throwing myself onto my bed, I screamed into my pillows. Nobody prepared me for this. I couldn't love somebody and lose them - not again. Not after Mom and Brandon. I couldn't. I didn't have it in me. Not to do this. To be there while they self-destructed. Brandon gave up. I couldn't even remember my mom before she got sick anymore. Brandon didn't want to fight, and that hurt. Jackson wanted to keep fighting, and that hurt. None of this was my choice. I just had to accept whatever decision he made and figure out if I could handle it.

How could I prepare for this? Plan for it?

A knock interrupted my thoughts. "Beni?"

"I want to be alone," I called, rolling over to curl up on my side.

"I'm coming in anyways," he informed me, letting himself in. He sat on the edge of my bed. "All I meant was - don't make big decisions without Jackson. One of the most important parts of a relationship is communication. Don't go making big decisions for him."

Wrapping my arms around my legs, I sighed. "I just want to be prepared."

"Honey, nothing's gonna prepare you for somebody like Jackson," he told me. His lips curved into an almost smile. Something fond and sad. "He reminds me a bit of your mother - not that I know him very well, mind you, but he's got a plan for himself, and if you let him, he'll run you over to get what he wants. Your mother always knew the next step - when it was time to get married, to buy a house, to have children...she always knew when we needed to do whatever she knew we ought to do, and with people like her - like Jackson, it's easy to let them pull you along."

"I don't want him to hate me."

"Oh, Beni, he's not gonna hate you," he assured me, wrapping an arm around me.

He seemed so certain, but we hadn't even been dating when Mercy happened. Everything moved too quickly. Worse, even though I had seen him - even though everyone said he was in stable condition, a part of me feared Jackson wouldn't wake up at all.

Chapter Thirty-Seven

Brandon hated cards. People sent them, signed with a half-illegible scrawling inside if they'd bothered to say anything at all. Sweets - often inedible to him - came a close second. Nobody thought to send the high school guy dying of cancer - down a leg and stuck in bed - flowers or a Teddy Bear. Even dying, nobody considered he might like something soft or beautiful. Only bit of either he got came from Scott. A pastel pink bear lobbed at Brandon's head after my brother complained about the injustice for almost a full week.

Jackson wasn't Brandon. He didn't rage like Brandon did at first or go numb when knocked down, but then again, Jackson had a bone condition not less than six months to live. Still, a card alone seemed too little. Buying daisies - because they looked happy, right? - a small lion, and a card, I walked into the hospital. Same too clean smell. How could a place feel sick and dead sterile at the same time? Not a strong smell, but my nose caught it and I swallowed the instinct to gag with each breath.

His voice reached me first "That's just dumb! I'll be perfectly fine by next season."

My stomach lurched. Stumbling, I caught myself before I dropped the flowers. He couldn't. If he played again, he would end up right back here. All along my arms, goosebumps rose. Off the ice, I ran from these sorts of talks. The ones that mattered. The ones where I was the voice of reason. What right did I have? I ignored presidence and joined the guy's side when all the other girls moved on to other sports. When people questioned me, I dug in, keeping my head down. Kept playing. How could I tell him to quit?

He loved hockey. Lived for it - same as me, but also - the selfish part of me remembered the hate in his father's eyes. If he left hockey behind, would he leave me too? Or would he expect me to give it up for him? I couldn't. I wouldn't even if it meant losing him, and didn't that mean something? Did I not like him enough?

Ducking, I pushed against my instincts. With a smile forced onto my face, I knocked, and both Duke brothers stared at me. Jackson looked better. Or maybe that was him being conscious. Bright green eyes and a blinding smile focused on me.

"Beni!" he exclaimed, and scooting to one side, he patted the spot beside him on the bed, but as I crossed the room, his smile grew. "Oh shit! Did you bring me flowers?"

"Daisies," I offered.

He held out his hands, grabbing them and swirling them around to set them on the table beside him. "I'll forgive you not being at my bedside when I woke up I guess."

Tanner scoffed. "You woke up in the middle of the night complaining about your foot itching. Only Dad was around for that."

"Cause he kicked you out," Jackson noted, but despite his argument, he kept smiling at me. "Come on, Seaver. Kick off your shoes and cuddle my poor injured body. I'm cold, and you're a furnace."

"I can get the nurses to bring another blanket," his younger brother informed him even as I did what he asked. Taking whatever he offered while I could.

I took the lion from my bag before letting it drop to the floor. "Also got you a friend. In case you get lonely when Tanner has to go to school."

Throwing an arm around me, Jackson tugged me closer until our hips pressed together, and he kissed the side of my head before settling the lion on his monitor. "Look at me! Flowers and a new friend, and Dad said I'd have nothing but broken bones to show for my hockey career."

"You have multiple rib fractures," Tanner retorted.

But Jackson laughed, leaning on me. His hand was colder than ever as he held me. One hand wrapped around my shoulders, sneaking along the collar of my jacket as the other took my closest hand to him in a weird handshake-like hold. Even as the monitor steadily beat, the coldness screamed about how close he'd come - all the blood he'd lost when his spleen ruptured. He could have died. Jackson could have died, and even thinking the words left me choking as my vision blurred,but I did my best to swallow my tears, jokingly smacking his hand from my shoulder.

"Stop trying to steal my body heat like a creeper," I teased even as I slouched down and cuddled closer to his side.

"You mean going for the boob," Tanner drawled, causing Jackson to gasp and press his hand to his chest like a scandalized southern belle as my face heated. "You aren't as subtle as you think."

With a less than dignified scoff, Jackson rolled his eyes. "Don't be jealous. Not our fault your girl's helping move her ex into the guest room instead of here."

"I'm perfectly alright with Ryan moving in. What I'm not fine with watching my brother paw at my friend - girlfriend or not," Tanner announced as he crossed his arms over his chest. He looked disturbingly like their dad, but for all the complaining, everyone seemed happy, so I wasn't about to comment. "Whatever - I have PT today. I'll be back in an hour, so...get your giggles while I'm gone."

"Have fun!" Jackson called, grinning until his brother left. With a sigh, he sunk against me. "Love that jerk, but man, is it tiring trying to be all smiles."

Hugging him gently, I pushed down the flutters in my stomach at how he curled into me. "I'm sure he'd understand if you weren't."

"Yeah - I know, but it's hard to think about this being the end of hockey without him pointing it out. He's in a wheelchair, and he's worried about me. I must be a terrible big brother," Jackson murmured.

"So...you're not going to play next season?"

Jackson laughed. "You suck at pretending you're not relieved, Beni. Yeah, I'm done." Squeezing me, I resisted the instinct to squeeze back; instead, pressing a kiss to his forehead for fear of hurting his ribs. "I always thought I'd be fine if I wrecked myself, planning to play until I was mangled but…" He sniffled and a wet laugh slipped from his lips. "It sucks. I'm horrible at everything else but athletics. Sports theory's as close as I get to anything academic. Math and physics only made sense on the ice."

"You could coach or do sports therapy," I suggested, but he shook his head.

He sighed. "Think you can deal with dating Jackson Duke the model? That bastard didn't screw up my face."

Taking his face in my hands, I forced him to meet my eyes. "I like you. I want to date you - Jackson Duke, and whatever you want to put after that, I'm in."

Jackson's face scrunched up, and with a sharp inhale, he tugged me forward, bringing out lips together. My heart fluttered in my chest even as the brief touch. When he pulled back, he curled against me once more. "I'm going to be so annoying. Showing up at all your practices like an addict."

"You could always figure skate. Apparently that's Sean's back-up plan, and you're way better than he is. Plus, then you're only risking fall damage," I joked.

"I'm too old," he groaned.

A laugh burst out of me. "Old? You're sixteen. And didn't you do lessons?"

"For a hot second in middle school."

I rolled my eyes. "You're a competitive jerk. Don't pretend you weren't showing off on our date."

"Some people woo a girl with chocolates. Not this guy. I showed off my skating skills," he said, gesturing at himself with his thumbs. "Crap, I'm lucky I found you. I've got a really weird way of flirting."

Brushing off his obliviousness to the girls who adored him before I ever came into the picture as either due to the drugs they had him on or winding me up to get a compliment, I hummed softly, trying to find the right words before giving up and just going for it. "I think you were pretty brilliant at it actually. Anyway, you don't have to decide anything now."

He nuzzled into my side. "Would you take lessons with me in the off season?"

"If you want me to - but we both know I'd probably be a hazard."

With a soft sigh, Jackson smiled at me. "Anything worth having has its risk."

Epilogue

When time rolled around for Nationals, Jackson hadn't recovered enough to come even just to watch, but he didn't miss much. We lost that year. On the plus side, we won my senior year - though Jackson always pointed out that would've never been the case if he had still been able to play. Afterward, Port Edmond's rivalry with the St. Raphael's Lion even once again.

Ande ended up playing for the Bruins. He married Ryan the same year, and he was still playing for them when Ryan graduated from med school. Dr. Duke actually scouted him. As much as I wanted to credit it to a desire to give back to someone from his community, Tanner retorted that his father enjoyed having a connection to bring in well-known athletes for the pediatric wing.

Sean stopped playing hockey after high school. He ended up going abroad his junior year and falling in love with South Korea. Ironically, the first job he got out there was as a hockey coach for a group of kids in Seoul.

On the other hand, Geoffrey played a bit in college, but he stopped his sophomore year after breaking his leg. Dedicating himself to tech, he ended up moving out to New York City. Even all the way out in Seoul, Sean mocked Geoffrey for the decision, but we were all happier he ended up there than in California. NYC was a train-ride. California seemed like another world. Plus, he could pop up to Boston every now and then for my games when the Boston Pride recruited me.

Northeastern gave me a scholarship, and with Jackson at Harvard, Boston seemed an awful lot like Port Edmond. After everything we'd been through getting together, the biggest hiccup we'd faced might've been explaining our decision to get an apartment together post-university to my dad. It made sense. The Pride picked me up, and Jackson trained out of Boston with Sadie as his pair. They got all the way to the Olympics in my junior year, but he decided to go solo after they placed sixth.

"If I have to go with anybody to the next Olympics," he told me, "it'll be you or nobody."

Rolling my eyes, I threw a piece of popcorn at his head. "Not a great chance then."

Jackson said nothing. He gave me a smug knowing look, and at the time, curled up in my dorm room watching a game, the idea of not only getting recruited but qualifying for the Olympics so quickly seemed too good to be true. However, with the challenge set, I could be just as stubborn as Jackson, so after a scout approached me about the Boston Pride, Jackson smirked. His hands in his pockets as he sauntered over to bump my shoulder.

Like a smug cat, he preened. "You know - now that you've got a contract...it wouldn't be too hard to put your name into the ring for the US women's hockey team."

"I haven't even played a game yet," I retorted.

His eyes narrowed. Raising a single brow, he asked, "What was the last four years?"

I shoved him back. "It's not the same."

"Odds are in your favor, Seaver. It'd show some initiative."

So - I joined the Pride, moved in with Jackson, and qualified for the Olympics. Which was great, but the competitive spirit in me saw my first Olympics, and as the United States came into it as the defending champions, I couldn't help but want more.

"You realize I'm almost definitely going to get a medal," I informed Jackson part-way through.

His nose wrinkled. "So? I'm a favorite for gold too."

"Yeah...but if I get a medal my first time around, that kind of means I win."

Jaw dropping, he feigned a horrified gasp. "How dare you!"

"Still - not wrong."

He ran his hands through his blond hair, rolling his eyes. The Olympic village churned with constant energy. Everything moved between partying to preparing to make history, and sometimes the two mixed in a strange almost bacchanalian insanity. Not for the first time, I appreciated being part of a team. So many people handled having all that pressure just on themselves. Jackson, as usual, remained at ease.

"Fine," he replied, smirking. "We both win gold, you win."

Beating out Canada in our final game, the United States women's hockey team won gold. A few days later, I watched Jackson's final skate. Jackson flew across the ice - jumping, dancing - a whirl of color and grace which slowed as the crowd cheered. Flowers flew through the air, but my eyes jumped between Jackson as he bowed, his chest heaving before his eyes lit. I couldn't take my eyes off him. The cheering, the lights, the cold of the rink - nothing else mattered. Everything faded to just him, so when he leapt to his feet, grabbing something from his coach and jumping the barrier to where I sat, I moved to hug him before he dropped to one knee.

"We both won gold, so you win at life. Say you'll marry me, so I'll have won too?" Jackson asked, holding up a gold band with an inset diamond. All the air rushed from my lungs. Blinking back tears, I nodded like a bobble head until he stood, wrapping his arms around me. "That a yes?"

Half-laughing, half-crying, I whispered, "Yes." When he chuckled, I pulled back and kissed him. "I love you, you jerk."

"Love you too, Beni."

www.ingramcontent.com/pod-product-compliance
Lightning Source LLC
Chambersburg PA
CBHW070533260626
47161CB00002B/369